NEMESIS
BRENNUS
CONQUEROR OF ROME

BOOK TWO
C.R.MAY

This novel is a work of fiction. The names, characters and incidents portrayed in it, while at times based on real figures, are purely the work of the author's imagination.

It is sold subject to the condition that it shall not by way of trade or otherwise, be lent, resold, hired out, or otherwise circulated without the writer's prior consent, electronically or in any form of binding or cover other than the form in which it is published and without a similar condition including this condition being imposed on the subsequent purchaser. Replication or distribution of any part is strictly prohibited without the written permission of the copyright holder.

Copyright © 2015 C.R.May
All rights reserved.
ISBN: 1511479892
ISBN-13:978-1511479899

Dedicated to the Celtic peoples of Europe and beyond

Panic stricken by the unexpectedness of the invaders' expedition, by their numbers, by the huge size of their bodies and by the strange and terrifying sound of their voices, they forgot their training in military science and hence lost the use of their valour.

Cassius Dio - Roman History

ONE

The moon slipped free of the cloud and the man froze. Twenty paces before him the guard was grinning as his head swept in circular patterns, the wan light reflecting dully from the polished bronze of his armour. A small shape, a solid point of black amid the gloom, flitted past in the chill air and the giant Aeduan caught his breath as the Roman's gaze swept through and beyond him as it followed the erratic flight.

Berikos' eyes flicked down as he judged the distance between them, but he quickly discounted the idea of a sudden rush forward. The bat was moving just too quickly, its flightpath too difficult to predict, and he slowly turned the blade of his dagger until the pale reflection disappeared with a final flicker.

The guard's gaze passed across him once again as the dark shape sped past on its circular beat, and Berikos closed his eyes briefly lest the glint in them betray his presence. Senses heightened, nerves taut, Berikos felt the air move against his face as the rhythmic sound of tiny wings split the air only inches away.

Desperate for the life-preserving shadows to return, he cautiously stole a look. Rolling his eyes skywards, hope returned as the after part of the cloud, its greyness edged in silver, began to nibble at the moon's rim.

With agonising slowness the cloak of darkness deepened, and he gripped his blade tightly and crept forward with feline stealth. Twenty paces, fifteen...

He must see me.

The gods continued to show him their favour and the guard's head flicked up, the bat climbing suddenly as it homed in on a large, silvery moth. Ten paces, and the warrior knew he must strike. His gods were with him he knew, but they could also be fickle and they craved entertainment; it would not do to press them too far.

Now!

Berikos leapt forward and a heartbeat later the edge of his knife was pressed firmly against the olive tones of the guard's upturned throat. As the man went rigid and his eyes widened in terror, the Aeduan spat softly through gritted teeth.

"A single noise from you and it will be your last. If I hear so much as a nervous gulp or a squeaky fart you'll find yourself with another mouth, a big red one. Do you understand?" He leaned in and increased the pressure on the blade to lend his words emphasis. "We are going to cross the field here and you are not going to try and run, because if you do my friends will pepper you with arrows before you can get more than three paces, *intelligo?*"

The guard moved his head almost imperceptibly as he struggled to overcome the fear of the cold steel pressing against his windpipe.

Berikos reached down and drew the man's own dagger from its sheath and tucked it into his belt. He hissed into his ear.

"Any more?"

The guard gave a slight shake of his head and Berikos grabbed a handful of his tunic and twisted it into a tight ball as he prepared to push the man before him, back into the safety of the trees. As he made to drop his dagger to the man's side a nearby door opened suddenly, washing the area with the buttery light from the fire within. Berikos pulled the man to him and increased the pressure of the blade as the sound of animated conversations carried to them. A sudden shout made both men start.

"Marcus, shut the door. This isn't a barn!"

Marcus let the hem of his tunic drop as he leaned across and tossed a light-hearted comment back into the room. The answering jeers were cut short as the door closed with a clatter and the newcomer hitched up his clothing once again as he splashed noisily against the outside wall. Berikos and his captive tensed as Marcus threw a comment over his shoulder.

"It *is* a cold night, Atilus. Glad I'm in the warm."

Atilus rolled his eyes towards Berikos who shook his head, hoping that the night was cold enough to draw the man quickly back to the warmth of the fireside. Berikos attempted to slip behind Atilus as Marcus glanced across but, with mounting despair, he knew that the action was futile. He was bigger than most Celts, and often found that he stood almost twice the height of these men in the South. In desperation he flicked the braid of his hair forward and snuggled into his bemused captive.

As Marcus reached out for the handle of the door, the Aeduan cursed inwardly as the man paused and leaned forward, squinting into the shadows.

"Have you got someone there with you?"

Berikos whispered a warning into Atilus' ear as the man's superior took a pace towards them, easing the pressure of the blade just enough to enable him to make an edgy reply.

"No, sir."

The man hesitated for a moment and seemed on the point of returning to the hut when an innate sense that something was not quite as it should be caused him to move towards them. He spoke again, angrier now.

"Yes, there is. You are on guard duty, if it's that woman again you'll be in some serious shit, lad!"

Atilus tensed as Berikos increased the pressure once again on the dagger and wound his body in preparation to strike. As the Roman unknowingly left the safety of the light, a dark shape detached itself from the shadows and padded stealthily across the courtyard with a litheness which belied its size. Suddenly the moon slid from behind the cloud to bathe the scene, and Berikos was finally revealed by its watery light.

Marcus' expression changed instantly to one of shock, and he drew in a breath to shout a warning as, unseen, the wraith-like figure rose to stifle the cry with a meaty hand. A moment later the Roman's eyes shot open in surprise and horror as his head was snatched violently back and a blade flashed to slide across his upturned throat.

Druteos moved his dagger down and plunged it into Marcus' heart, gripping the body tightly as it shook in its death spasm. As it fell, lifeless, the Horsetail hoist the body across his shoulder and shifted its weight. He shot his friend a look as he loped past and grinned.

"I am sorry to spoil your fun, but we really do need to go."

Berikos realised that he was still cuddling into the terrified guard and, leaping back with a frown, he hissed a reply.

"If you mention this to anyone you'll join our friend there!"

Druteos smirked mischievously and, ignoring the gouts of blood which were still pulsing from his victim's neck and chest, the big man doubled across and let the corpse slip unceremoniously to the ground in the deep shadow of a wood pile.

With a final, furtive glance about the clearing, the Celts pushed their captive ahead of them and were swallowed by the darkness.

Behind them, the never ending circle of life and death continued to stalk the night on serrated wings. Vaporous tendrils rose gently in the cold night air from the dark stain on the wall and the small pool which had collected at its base.

Albiomaros lifted his nose and drew a great breath before letting it go with a sigh. "Smell that? We are nearly home."

A rumble of laughter came from the column as the men shared looks which told of their gratitude and relief that they had managed to survive the task set by Brennus and come safely back to the army.

A finger of light broke through the graphite clouds to point accusingly at the war-weary city of Clevsin, huddled on its ridge above the valley floor. The army of the Senones were encamped on the ridges opposite they knew, waiting for them to return with the results of their mission to the southern city of Rome. With the army now a short gallop away they were finally safe from ambush or pursuit, and Solemis allowed himself a small self-congratulatory smile at having largely fulfilled his task without losing a man.

At his side, Albiomaros turned his head, throwing a question back along the column with a smirk.

"Do you think that your friend made it home, Berikos?"

The laughter redoubled and their chieftain glanced back with a grin as the men puckered their lips and made a series of loud kissing noises. He looked across to the Aeduan and was gratified to see that the man was chuckling happily along with his adoptive clansmen. He was glad. The man had proven to be a popular and useful member of the war band ever since they had released him from slavery several weeks before. They had quickly discovered that the man's great size and strength was matched by his cheeriness and easy-going nature and he and Albiomaros in particular had soon struck up a great friendship. Druteos chipped in as the horses trotted on.

"The last time that I saw him he was running back towards Rome. Mind you though," he added as the men smiled in anticipation, "it was not as fast as I would have run if the ugly bastard had slobbered all over my neck!"

They all laughed again as Solemis reflected on the Roman, Atilus. It had been a mistake to risk the lives of his men to capture him. He had already suspected that the Romans would wait until they had regained Etruscan lands before either attempting to overtake his small band

and overwhelm them or, as had transpired, sent a number of their equites on ahead to lay in ambush for their return. It had been plain enough from the treatment meted out to them outside the city walls that they were regarded as a curiosity at best, an amusement for the citizens to mock and gape upon as they took their leisure on the Field of Mars. He thought that his judgement had been sound at the time but, to their surprise, the captive had quickly regained his humour once he realised that he was not to be killed out of hand and they had grown to admire his confidence and self-assurance. It had lent the enemy a human face and, having learnt little of use from the encounter, Solemis resolved that he would not suffer a prisoner to live again if the time came.

They had left the paved surface of the via cassia with reluctance soon after passing beyond the River Tiberis. Tired and keen to return to their homes and families on the eastern side of the Apeninnus after a long summer away, the solid footing had offered the ideal route home for the weary men. The rapidly shortening days had already added a full day to their journey back to Clevsin, but none had demurred as Solemis had led them across the fields and taken the muddied track which shadowed the roadway. Within hours they had discovered the expected ambush party ensconced within a small settlement which stood hard on to the road. Securing their horses on the far side of the ridge they had crept forward to observe the enemy force from the safety of the deepening shadows as the sun had dipped, an indistinct smear to the West.

A full century of equites had left Rome the day before the Fabii brothers had ridden out to deliver the senate's reply to their demands, and Solemis had immediately suspected that they had been under orders to intercept the Senone party on the road home. He had been exercising his mount alongside Albiomaros and the looks which a few of the riders had cast in their direction had left him in little doubt that they could be expected to meet again, and soon.

Thankfully, the momentary slip of their much lauded *disciplina* had alerted him to the danger, but he had wanted to be certain that they were the same men, and he chastised himself as he realised that he had put his own clansmen in harms way to do so.

Whoops of joy came from ahead as a party of riders clattered down the via cassia towards them, and Solemis' thoughts came back to the present as the answering shouts of recognition from his own party rose into the chill air. Led by Galatus, the clansmen who had remained behind with the army broke away as they drew near and circled the column, beating spears against shields and announcing the return of their chieftain in a whirl of ululating mayhem.

Galatus finally steered his mount across and fell in step alongside his chieftain as the rest of the clan exchanged animated greetings to their rear.

"Welcome back Solemis!" He cast a quick glance back along the column as he did a quick head count and shot his leader a delighted grin. "You are all here. How did it go?"

Solemis shared a look with Albiomaros and blew out his cheeks. "We all survived, that is the main thing." He nodded towards Galatus' long sword as it bounced at the horses flank and shot him a wolfish grin. "I should keep a sharpening stone nearby, though. We will be busy again next summer."

A flash of joy animated the warrior's features as he digested his chieftain's remark and Solemis looked back towards the city as a low rumble rose from the Senone army there, rising to a roar as the news of their return was passed from man to man.

The three men shared a look and laughed.

"Time to go home!"

Grins and good-natured catcalls welcomed the Horsetails as they rode through the camp, and soon Solemis was dismounting and walking up the rise. Ahead, Brennus was perched upon a rock, swigging from a small amphora of wine and reaching into a bucket which lay cradled between his legs. He threw Solemis a grin as he approached, before launching another stone at the head of Zilach Porsenna's helmeted head which still stood impaled on a spear point nearby. Solemis chuckled and threw his chieftain a light-hearted comment as the pebble arced low and missed the helmet completely.

"You should be able to hit that helmet with your eyes closed by now. Have you not moved since I have been away?"

Brennus returned the smile and indicated that Solemis come and stand beside him with a jerk of his head. They clasped forearms in the warrior greeting and exchanged a look which confirmed the high regard in which each man held the other. Brennus scooped another pebble from the pail and took aim as he handed the amphora across.

"I have a new target now. I can only take a swig when I get one to stay in."

Solemis looked across and laughed as the pebble bounced away from the gaping maw of the old zilach. Brennus cursed at his side and eased himself from his improvised seat, flexing his back with a grunt.

"It started to hang open a few weeks ago, every morning now it is open a little bit more. I was considering taking two swigs for every tooth that I could dislodge but they are still too firmly fixed to the gums."

Solemis ran his gaze over the head of the old ruler of Clevsin. Crixos, chieftain of the Crow clan, had led the charge at the second battle that summer and personally killed the zilach, before the Roman, Numerius had avenged him. The Roman intervention had broken the Laws of Nations and Solemis had travelled to Rome in a forlorn attempt to bring the man to trial. Solemis rubbed his chin as he took in the macabre remains. The skin of the zilach had drawn tightly over the cheekbones and taken on a yellow, waxy pallor. Shrivelled eyeballs stared unseeing from the shadowy depths of their sockets and ropes of torn skin and tendons hung from the severed neck. Without doubt, the zilach had seen better days.

Brennus placed a hand on Solemis' shoulder and indicated the small house which stood nearby as he lowered his voice.

"Come inside and eat; I have other news for you."

Solemis followed on as Brennus beckoned to the remaining Horsetails with his arm.

"Come and eat, boys. You all deserve it."

As his clansmen threw themselves noisily from their mounts, Solemis racked his mind. It was unlike his leader to be reluctant to voice any opinion or fact, and he wondered at the tone which he had used. As the men rushed up and edged behind them in a rowdy mass, Brennus snatched up two hunks of beef from the table there and indicated that Solemis follow him through the smaller door at the rear. Stooping low the men passed through and Solemis flinched as he was hit immediately by the sweet smell of death. Brennus appeared not to notice, and he handed a hunk of meat across as a black haze of flies buzzed around them.

"I will burn these now, but I wanted you to see the lengths which we went to in our efforts to discover who killed your father." Several corpses lay in a tangled heap. Each had been flayed and the shrivelled strips of skin lay discarded in a smaller mound nearby. Brennus tore off a mouthful of beef and waved a fly away with his hand as he chewed. He indicated the buzzing pile of pink, grey and white with a flick of his head.

"These were the black riders."

Solemis looked at him.

"You are sure?"

Brennus snorted.

"One man might be brave enough to hold out as his skin is slowly stripped from him but I doubt that they all would."

Brennus tutted and flicked several flies away from his face.

"Let's go back inside. These things are driving me mad!"

They ducked back through the doorway and the big chieftain closed it and pulled a heavy curtain across. Solemis shrugged.

"They tried to kill you outside Alesia and they were probably the ones who stirred up the Helvetii against us in the mountains. They deserved to die, but why are you showing me?"

Brennus fixed Solemis with a hard stare.

"As I said, men tend to tell the truth as the skin comes away, if only to hasten their end. They all denied that they knew anything of the death of Connos."

Solemis looked at him with disbelief. His father had been cut down from behind in the hills behind their settlement the previous autumn. The clan had swept the area and interrogated the local Etruscan population. They had all agreed that the black riders had been there and that they had come from Clevsin. Added to the previous attempt on Brennus' life, it had been a reason for the punitive campaign against the city that summer and now it would seem that they had been mistaken after all. He shared a look with his chieftain as he fashioned his thoughts into words.

"If they didn't do it. Who did?"

They awoke to a sky as grey and hard as iron. Bitter winds were stripping the last of the leaves and scattering them in waves as the army of the Senones broke camp and prepared to depart from the scene of their triumph. The great festival of Samhaine was almost upon them and they had reluctantly conceded that they would spend this auspicious day away from their families. Although they now lived hundreds of miles away from their ancestral home in the North and the bones of their kin who remained there, the druids had assured them that the spirit world knew no physical boundaries and the souls of their ancestors would be attracted to them wherever they lived.

To a man they felt disappointed that they had missed the chance to display the spoils which they had plundered from the city as their forebears walked among them, but such was the discipline that Brennus had imposed on the tribe that none had complained.

Solemis bit down on a hard crust as he watched his men dismantle the tents and toss them upon the cart. Each clan had been provided with the means of transporting the booty which they had gained over the course of the summer and, although it had been necessary, Solemis regretted that it had removed the sense of martial menace which had accompanied the clans on their arrival.

It was, of course, a small price to pay for the fact that the clans were now fabulously wealthy. The Horsetail's share belonged to Solemis as the chieftain. He would hold a great feast on their return and distribute *potlach* to each man in recognition of their bravery and fighting spirit during the course of the two battles that summer. Not all men, he knew, were inherently brave, but no man wished to appear anything less in the eyes of his woman and children, and the distribution of *potlach* before the fully assembled clan was an important means of kindling fighting spirit.

The sound of hammering came from the ridge line and the Horsetail chieftain looked across and watched the men completing the giant cages as he gnawed idly on his crust. The legs, arms and heads of the giants were already complete and the last of the timber and brushwood was being stacked against the base. He glanced up and sniffed the air. Snow was in the offing, and soon. It was good that they were leaving this day. His ride to Rome had cost them a full month, the time it would take them to transit the mountains now that they were restricted to the pace of the wagons, and the sense of urgency to be away from this place was writ large on the faces of those around him.

Within the hour the wagons had collected in the valley bottom and the men were ringing the cypress grove in their war gear. The knot of trees stood hard on to the site of the second battle of the summer and they all knew that it had been a major factor in the overwhelming victory that day. It had shielded the Crow clan as Crixos had led them in the charge which had routed the Etruscan left wing and wiped out the zilach and his commanders. The enemy phalanx had broken and run the moment that their banners had been beaten down and, although Crixos had fallen in the attack, each man there acknowledged the debt which would need to be repaid to the spirits which inhabited the place before they left for home.

The warriors parted as a group of druids escorted a party of sullen men down from the ridge line. The Etruscan captives had been held within the bowl of a steep depression ever since the battle, surviving on spoiled food and scraps, and the smell of loose bowels hung about them like a shroud. Despite their pathetic state the Senone warriors glowered at them as they passed, heads hung low in shame. They had all witnessed the collapse of the army of Clevsin; no Celt would allow himself to be taken alive if it was within his power to fight on, and they knew the captives to be less than men, men without honour.

Before them the branches of the trees were festooned with ropes, the loop which terminated each one confirming the fears of each man who risked a glance. As the druids began their dedication to Lug, the men were led forward and the massed ranks of Senone warriors set up a low keening sound as the grotesque fruit sprouted on the boughs.

Soon it was finished and the army moved across to the river. It had been the focus of the battle, the place where Brennus had led the army in its fight, and the druids collected there as a further hundred downcast captives were led down the slope towards them.

The tributary had been little more than a collection of shallow pools during the heat of the summer but the autumn rains had restored it to its glory and the central pool was now wide and deep. A score of the druids waded into the shallows and called to the chosen warriors to hand them their shields.

The men had been chosen by their chieftains as a reward for their bravery in the great battle and the faces of the selected warriors shone with pride as they handed them across, basking in the congratulations of their clansmen and friends at the honour shown to them.

The first of the Etruscans were led roughly to the bank as the chief druid intoned a dedication to Teutates, the god of the tribe. The guards shoved them forward into the shallows, and the terrified men were immediately gripped by a pair of russet clad druids. As he was forced forward with a scream, the druids pressed down with shields and waited for the frantic thrashings to lessen and grow still.

Each man met his end as his character dictated. Denied any chance of escape by the mass of Celtic warriors which pressed in on them, most remained stoic to the end, but a few offered wealth for their lives and fewer still managed to find the will to fight and die which had deserted them in battle.

As the sun drew itself a full span above the hills to the East the sacrifice to Teutates were completed and the army moved up to the ridge.

The wicker men had finally been completed the previous evening and the carpenters stood ready with the final cover which would seal the hatch at the base.

There were five of the wicker giants lining the ridge, each one facing towards the city perched on its rocky outcrop. As the army set up a low rhythmic beat using their spears and shields, the remaining prisoners were led across the ridge line to have their worst fears confirmed. They were not to be released; that morning's sunrise had been their last.

Casting wistful looks towards the safety of the city walls across the vale, the Etruscans descended the slope in a shuffling mass. The druids moved forward to parcel the ragged column into five roughly equal groups, and they were herded towards the base of the wicker men by spear wielding Celts. Resigned to their fate, the men struggled to overcome their feelings of dread and pulled themselves into the body of the giants. Crammed full, the wooden bodies began to sprout arms, legs and heads as the increasingly terrified inhabitants clawed at the last vestiges of freedom. A haunting wail came from the prisoners as druids moved forward with brands and began to thrust them into the kindling at the base of each giant. Soaked in fats, the bundles caught immediately and within moments wispy tendrils of smoke began to rise into the morning chill. As the men above began to howl and moan in terror, the first fronds of flame flickered from the faggots and suddenly the fire took hold with a deep *whumph.*

The chief druid cried the dedication to Toranos as the flames rose higher to engulf the lower legs of the wicker men and the Senone warriors filled the air with the staccato beat of their weapons. The first traces of liquid began to seep from the base of the giants as the terror stricken sacrifices lost control of bowels and bladders, the physical manifestation of their fear sputtering and hissing on the burning wood below.

As the flames rose to engulf the men, the victorious Senones turned away to collect their mounts for the long ride home. Solemis found himself near to Brennus and the chieftains detached themselves from the swirling mass with unspoken accord.

They stood for a while in silence, each man comfortable in the other's company. An amphora of wine lay discarded from the previous evening's celebrations and Solemis nudged it with his foot. To his surprise it still felt heavy and he hooked a forefinger through the circular handle and scooped it up. Brennus came back from his thoughts and Solemis handed the wine across with a tired grin. As the leader of the tribe took a deep pull from the broken neck, Solemis ran his eyes across the valley before him. It was, he knew, the scene of his people's greatest triumph, the most complete victory of their arms in the history of the tribe. Bards would spend the winter moving from clan to clan as they collected the tales of the fighting here, entertaining them all with their compositions.

The druids would add another glorious episode to the record of their tribal history, Solemis reflected with pride. He had been there, he had played a pivotal part in the battle. The heroic defence of the left flank by the Horsetail clan was sure to prominent in the accounts. He had brought unprecedented fame and honour to the clan in his first year as chieftain so why did he feel so despondent? Solemis sighed as he took the amphora from his leader before gulping down the dark liquid. Brennus caught his mood and clapped him on the shoulder as men led his mount across to them.

The wicker men were roaring torches now and the terrible screams had petered out. The victory had been gained and the gods propitiated. It was time to go home.

Solemis walked across and smiled weakly as he took the reins from Albiomaros, his *blood genos*. Hoisting himself into the saddle he walked the horse to the head of his clan and turned its head to the East.

As the army put the devastated valley behind them, he glanced down as the first petal of snow appeared on his sleeve.

TWO

The senators reclined in warmth as the world outside shivered. It was the coldest winter in living memory and the tribune reflected on the changes it had wrought to the city as he waited impatiently for the concluding debate.

The first snows had fallen on the incredulous population soon after the Senone delegation had departed the walls and ridden north. At first people had laughed and stared in wonder at the unseasonal fall, but as the snows had begun to collect to drift among the gilded statues of the forum their humour had slowly given way to unease. Cold snaps were not unknown in Rome of course. The occasional wind would sweep the frozen air in from the peaks of the Apeninnus and Chione would scatter her deposits across the seven hills. This year however, the winter had gripped the city like an angry bear and the snow nymph had come to stay.

The citizens had quickly lost their sense of levity as the simple need to survive had preoccupied their waking thoughts. The shortening daylight hours saw a steady procession of carts and individuals leaving the city before dawn and returning with their ever decreasing loads of fuel to feed the home fires. Country folk had taken advantage of the desperation among the city dwellers and a cartload of good quality firewood would have brought them a healthy profit had it not been for the need to pay the local thugs to protect them, usually from the depredations of the very same men. Very soon even this supply had lessened and dropped away as the continuing snowfalls made the roads impassable and the dangers of the city had outweighed any potential for profit.

Yet another patrician was on his feet bemoaning his lot, and Numerius shifted and he listened with disgust. Many of the small workshops which littered the city had closed due to the lack of fuel to feed the fires and furnaces; rents were falling in arrears. The men who worked in such places remained huddled together with their families in the unheated rooms of their insulae. Numerius knew that unless the thaw came soon many more people would start to die of hunger and cold. Already, scant wood supplies had had to be reserved for bakers ovens, and the situation in the poorer areas of the Quirinal was already grim. Increasingly, the hoodlums who were sent by these wealthy landlords to extract rents from the unfortunates were finding whole families dead and beyond caring upon forcing entry to their squalid rooms.

The master of debate caught the senator's eye, and a raised eyebrow at the hopelessness of his cause was enough for him to conclude his address and resume his seat with a self-satisfied grunt. Many there would sympathise with Sulpicius. The gods knew that they were all losing money this accursed winter. Trade had all but dried up as the roads had succumbed to the great freeze. The citizens had watched in wonder as the waters of the

Tiberis itself, the sacred river of the city, had slowly grown sluggish and finally stilled completely as a thick crust of ice gripped the vital artery.

As military tribunes Numerius, along with his brothers Quintus and Caeso, had used the power invested in them to raise a legion of men to keep the road open to the port of Ostia, eighteen miles downstream. By their efforts, grain supplies from Africa had kept flowing into the city despite the cold, and Numerius shook his head in disappointment as he looked back towards Sulpicius.

Quintus Sulpicius Longus had been, like the Fabii brothers themselves, elected to the position of military tribune of the city, but there the similarity ended. Grasping and conceited, Numerius watched as the man sat basking in the congratulations of his friends and he snorted in derision. They could stand the shortfall, and besides, their homes were warm and the public baths still functioned, what did he expect people to do? Many had already sold anything they had considered to be of value at a knock-down price in order to feed their fires and children and were left with nothing. These were fellow Romans after all; most men there realised that a little consideration, a little nobilitas indeed, was expected of them in the current situation.

Despite the icy grip of winter, the Senate House was full, the air thick as the confines of the debating chamber added the body heat of almost three hundred of the nobility to the effects of the underfloor heating. Lamps and torches contributed further to the heat in the room as they fought back the gathering gloom of the short winter day, and Numerius was beginning to find the aromatic scent of the incense which wafted across from the braziers cloying and overpowering. He could wait no longer and he rose from his seat and held the master of debate with a look until the man inclined his head in his direction.

Numerius returned a small nod of thanks and waited patiently as the hubbub made by scores of conversations slowly stilled before beginning his address.

"All of you are aware, I am sure, of the seriousness with which I discharge my duties and responsibilities as a *tribunus militum* of our great city." He paused as a titter arose from the direction of the men of the Sulpicii and their allies. The master of debate shot them a stony glare and held it until they had composed themselves. The gens was a traditional ally of the exiled dictator, Camillus, and thus a natural enemy of the Fabii. Numerius' family had been one of the leading movers in the prosecution of the old general for embezzlement of public funds, the money from which, he now knew, had been used to persuade the Gauls to migrate across the Alpes. Numerius drummed his fingers lightly on a fold of his toga as he waited for the interruption to fade. Finally all was still and he continued.

"As I have already said, before I was interrupted," Numerius shot the men opposite a look of exasperation and they smirked with unconcealed delight. "The Fabii take their responsibilities extremely seriously. It is not our way to occupy the floor of this great house and the precious time of the honoured senators within with tales of woe about the inability of the dead to pay their rent on time." An audible gasp escaped the lips of Sulpicius, and the benches around him were swept by a wave of muttering at the slight. Senators rose to their feet and sought to catch the eye of the master of debate as laughter, catcalls and jeers filled the room. The man flicked up his hand and swept the chamber with an icy glare and, one by one, the senators returned to their seats. The master of debate fixed Numerius with a stare and raised a brow as he indicated that he continue with his address. The message was clear. Both sides had scored hits and the game was square; if he had a point to make he had better make it now or lose the opportunity. Numerius suppressed a smile.

"Despite the fact that people are dying in the great cold, work must still go on. I refer of course to the urgent repairs which have been delayed for lack of funding to the city walls." Further catcalls broke out and Sulpicius crossed his arms and shook his head from side to side in great exaggerated sweeps as those around him hooted and jeered. He pulled himself to his feet and waited for permission to speak but the master of debate averted his gaze and the senator cast an amused glance at his allies and slumped theatrically back to his seat as Numerius resumed.

"I must reiterate the points which I have made on earlier occasions to you here. The Gauls promised to return in the spring and I believe them to be men of their word. They *will* return and we must be fully prepared to meet them. I have met their leaders and seen the army in battle, as have my brothers. Their weaponry is of the highest order and their military acumen is only matched by their ferocity." The Sulpicii and their allies were feigning disinterest as they stared around the room or smoothed the folds of their togas but Numerius pushed on. "I hope and believe that the army of Rome will defeat these invaders before they reach the city but we would be failing in our duty to the citizens who rely on us for their ultimate safety if we did not take precautions against the unthinkable." A gasp of shock rolled around the debating chamber and Sulpicius shot to his feet once again. This time the master of debate appeared to share the feelings of the majority in the room and he indicated that Sulpicius speak with a curt nod as Numerius regained his seat. His brother, Quintus, winced at his side and, leaning across, pursed his lips as he let out a low whistle. "A bit strong brother, if you don't mind me saying. That was a mistake." Numerius grimaced slightly as he reluctantly recognised the truth of Quintus' judgement.

The men of the senate, in fact all those in the city, still held the view of the barbarians from the North which the Fabii had harboured themselves on the road to Clusium the previous summer. What possible threat could a horde of hairy-arsed savages pose to the army of Rome? Their animal charges would dash themselves upon the walls of Roman *disciplina* like storm waves upon a cliff face.

Numerius stole a look across to Sulpicius as he gripped the folds of his toga in the classic pose of a statesman, thumbs tucked behind the fabric, chest puffed out, chin slightly raised, and his heart sank. He had miscalculated badly and lost the day. His enemy began to speak with the calm assurance of a man who knew that the chamber was with him.

"I thank my friend for the concern which he shows for the future of the city, I really do, but I would suggest that the awe and dread in which he holds these barbarians is rather misplaced. I myself, and many of you here today, also saw what can only be described as a collection of their better sort, when the delegation was lodged on the Field of Mars last autumn. Well," his face broke into an amused smile as he looked about the room, "if that was an example of their finest, I think you will all agree that we have little to fear!" A peel of laughter rolled around the room and Numerius sat in stony silence as he noticed that even his natural allies were struggling to suppress a smile. Sulpicius continued, revelling in the moment.

"What a collection of curios they were!" He made a face and nodded as the room dissolved into laughter. "They were large, I will grant you that," he smirked, "but I thought for a moment that I had stumbled upon a travelling troupe of entertainers! Most of them seemed to sport more hair than my horse and more jewellery than my wife!" He leaned forward conspiratorially as the laughter redoubled. "And my wife, as my bookkeeper can confirm, is extremely fond of jewellery! There was one in particular I seem to recall, as big as Hercules with white spiked hair and a semi-naked body painted in bizarre blue swirls. Now he," Sulpicius suddenly drew the humour from his voice as he emphasised his statement with a stab of his forefinger, "he, I pledge before you all now, I will sacrifice on the altar of Hercules myself if he ever returns to our city!" He raised his voice and looked across to the Fabii as they fidgeted uncomfortably. They were the descendants of the god and the significance of the moment was not lost on those in the chamber. Sulpicius would do the deed and honour their ancestor himself if the Fabii felt unable. As his supporters cheered at his side, Sulpicius drove home his advantage.

"We have no fear of these barbarians, Numerius. I propose that we appoint a commander for the defence of the city here and now so that we are not caught unawares when this rampaging horde descends upon us."

A trim senator with a shock of black hair rose immediately and caught the eye of the Master of debate who nodded his consent.

"I nominate Quintus Sulpicius Longus, tribunus militum, as commander of the army of Rome."

The master of debate raised his brow and scanned the ranks of men. He did not have long to wait and another senator shot immediately to his feet. Numerius knew that he had stumbled into a neatly laid trap.

"I second the nomination of Quintus Sulpicius Longus, tribunus militum, for the appointment as commander of the army of Rome."

Loud cheers greeted the announcement, and Numerius chewed his lip in frustration as the master of debate scanned the ranks of the nobilitas seated in an arc before him.

"Are there any further contenders?"

All eyes were turned his way and Numerius indicated that Quintus propose his candidacy with a single jerk of his head. His brother rose and Numerius sensed the reluctance in his movement, but his sense of demanded that he oppose what was beginning to look more like a coronation than a democratic vote.

The nomination was quickly seconded and the master of debate paused and peered about the ranks of senators but no further nominations were forthcoming. He raised his hand and waited until the hubbub subsided.

"Very well, we will take the vote. Those in favour of the appointment of Numerius Fabius Ambustus as commander of the army of Rome for the coming campaigning season?"

Numerius stared straight ahead but, although he was surrounded by the upright figures of his family, friends and allies, experience told him immediately that the noise had been too slight to indicate that they may carry the day. A pair of aides moved their heads in a nodding fashion as they counted the number of senators on their feet. Within moments they seemed to be putting their heads together as they confirmed that their tallies agreed, and Numerius sucked at his teeth in disappointment. The master of debate nodded his thanks as the numbers were reported to him and he cleared his throat.

"The number in favour of Numerius Fabius Ambustus is one hundred and seven."

The announcement was greeted by loud cheers and catcalls from those gathered around Sulpicius, and Numerius exchanged a brief nod of congratulation with his opponent. He recognised that the victory belonged to the guile of his opponent as much as his own bungling performance that day. They were all of Rome after all. He would serve where needed when the time came, as he was sure that it must. The master of debate called for those in favour of Sulpicius to stand and confirm the appointment, the perfect acoustics of the chamber allowing his voice to carry to the furthest reaches of its vaulted magnificence despite the background noise.

A forest of white rose before them and the Fabii rose to leave the chamber as their opponents savoured the moment of victory.

As they passed back through the high bronze doors of the debating chamber the chill wind snatched at them from the forum beyond. Caeso turned to his brother as slaves hurried forward with their *paenula*, the heavy, hooded cloaks of deep winter.

"What do you propose to do?"

Numerius gave a shrug.

"Serve where I am sent, of course. What else can a proud citizen do?"

He turned back as his guards came to his side, ready to escort him back to his home on the Aventine. It had been one of the few benefits of the cold spell that even the *latronum*, the robbers and cut-throats who usually infested the roads and passageways, were holed up somewhere warmer, but it still paid to be sure. He made to leave but paused and turned back as his brothers' men came to their sides.

"I think that Licinia and the girls will be spending next spring and summer at the villa near Ardea. Perhaps you should consider similar arrangements for your own families?"

Numerius left the shade of the porticoed building and stared across the forum to the temple of Jupiter crowning the Capitoline opposite. The sky above was a steely cobalt, as hard as the ice which surrounded them all. Away to the West the sun lay on the horizon as another short winter day drew to a close. There was, he mused, a beauty to the world which was incomparable, even in the depths of the hardest winter.

Snow was falling again, and the hunched forms of a gang of slaves could just be made out on the roof of the building. Several roofs had already given way under the weight of snow in the city and the priests there were taking no chances. Numerius approved. Several of the men had already slipped, or been blown by sudden gusts, to their deaths but this was no time to draw the anger of the Greatest and Best. He shrugged; they were only slaves after all.

Pulling the hood tighter, Numerius lowered his head and trudged off across the deserted forum.

*

The decurion sniggered to himself as he led the men of his *turma* into the town square. Despite his weariness he turned his face to the optio who rode at his side and flashed him a smile.

"We appear to have found the forum. Let's hope that the general's home is as easy to find."

The optio chuckled and returned the smile as the pair took in the rusticity of the place. The grandest building in the 'forum' was a small porticoed building which appeared to be the temple of Jupiter. Constructed from fine creamy limestone, the temple was a scaled down copy of the building which towered above Rome herself and Lucius suspected that it was a gift to the town from their newest and most illustrious resident. Three smaller temples were ranged at intervals around the forum, the age and design of which harked back to the foundation of the town by Greek settlers centuries before. Urging his mount forward, he led the men past the grim line of skeletal trees and up to the door of the house.

Barely more than twenty miles south of Rome, the provincial town of Ardea lay at the terminus of the road to which it had lent its name. In summer the journey would have been a pleasant day's ride but the men of Lucius' turma had taken two as the horses had beaten their way south against the elements. The snowfalls which had plagued the land had finally ceased but the temperature had remained resolutely below freezing and the surface of the via ardeatina, despite the almost complete absence of traffic, had resembled a sheet of burnished silver. Movement had quickly proven too hazardous on its polished surface, and after they had lost a man to a bad fall whilst they still remained within sight of Rome itself, they had abandoned the road and taken to the fields alongside. Thankfully, the frigid winds which had characterised the winter so far had tended to pile the snow into deep drifts as soon as they encountered an obstacle of any sort. By following the valleys which had formed between these drifts, the Romans had managed to weave their way south without further mishap.

They had sheltered for the night in the relative comfort of a barn on one of the many small farms, the *villa rustica* of the countryside which fed the metropolis to the North, and Lucius had been surprised at the quantity and quality of the foodstuffs they had been able to purchase there. The inhabitants of the great city had lost their connection with the land and with it the ability to supply their own food. A city dweller all of his life, he had realised for the first time how thin the veneer of civilisation actually was. At the present time he had been left in little doubt that the benefits of rural living could outweigh the attractions and entertainments of city life by some margin.

Early afternoon on the second day had brought the welcome sight of the *agger,* the fortifications which protected the town, into view on the horizon. Soon after they had passed through the gate, and away from the blinding whiteness which had tormented their eyes for the entirety of the journey.

Now, they stood before the inauspicious gate which led into the island of *Romanitas* which, they had been told by those who had visited the villa of Camillus before them, was the home of the general.

Lucius rapped on the door with frozen knuckles and moments later a small shutter was thrown back and a face appeared.

"Yes?"

"Lucius Antonius Creticus, decurion. I carry a communication for the attention of Marcus Furius Camillus from the commander of the army of Rome, Quintus Sulpicius Longus."

The face before him sniffed, seemingly unimpressed at the news, and he moved closer to the barred opening as his eyes flicked to left and right. Satisfied that the decurion and the men of his turma were alone, the guard regarded him for a long moment before the shutter slid closed with a bang. The door remained closed to them and Lucius exchanged a glance with his optio as the sound of *caligae,* the hobnailed sandals of the Roman legions, carried to them from within. As a freezing gust snatched at them in a final mocking assault, the locking bar was thrown back and the door opened to admit them into a large open courtyard which stood before the building proper.

The grim-faced guard stood to one side and motioned them inside with a jerk of his head and Lucius led his men inside in column. Facing them, on the far side of the courtyard, twenty men armed with circular shields and heavy spears had formed up in a line across the formal entryway to the *domus* and the *atrium* beyond. Arranged on either side of the space, groups of archers had taken position on a series of raised platforms which had obviously been constructed there for just that purpose. A single glance at the manner and bearing of the guards present was enough to tell the decurion and his men that these were experienced soldiers, tough veterans of the siege of Veii and beyond, undoubtedly the general's personal bodyguard who he knew had elected to follow the dictator into exile.

The doorman fell into step beside him and indicated an extensive stable block which stood off to one side.

"You can leave your horses with the slaves over there." He nodded down at the swords which hung at their sides, "and your weapons, too."

Lucius' hand moved instinctively to the handle of his sword but the guard raised a brow and shot him a look of pity.

"If we had wanted you dead, lad, you would already be fumbling for a coin to pay the ferryman."

THREE

The men of the Roman phalanx shifted nervously as the wall of muscle and bronze bore down upon them, screaming their war cries. Instinctively the men in the leading ranks drew closer together, as if the mere act of coming into physical contact with their neighbours would enthuse them with a collective strength.

At the head of the onrushing horses, Numerius ran his eyes along the wall of shields and spears before him and allowed himself a small moment of satisfaction.

The men of his century were clearly afraid of the wall of death thundering down upon them and that was good, he mused, they had every reason to be. But at least they were following his orders now as they began to accept that it was the only way which they could hope to survive.

Almost upon them now, Numerius savagely yanked his reins around and drew up in a cloud of dust and grass. As the following riders wheeled their mounts alongside his own, he craned forward to stab down behind the raised shields of the front rank. The lines wavered but stood firm and moments later he felt a sharp blow to his groin as a cloth-bound spear shaft lanced out in what would have been a killing blow.

The Roman commander disengaged, wheeling his mount as he watched the phalanx begin to push forward into the flanks of the remaining horses. Unnerved by the noise and battered by the shields of the soldiers, all semblance of order fell from the attacking force of riders and they were taken down by well aimed thrusts as the horses turned and twisted in panic.

Numerius climbed wearily from his own horse and returned the grins of the delighted footsoldiers.

"Excellent! Absolutely excellent!"

Numerius' grin widened and the men beamed with pride as he stalked across.

"That's how you do it! That's how you break a charge by barbarian horsemen. With good, Roman *disciplina!*"

He reached to the canteen at his waist and unstopped it. Throwing back his head he emptied the last of the watered wine and sighed with contentment. Upending the now empty container over the grass, he shot the men nearest him a smile.

"It looks like our games are over for the day."

A wave of laughter, broken by cheers and good-natured catcalls rippled along the line as he called out to them.

"One more practice and I will buy the drinks."

The sun was lowering in the sky away to the West in a wash of orange. It had been a long and tiring afternoon, but Numerius reflected with pride on the progress he had made with his century in the short time that the gods had allowed them to prepare.

The winter had seemed interminable. Month followed month without a break from the flesh numbing cold as life in the city retreated and awaited the return of spring. It was a source of great pride to him that the men of Numerius' century had taken it upon themselves to keep the road to Ostia open throughout even the darkest days. Working on a rotating basis they had ensured that supplies from the warmer lands to the South had reached the city and he knew that they had played a large part in avoiding a catastrophe. Nevertheless, the more vulnerable members of society, the old, very young and the poor, had died in their thousands, to be burned en-masse at a weekly held pyre to conserve the dwindling supplies of fuel. It had been, he reflected, one of the few benefits of the constant freezing temperatures that the bodies of those which it claimed could at least be stored in simple storage sheds.

When the thaw had finally arrived it came with a rush, almost overnight transforming the alleyways and thoroughfares of the city from impassable fissures of sheet ice and snow to a raging torrent of melt water. Buildings damaged during the freeze were inundated as the waters poured through, adding to the sense of misery which had gripped the city, but the grit and determination which characterised its citizens had returned with the sun and Rome had quickly shaken herself and got back to work.

A crow cawed overhead as it passed away to the South and Numerius' thoughts returned to the present. Handing his reins to another he hefted his spear and pointed along the midline of the formation.

"Those on the left are with me, the rest form in front of Cassius. Let's have one last go and then, home."

As the men swarmed around him, those assigned to the command of his optio retreated to the edge of the field. Shuffling into their ranks, they faced each other across the field and Numerius glanced across and called to one of his men.

"Secundus, pass the bags forward to the men in the second rank."

The man screwed up his face and reached behind him to scoop up several bags which sagged ominously. Within moments they had been swallowed by the ranks and Numerius called across the heads of the men before him as they waited for the order to begin the advance.

"Second rank. Remember to concentrate on the central point. Everybody else, mark where it lands and follow up with spirit."

Numerius raised his chin and looked out across at Cassius' men. They had begun to move forward and he too inhaled and gave the order to advance. As the final exercise of a long tiring day, he had ordered that neither phalanx break into the customary charge as they neared each other. It was to be one last scrummage, a last 'push of spear' as the men called it, before a well earned drink and a bellyful of hot food back in the city.

The distance between them quickly lessened until he felt the surrounding men brace as they prepared for the shock of contact. It was the perfect moment, and he snorted with amusement as the saw the contents of the bags sail across the gap to spatter the opposing formation. A heartbeat later the shields met with a bone jarring crash and Numerius was elated to find that Cassius' phalanx had held its discipline despite his underhand efforts at disruption.

Well-matched and unable to use their spears to break through, the pushing contest quickly reached stalemate and Numerius called a halt. "That's enough for today, well done everybody." He called across to the front ranks of the formation opposite, as his men pointed and hooted with laughter at the horror stricken men. "Especially the men who were hit by shit. Well done. Remember that we will soon be facing a barbarian army who will use guile and shock tactics to break our formation. I have witnessed a single warrior accompanied by two Greek war dogs shatter a phalanx, but you held firm."

Numerius raised his voice and the men cheered his words.

"We are ready for them. Let them come!"

*

Lightly joined at the wrist by a simple chain of woven hair, the young couple slid from the bank and carefully waded into the waters until they lapped about their waists. Swollen by the last of the melt water from the nearby mountains, Aia gasped and laughed nervously, instantly chilled by the waters which swirled around them as the grinning throng lined the bank and jostled each other for a better view. All adults from among the people of the Horsetails and Aia's clan, the Crow, had contributed a few strands to the weave which symbolised the joining of the two clans in the physical forms of Solemis and Aia.

The melodic tinkle of small bells filled the clearing as the women called the water spirits to them and drove away their malevolent kin.

It was the culmination of the rites that day, and the people instinctively checked and rechecked the silver in their hands as the moment approached.

Brennus, war chieftain of the Senones, stepped forward into the shallows as an expectant hush fell upon the gathering.

"Water spirits accept my sacrifice to you. Hallow their union with health and happiness, warlike sons and strong daughters, that their roots burrow ever deeper in this land."

Reaching inside his purse, he scooped out a handful of gold coins and let them tumble into the cup of the helmet. Most of the men had been to see the helm of Porsena, perched atop the grisly head of the old Zilach of Clevsin after the battle the previous summer, and every man present that day was aware of the honour which the chieftain was showing to the young couple. Brennus lowered the magnificent object beneath the surface and stepped away.

As dozens of clansmen and well wishers from allied clans moved forward to lower sword and spear blades taken from their Etruscan foe into the chill waters, the people on the bank tossed their own pieces of silver into the watercourse where they straddled the couple like rain. As the last of them fell, Solemis glanced across at his new *gwraig,* the woman who would bear his children.

"That's enough for me; if I stand in this freezing water much longer I won't be able to complete the most important ritual," he chattered with what would have to pass for a frozen smile.

Aia giggled as they moved back to the bank and Brennus stood aside as they walked between lines of chanting warriors, back towards the settlement. The smell of wood smoke and roasting flesh drew them on and, as the excited chatter of their guests rose in their wake, Solemis and his gwraig crested the rise and moved towards the smiling figure of Caturix. Aia's brother had become the chieftain of her clan on the death of their father, Crixos, at the battle outside Clevsin, and Solemis' good friend smiled as he held out the twin handled cup for them. Taking a handle each they drank together from the vessel in an action which symbolised the moment when Aia passed from Crow clan to Horsetails.

Caturix pushed open the door to the roundhouse and a great cheer rent the air as Solemis swept Aia up and carried her inside.

"When do we ride?"

Brennus shot Solemis a wink as his reply caused a ripple of good humoured laughter to run around the group.

"As soon as you regain your strength."

The sun was lowering in the West, washing the sky there the colour of blood. The group of men clustered around the fire knew it to be a sign from the gods and they hoped that it was Roman blood which they could see there and not their own. They had spent the winter cooped up in their settlements as the snows fell and the winds blew. Throughout the darkest months all but the most urgent journeys had been curtailed as the clans huddled about their hearths and listened with pride as the warriors told of the parts they had played in the previous year's fighting. With the coming of spring, thoughts had turned to the upcoming campaign against the new enemy in Rome, and messengers had crisscrossed the gentle hills of Umbria as the clans gathered their strength and prepared for war.

The uncertainties of the coming year had caused Solemis to bring forward his wedding plans as it became apparent that the new enemy in Rome would prove to be a much harder foe to defeat than the Etruscan one the previous year. He had seen the city of course, and knew it to be formidable. Perhaps more than most of the Celtic leaders there, Solemis realised that the confidence bordering on arrogance of the men that they had met so far was not entirely misplaced.

Their stores and pens groaning with Etruscan grain and cattle they had been in a good position to hold such a feast and Brennus had wisely chosen the day to assemble the leaders of the clans to plan the forthcoming campaign. He tore a mouthful from the hunk of beef in his hand and wiped the grease from his chin as he spoke again.

"The only decision we need to make is if we are to split our force before we approach the city. The Umbrians tell me that there is a pass with a good road further south which leads directly to Rome. It will give the Romans a headache and ease our supply problems but it will also divide our force in unknown territory." He ran his eyes around the group as he paused and waited to hear their advice. Sedullos was the first to speak and the eyes of the chieftains lit up with pride as he came straight to the heart of the matter.

"We can put twenty-thousand warriors into the field, men who tore the heart out of a southern army only a few months ago. How many men can the Romans field?"

Brennus grinned.

"Everyone agrees, Etruscan prisoners, Umbrians and their neighbours the Piceni, that the core of the Roman army numbers six thousand. They can field more if they consider it an emergency and they have a treaty of mutual aid with the surrounding cities, but I have thought of a plan to keep them occupied as we approach. From what Solemis saw when he led our delegation to the city last year, they seem to think that we are some kind of curiosity sent for their amusement, like dancing bears or fighting dogs." He grinned wolfishly as they all chuckled at his conclusion. "They are about to discover that these dogs have a nasty bite!"

Caturix cut through the laughter.

"Are the Umbrians offering to supply the army which moves through their land?"

Brennus nodded as he picked at a strand of meat lodged in his teeth.

"The Umbrians and Romans have a bit of a strange relationship. They seem to fight most years but never let that interrupt the trade which passes between them. The road which they have offered to lead us to they call the *via salaria,* after the salt trade which is its main reason for being there." He shrugged. "It's not as well made as the road which led us all across to Clevsin last year but it is perfectly passable, especially by mounted warriors." He flicked a look up at Solemis. "I was thinking to send Solemis' Horsetails across with a strong force of mounted men while I lead the main army back across the via cassia which we used previously. It's more direct and the quality of the road will enable us to resupply the army easily from home if we need to." He glanced about as he waited for their response. Solemis made to speak but Sedullos cut in again.

"What would Solemis be doing with all of our mounted men? Is it wise to strip the army of its eyes and ears?"

Brennus shook his head.

"I am only thinking of a force of," he pulled a face and looked across to Solemis, "five hundred or so?"

Solemis nodded that he agreed with the size of the detachment. After the actions the previous summer, all the war leaders had recognised that the Horsetails and their chieftain had become the premier mounted warriors among the clans, the best of the best.

"Five hundred is a good number. It is large enough to be considered a mounted army but not so large that it would be too difficult to move quickly and live off of the land." He grinned. "I can do a lot of damage with such a force."

Brennus met his gaze and nodded in agreement before continuing to outline his plan.

"It was a good question, Sedullos, and you would be right to worry if all of the mounted warriors left us, but most of the mounted men will remain with the main army. All I want is a fast moving column to cause as much havoc in the region of the city as possible as we approach. All of our information confirms that the Romans do not have a large number of mounted warriors. They rely on the phalanx to crush their enemies like the other people here in the south, so a mounted force causing mayhem in their rear should be able to draw these away from the city." His eyes sparkled as he threw them a cold-hearted smile. "Rather than losing our own outriders we shall be denying the Romans the use of their own. They will blunder forward until we can take them at a place of our choosing." He took a swig of cervesia and swept the cup in a circle. "These phalanx formations that they use in the South are ridiculous." He paused as he made a fist and pushed it into his stomach. Belching softly he continued. "Thousands of men gathered together in great squares, trundling all across the field. Only a small number of them actually get to fight and they need to agree a suitable place that is large enough and level enough for the battle beforehand or they can't fight at all." He leaned forward and held them with a stare. "I am told that these Romans are the most dangerous of the races which live here in the South. Beat them, and beat them well, and we can live here in peace forever."

The group nodded their agreement as Solemis asked a final question.

"When do you want me to leave?"

Brennus threw him a mischievous smile and arched a brow.

"I take it that everything went according to plan in the roundhouse earlier?"

The group laughed at his discomfort, and Caturix made a ribald suggestion as Solemis nodded with a self conscious scowl.

The chieftain of the tribe grinned.

"Why are you still here then?"

Their laughter was interrupted as the first signs of a disturbance near the entrance to the settlement carried across to the group. Instinctively their hands moved to their sword hilts as they craned their necks to see above the packed revellers. Armed warriors were hurrying across to reinforce the men on duty there and Solemis called out as Albiomaros came by.

"Genos, what is happening?"

The big man, the new champion of the clan, held up a hand to indicate that there was nothing to fear.

"It is Anastasios and his sons," he shot them a smile as he passed. "I will go and save them from a lynching!"

Solemis turned back to explain.

"They are Umbrians who live in the next valley, good people. I have been befriending them over the course of the winter."

Brennus nodded that he approved. It was still natural for the Senone people to see any southerners as their enemies but that would need to change if they were ever to become accepted in these lands.

"You had better get down there, Solemis. We can speak later. Having your neighbours lynched at the wedding feast is perhaps not the best custom to introduce down here!"

Solemis flashed a grin and followed on in Albiomaros' wake. Ahead, he could see that his friend had placated the armed warriors there and was embracing Brizio, Anastasios' eldest son. With practically the entire leadership of the tribe congregated in one small valley it was natural that many of the warriors were a little on edge. War was looming and an overwhelming attack here could see the Senones decapitated at a single blow. As the crowd relaxed once again and edged away, Solemis walked up to the group and smiled in greeting.

"Anastasios, you are welcome here." They gripped forearms in greeting as Solemis acknowledged the man's sons with a nod. "Brizio, Rodolfo, welcome to my home."

The Umbrian was holding the reins of a fine looking horse which flared its nostrils and tossed its head as if it was fully aware that it was the centre of attention. Anastasios smiled again and presented the reins to the delighted Senone.

"Solemis, I would be honoured if you would accept my wedding gift to you."

Solemis grinned with delight as he took the proffered reins, moving forward to run his hand along the animal's head and neck. As black as jet, the horse shone with a deep lustre which seemed to lend a silky liquidity to its movements.

"Anastasios, it is I who is being shown honour here, as you well know. He is beautiful. You have my thanks, it is a noble gift worthy of you and your family."

The Umbrian beamed.

"He is no ordinary horse, my friend. This horse has been specially trained for war by my son, Rodolfo, the greatest horseman in all of Umbria."

Solemis was still admiring the sheen on the flanks of the animal but looked across to the young Umbrian and smiled.

"You have my thanks also, Rodolfo. What is his name?"

Rodolfo smiled brightly at the compliment. He was sure now that the gift would have the desired effect on the Celt and he began to move the conversation in the direction that he had intended if the opportunity arose.

"I named him *Tantibus,* what you call a nightmare I believe, when he was a foal." He chuckled and moved across to caress the horse's ears as he spoke. The mutual affection between man and animal was obvious. "He *was* a nightmare to handle at first and I thought that I had finally met my match, but I persevered and one day I realised what the problem was." He laughed as he took a handful of grain from a sack and let the animal munch contentedly from his hand. Rodolfo flicked a look back at Solemis as he continued. "Big, bad, Tantibus, the terror of the corral. The horse that they said was untrainable and vicious. That same Tantibus was afraid of his own shadow!" He laughed again as the horse nuzzled into him. "Sometimes it happens when a stallion is the natural leader of a herd. He sees the shadow as a rival and will never turn his back on it." Rodolfo shrugged. "Sometimes he is still wary of it, but not so much now. Now he is fully grown he is not so concerned, he knows that no other horse is his equal."

Solemis reached inside the feed sack and offered a handful of oats up as he repeated the name to make sure that he had it correctly.

"Tantibus?"

Rodolfo nodded.

"It would be no problem if you wanted to change his name. He is very intelligent, he would pick it up in no time."

Solemis snorted and shook his head as he ran his hand across the downy muzzle of the horse.

"No, Tantibus is a fine name. We shall keep it, eh boy?" He glanced back at Anastasios as Albiomaros' laughter boomed out across the valley. Berikos had come down to see the horse and the pair of them were already sharing a joke at someone's expense.

"You said that Tantibus is a war horse. In what way?"

Anastasios' eyes widened in surprise.

"He has been specifically trained for war. He will bite and kick the enemy at your command as well as many other things. I know that you are fine horsemen, I assumed that you would have similar horses in your own army."

Solemis shook his head in wonder as he struggled to control his excitement. His own horse obeyed his commands, but that was all. Already they had bested the southern horsemen at every turn, such horses could make his clan invincible. He turned back to Rodolfo.

"How long will it take you to supply me with a dozen such horses?" Before the Umbrian could answer, Solemis added. "And I would need you to train the riders. Silver is no object, but I will need it done immediately."

Smiles spread across the faces of the Umbrians and it was obvious to Solemis that they had known all along that the Celts did not possess such mounts. He had reacted as they had expected him to and he knew that the price required for the horses would not be in precious metal. He grinned as his neighbours shared a look of satisfaction; it seemed that the young Umbrians also had a taste for war. Rodolfo sucked in air as if deep in thought.

"Twelve fully trained war horses." He shook his head and pulled a face. "I could not supply so many my friend before, what," he paused and shared a look with his kinsmen before turning back with a wicked smile, "noon tomorrow? I have to celebrate a neighbour's wedding tonight and I may not make it home until morning!"

They shared a laugh as Solemis indicated that they follow him with a flick of his head.

"Come and share my food and drink. I will introduce you to Brennus and the other clan chieftains. If we are to ride to war together it is the very least that I can do."

FOUR

The brothers exchanged a worried look. The land was now little more than a green and yellow smear to the East; very soon it would dip below the horizon completely. They knew that Tereno would be testing the providence of Manannan if they ventured any further.

The older man laid a kindly hand on the boy's shoulder and he turned and instinctively watched his father's lips.

"Terkinos, shin up the mast and take a look around. Sing out if the coastline grows any fainter."

Tereno's face broke into a smile and he winked at the boy.

"What? You thought that I missed that look?"

Terkinos flashed his father a smile and shimmied up the *Dolfinn's* stubby mast. The wide sail was flapping like a mad thing in the fitful wind, but once clear of the greasy woollen sheet the air was as clear as spring water and he felt that he could see to the ends of the earth. The last dark grey clouds, torn and shredded by the great storm which had battered the coast for most of the previous week, were hurrying away to the south-west, and Terkinos gulped down a lungful of the salty air with a sigh. Despite the danger, he had imbibed his love of the wild seas off Iberia with his mother's milk, it was in his blood now, a very part of his being.

Curling his legs around the trunk, he gripped the masthead and squinted ahead. Turning his face back to the deck he called out in his distinctive burr.

"It looks like they are slowing down again and one of them is waving to us to hurry along with his flipper!"

A deep rumble of laughter came from Tereno as he shielded his eyes from the glare and stared upwards. "Yes, son, Sea Wolves are very helpful like that. They always show me where to fish," he exchanged a grin with Terkantu as his eldest wrestled with the steering oar. "At least, they do when the faeries are too busy!"

His youngest son was ever the joker and popular with all in the settlement, despite his deafness. It had been almost five winters since the accident now and they had come to accept that his hearing would never return, although they gave thanks daily at the shrine to Manannan that the sea god had allowed Terkinos to return from the depths. It had been on one of the boy's first trips to sea that the accident had happened. A sea monster had been caught in the net and young Terkinos had been swept over the side as the grab lines ensnared his legs. Carried beneath the waves, his horrified father and brother had all but given him up for lost when Manannan came to his rescue. Terkinos had resurfaced, badly cut and bleeding from both ears and, although the lacerations had healed to leave his body a crazy web of scars, the damage to his hearing had been total and permanent.

Tereno looked at the sun and pursed his lips. It was midmorning now and the days were already growing noticeably shorter. He would have to turn back very soon whether there was a rich shoal of *sardinas* ahead or not. The mighty storms which swept in to lash the coastal settlements at this time of year rarely came alone. They could expect another at any time and he wrestled with his conscience. He was placing his family in danger, but it really did seem as if the Sea Wolves were leading them on.

They had been just off the coast when they had picked up the trail, the screaming tumult of gulls marking the position of a rich shoal to any fisherman with a practised eye. It had been Terkinos who had first spotted the pack of wolves herding the shoal before them, and they had held off to wait until the great sea hunters had eaten their fill and moved away. Caught up in the chase, they had not noticed how far they had sailed until it had almost been too late, and Tereno spat over the side in disgust as he came to what he knew to be the only sensible decision. The wind was rising again and spindrift was beginning to curl from the crests of the rollers. He cursed and banged his fist on the mast to gain his son's attention. The young man looked down and Terkinos mouthed his decision. "Terkinos. Come down, we need to turnabout. Even a deck full of sardinas are not worth our lives."

Terkinos nodded that he understood, and his father paused and looked on him with pride. He was as fine a looking man as any in the village and certainly not the fool that some of the village children seemed to think. A decade at sea had shaded his skin a golden bronze and corded his arms and shoulders with layers of muscle. His hair was testament to his mother's people and the dark strands whipped forward in the gusting breeze. Despite the lad's handicap, he would find him a fitting *gwraig* if he had to search every village along the coast. He sighed and looked back to Terkantu.

"Bring her about. Let's get back, it will take the rest of the daylight hours to tack into the teeth of the headwind as it is."

Terkantu nodded and braced as he pulled the big oar into his chest. The bows of the *Dolfinn* slowly began to come about as Tereno unlashed the braces and prepared to heave on the spar, altering its angle to the wind. He glanced up at the masthead, surprised that his son was not back on the deck, and kicked the mast to gain his attention.

"Terkinos come on, let's go. I need you to play out the other brace."

He shuddered as a dark cloud moved across the face of the sun, throwing them into shade. As the watery light faded, he felt a knot of anxiety tighten, and he chastised himself for being led out to sea during the season of storms. His mood had darkened as suddenly as the day, and he snapped out impatiently as his sense of anxiety grew.

"Terkinos, get down here, we need to go!"

To his surprise his son barely seemed to acknowledge his words and he quickly returned his gaze ahead of the boat. Terkinos jumped up and slapped his son's foot, angrily.

"Terkinos!"

The boy moved his head to one side and called down without shifting his eyes from the sea.

"There is a raft of some sort ahead of us, the wolves are circling it."

Tereno wrinkled his brow and exchanged a look of exasperation with Terkantu.

Terkinos finally looked down and the pair could see the bewilderment writ large on his face. A feeling of dread crept upon him as he began to sense the hand of the gods in the events of the day.

"A raft? Is it empty?"

The boy shook his head.

"There is a druid standing on it. She's waving at me!"

Catumanda made to open her mouth and winced with pain. The iron-like taste of fresh blood played on the tip of her tongue and she instinctively flicked it forward to moisten her parched lips. Forcing her eyelids apart, an involuntary groan escaped her as the cracked and taut skin protested at her movement. A shadow detached itself from a corner of the room and a blinding light flashed for a heartbeat as a door was swiftly opened and closed. She rested her eyes again but a kindly voice at her elbow made her start.

"Hello, druid. My name is Ama."

Catumanda opened her eyes once again and blinked a she attempted to focus on her visitor. The woman smiled reassuringly and began to dab the druid's cracked and swollen lips with a small damp piece of wool. Catumanda sucked hungrily at the fluid but Ama laid a hand on her brow and made a soothing sound.

"There, there…slowly, slowly," she purred, "you are not the first person we have saved from Manannan's hall. Take a little at a time. If you drink too quickly it will kill you."

Catumanda nodded weakly that she understood and Ama's face broke into a warm smile.

"We will see how you are later tonight." She dabbed again. "Perhaps we can try some fish broth then. My daughter has gone to fetch the master, they will be back soon."

Ama rose and walked across to refill the bowl and Catumanda used the opportunity to take in her surroundings. She was lying in a bed, covered by what looked, and smelt, like a bearskin. The hut itself was not unlike the roundhouses she knew from home, although the walls here were made of stone, rather like the ones which she had seen in Ordovicia on her journey to the Spirit Isle with Ruffos and Clop.

Despite the pain it produced, she allowed herself a smile at the memory of her travelling companions and imagined them safely back in the valley outside Tigguocobauc. The big carter was unloading great cheeses of chedwr while his son and daughter played happily and Alwena compared the southern effort unfavourably to her own, onion flavoured, variety.

A circular hearth was piled high with burning logs and the sweet smell of pine pervaded the room as it burned, the smoke rising in wisps to blacken the roof of thatch.

Ancient leather hinges creaked as the door opened, and a rectangular pattern of light appeared on the earthen floor of the hut as Ama's daughter returned with their master.

Catumanda tried to push herself upright as the outline of a man appeared in the opening, but Ama had returned and she laid a hand gently on her shoulder.

"Stay down, mistress," she chuckled. "We don't want anything popping over the top!"

The woman's master had reached the bedside and Catumanda was overjoyed to recognise that he wore the garb of a fellow druid. The man laughed gently at Ama's remark and sat on the stool.

"I am afraid that your clothing was beyond saving when Tereno and his lads brought you ashore. I had them burned when a few of the women were washing the salt from your hair and body." He smiled again. "I had a supply of the same wool for my own robes and I instructed one of the women to use your old garments as a pattern before they were disposed of. They should be ready soon. But!" he exclaimed with a flourish, "I do have these." The druid held up Catumanda's crane skin bag and druid's staff. "How you managed to keep them from the shipwreck I can't imagine. The gods must have held you under their protection."

The man opened his mouth to launch into his next revelation but Catamanda placed her hand on his sleeve, causing him to pause. Her mind still felt turgid after her long sleep, but she craved the answer to two questions and her parched throat managed to rasp the first, despite the discomfort.

"Philippos?"

The druid slapped his forehead, melodramatically.

"Forgive me, the boy is well, considering. He is not yet up and about, but he has eaten." Catumanda winced again as her smile tore open her salt ravaged lips. The blood helped her to moisten her mouth and she pointed at him weakly.

"What is your name?"

He grinned and sat up proudly.

"I am sorry I thought that Ama would have told you."

A voice came from the shadowy depths of the roundhouse, and Catumanda recognised that it was the voice of a woman who was used to dealing with the grinding cheeriness which flowed from the man sat before her.

"She has just woken, master. Remember?"

The druid waved a hand in the air, lifted a cheek, visibly strained and farted with a grunt of pleasure.

"Of course, of course." He shook his head again in wonderment as his mind drifted to the act of her survival. "They told me that they found you adrift on the hatch cover of a large ship. You must have some story to tell, I can't wait to hear it!"

Her brother druid seemed about to ask, despite her condition, and Catumanda decided that she had grown beyond caring what his name was. Her skin was taut and painful, and a wave of nausea swept her as her body suddenly seemed to realise that it had finally stopped rising and falling with the motion of the waves. She moved a hand to touch him lightly on the sleeve once again and beckoned that he come closer. He lowered his head and smiled warmly.

"Was there something else?"

She licked her lips with a bloody tongue so that her voice would carry, before replying in a tormented croak.

"Go away."

Catumanda stood as Ama moved around her body, gently applying the balm to her sore and lacerated skin. Although still tight and as shiny as an autumn apple, the pain was far less now and she was beginning to feel her old self again. The druid's name, she discovered the next day, was

Olindico O Olinoco, although after enduring half a day of her tortured attempts at pronunciation they had agreed 'Lindo' would suffice.

He was sat now beside the hearth sharing a joke with young Philippos, and she looked again with pride on the boy. Despite the pain, it had been one of her proudest moments when she had learnt that he was alive and well. The faith which the lad had always displayed in her on the *Alexa* was touching, and her last promise to Hesperos that she would take care of the boy as they faced the power of the storm had been fulfilled.

The prolonged exposure to sun and sea had taken a terrible toll on her pale northern skin, but she was slowly recovering under the expert care of Lindo and Ama. Philippos of course had come through the ordeal in much better shape, his olive skin and youthful powers of recovery responding well to the care and good food which had been lavished on them since they had arrived back on land.

Ama moved around to the front of her body and knelt before her as she cradled the bowl in the crook of her arm. Catumanda chuckled to herself as the woman flushed and looked anywhere but straight ahead as she applied the unction to the folds of her skin.

Neither of them knew how long they had been cast adrift on the hatch cover, but it had certainly been many days. It had been over a week since the storm had blown itself out and they must have drifted north with the current for many miles.

The sodden wool of her clothing had rubbed large areas of her skin raw, and Lindo had prepared the balm using his knowledge as a druid. The application had become a daily ritual which she looked forward to, and Catumanda was pleased to find that the pain grew less each time.

She suppressed a giggle as Ama finally reached the area which the druid now knew she always put off until last. If Lindo's servant was anything to go by, the women here in the south were far more reticent about being seen naked than those at home. She herself had grown up in Camulodunon, and the young women there had certainly never bothered whether anything was 'popping over the top' or not.

Ama cleared her throat and glanced up, apologetically.

"I need to, erm...I need to do the cracks and crevices around the erm... around the, your..."

Catumanda could see the discomfort in the other woman's eyes, and she moved her legs apart and asked a question to take Ama's mind off her task.

"What is in the balm, Ama? I can smell honey, but there is something more."

Ama looked up, thankful for the interruption, and the druid choked off a laugh as she nodded downwards.

"I should look where your fingers are going if I were you," Catumanda reminded her. "Before both our days are ruined."

Ama's mouth dropped open and she quickly looked back as colour flushed her cheeks. Catumanda exchanged a smile with Lindo and spoke again to the flustered woman.

"Is it some kind of oil?"

Ama nodded vigorously as she quickly completed her task.

"Yes, it is the oil from a certain part of a fish. We mix it with the honey and it is good for many things."

Catumanda thanked her and slipped into the linen robe which Ama had found for her. Soon her skin would be healed enough to bear the weight and feel of wool and then she would continue with her quest.

Her dreams were infrequent now, but she knew that the gods would not be satisfied until she had visited each of the individuals or locations which had been revealed to her in the cave beneath the Spirit Isle. She wondered on the images again as she took her place with the others and spooned her broth.

The boy, Dun, had been the first, followed by the terrible head of the monster on the beach. She had thought for a while that they might be one and the same but they had only led her to the white cloud which had been revealed as the old Greek trader, *Alexa*. Despite her wretched condition, she had almost cried with joy when she recognised the man at the top of the mast of the fishing boat which had saved them. The raven haired man had first appeared to her in a moment of terror beneath ground in the Spirit Isle and she had been shocked to see his image included along with those of her dreams in the cave later. She had been led to this place. The gods could well have sent the fierce storm which had sunk the Greek ship, and she felt a stab of guilt that she might have been indirectly responsible for the deaths of Hesperos and his crew, men who had shown her nothing but kindness. Only the mountain of fire remained, and she wondered idly if it could be found here in Iberia.

Catumanda purred as the warmth of the soup relaxed her. She really was beginning to reclaim her strength and she looked across the flames to her host.

"How long will it be before my new moon blade is ready?"

Lindo shrugged.

"Quite some time, I would guess. I told the smith that you would not be needing it for a while."

She drew back her head in surprise.

"But you gave him the drawing which I did for you?"

The druid put his bowl down and looked at her with what she regarded as an almost fatherly eye.

"Catumanda, you are not up to leaving any time soon. There will be no ships passing through the Pillars of Hercules this side of spring. The seas along this coast are killers of men." He paused and arched a brow; "and women. You of all people should be aware of that fact. No, it's out of the question," he continued as the anger began to mount within her. "I have told everyone that you will be our guest here until next spring."

He picked up a fresh faggot from the pile at his side and tossed it into the flames, humming to himself contentedly as he arranged the bundle to his satisfaction with a stick.

Catumanda was a full druid now and she bit back a retort as her anger threatened to flare. The gods had led the fishermen to her for a reason and her brother druid should understand that. Besides, she would let no man tell her what was or not 'out of the question'. Ama and Philippos sensed the change in mood immediately, and paled as they watched her struggle to contain her emotions. She placed her bowl beside her as Lindo happily poked at the embers.

"How far is it to the metalworker's forge?"

The druid glanced up and the smile fell from his face as he finally caught the mood around the hearth.

"A full day's walk. Why?"

She nodded.

"Ensure that my new clothes are here at sunrise. We will set out after breakfast."

The trio paused as the path approached the crest of the spur and looked back at the sea. Despite the lateness of the year the weather was set fair, visibility stretching away for miles. Below them the River Dubro, shepherded within its steep sided valley, snaked westwards until it emptied its waters, ribboned with silt, into the sea.

Catumanda took a last look at the wide ocean and imagined the *Alexa* ploughing its way south only weeks before. Of those on board the wide bellied trader, only she had known that it was crewed by those about to die, and she smiled sadly as she brought a picture of the men back into her mind.

The brawny owner and his mate, Hesperos and Markos. She had watched as they grasped forearms in a final act of friendship as the killer wave had engulfed the ship. Arion, the gangly 'coxscomb', so proud of his silver beard rings and colourful *chiton* work shirts. Poor Hektor, never to lay eyes on the boy he would name for his own father.

She moved her gaze across to the fishing village which hugged the near shore. Cale was a nondescript collection of huts and animal pens much like hundreds of others along the coast. Fishing boats, their colourful upturned prows in ordered ranks as they lay on the beach as the nets dried after a day's work.

At least one family there had cause to thank the gods that the red haired druid had visited them. She had come to the home of Terkinos the previous evening. Despite her misgivings, the power of the spirits had been strong. These were, after all, Celtic lands, and she was soon harnessing that power, channelling the life force of mother earth and father sky through her body and into the raven haired boy.

His hearing restored, the debt repaid, Catumanda turned and put Cale behind her.

FIVE

The Bel Tree stood abandoned, still festooned in its gaily coloured streamers, as the men mounted their dark geldings and turned their heads to the East. It was the second day of summer and the people were still weary from the previous day's celebrations, but all were present as they collected together to wave their men off to war.

Aia moved among them, passing up cups of cervesia to the grateful warriors as they basked in the admiration of their clansmen and Solemis felt a kick of excitement as he watched her move. Her blood was late in coming, only by a few days, but she assured him that it was unusual and he sent a prayer to the gods that she really was with child. He smiled to himself as the men took the cups from her with self conscious nods. She was already a popular and valued member of the clan and if she was with child it was no accident, the gods knew he had tried often enough!

Eventually, her duties fulfilled, she came to his side and he bent low and, scooping her up effortlessly, they shared a last kiss as the women of the clan began to ululate and follow the slowly moving column. Pausing at the stream which marked the border of their lands the warriors turned back and raised their spears in salute. Their last wistful look up the valley took in all that they held dear in the world. Their *gwraig,* other clansmen and women, children running here and there, caught up in the excitement of the moment. One last look at the ochre caps of the roundhouses nestling among the greens and browns of the southern summer and Solemis turned Tantibus' head to the South and dug in his heels.

The road approached the border at a tangent before turning south for the last mile as it hugged the eastern bank of the River. Solemis led the great column of Senone warriors towards the crossing place ahead as he scanned the bridge for signs of life. A small hut lay off to one side, a thin grey line of smoke issuing from its roof line, and he watched it with relish as he waited for the occupant to come to life. Every crossing point here seemed to contain a man whose only function in life was to take silver from travellers for the mere act of travelling. It was a custom which bemused the Celts who seemed to value their freedoms far more than the people in the new lands. Finally a small figure emerged into view and Solemis exchanged a grin with Albiomaros as they saw the surprise and shock register on the face of the official.

The day was glorious, with all the bitterness of the winter months now but a rapidly receding memory, and their spirits were high as they gained the small stone bridge and clattered across. The River Anio marked the border here between the lands of Rome and those of the Umbrians and the chieftain reined in before the nervous looking man. He smiled, disarmingly.

"How much?"

The Roman shrank back, obviously hoping that one of his guards would challenge the column of shaggy giants who had appeared before their sleepy outpost and the Celts laughed at their reluctance to do so. They could hardly be blamed. Neither were obviously fighting men, and although they were well armed it was plain to all that they had allowed the more sedentary aspects of their duties here affect their waistlines. Solemis smiled again and cocked a brow. His command of the Latin tongue was now absolute and he was beginning to find to his surprise that he relished every opportunity which came his way to use it. It really was a quite melodic language.

"I asked you how much. Did you not hear me?"

Giving up all hope of aid from his guards, the Roman official looked back along the great column and cleared his throat as he replied.

"Ten *aes…*"

Solemis twisted in his saddle and cast a look back at the Umbrian, Brizio.

"Is that a lot?"

Brizio shook his head slowly in mock disappointment.

"An *aes* is a small bar of bronze. The Romans do not use coins like civilised people."

Solemis turned back.

"My friend tells me that is not enough."

The Roman sighed and he held out his hands.

"Fifteen *aes…*"

Solemis shook his head and drew his sword with a flourish.

"More."

With a final scowl at his statuesque guards the man sighed.

"Thirty *aes*. That is all that we have here."

The tax collector indicated that one of the guards fetch the bronze from the hut as Solemis studied the man. He fairly oozed the sense of superiority which had been so apparent in all of their dealings with the citizens of Rome so far. Even the common people had swarmed out onto the area known as the Field of Mars to gawp and poke fun at he and his men the previous autumn. He had not felt hatred towards the city and its inhabitants until this moment but the man's demeanour had caused a change within him. Solemis waited until the guard emerged with a bag of tablets and indicated that he hand it up to his clansman, Druteos. A glance back at the tax collector served to seal the man's fate.

"We are twice the size of you and your pathetic guards, wear finer clothing and carry superior arms and armour to that which I have seen worn by even those you call patricians, yet you look upon us like beasts and call us barbarians." He sniffed with disdain and the man shifted uncomfortably as he began to realise that he had been unable to keep the scornful look from his features. He was now in deep trouble and he knew it. Solemis continued.

"I was going to let you live to carry the news of our arrival back to your masters in the city, but I have decided that you must be a fool." Solemis' sword flicked out to take the man in the throat and he reached down and wiped the blood from the tip on the Roman's shoulder as he slumped forward, choking. The Senone chieftain glanced down at the figure which was settling onto the roadway and shook his head wearily as the blood pumped out to darken the dust there.

"The world has enough fools already. I dare say that you won't be missed."

The sudden act of violence seemed to spur the guards into action and, dropping their weapons they made off across the field to the rear of the hut. The field had been newly sown and the men in the column roared with laughter at the overweight Romans' attempts at flight. The clay soils near the riverbank were glutinous and soon the men were barely moving forward as their feet began to resemble balls of sticky mud. When one of the men fell forward into the ooze, Solemis grimaced as the entire column hooted and cried with laughter. He was the only Senone on the Roman side of the Anio and already the raid was beginning to descend into farce. He wheeled Tantibus about so that the men could see his expression and snapped an order.

"Berikos, Galatus, ride those bastards down and leave them nothing but a red smear in the soil. This is an invasion not a game!"

His clansmen nodded and kicked in as those close enough to hear their leader looked at the ground in embarrassment. Solemis called out across the bridge as Berikos began to wheel his mount across the field.

"What's funny?"

Solemis let the question hang as an uncomfortable hush fell upon the column. He let the silence stretch until even the cries made by the dying guards seemed to have lost their appeal.

"That's right, nothing. This is a war and the first of thousands has just died." He paused again and waited for Berikos and Galatus to regain their positions before continuing. "When you cross this bridge you will enter the lands of the Romans. They think of us as little more than beasts of the forest and if they don't yet hate us I aim to ensure that they very soon will. When you cross this bridge look at the man lying here and remember that if you treat this raid with anything less than total commitment you will end up just like him."

Solemis inhaled deeply. He was beginning to regain his composure and he was aware that he could easily go too far. Each man here owed allegiance to his clan first and foremost; these were not citizen armies like those in the South. They would fight for personal reward and reputation under a leader they followed voluntarily but he wanted to drive the message home. He had seen the Romans up close and knew just how dangerous they were.

"For many of you this will be a new kind of war and you will need to discipline yourselves more than you are accustomed to." He looked along the line and knew that he held their attention. "There is honour and reputation here for the right type of men but if you feel that your qualities would be put to better use in the main army you can leave now with my blessing and I will recommend you to Brennus. I have seen you all on the ride through Umbria and know that you are the right men for this. Prove it to yourselves."

Solemis waited patiently but no man moved and he nodded with satisfaction as he turned his mount's head back to the South. Urging Tantibus into a trot, he motioned to Druteos.

"Fire the hut and then toss the bronze in the river. Let's let them know that we have arrived."

As the first flames of the campaign flickered into life and licked at the eaves of the tax collector's hut, Solemis let his thoughts wander back over the events of the previous month. It had taken them a full month of hard riding to get them to the Anio. Skirting the foothills of the Apeninnus they had intercepted the via salaria and swung to the West as it climbed steadily before them.

The Umbrian senate had held to its word and it had seemed as if every man with produce to spare for miles around had made their way directly towards their intended route. Initially, the Umbrian brothers had been in great demand as interpreters until the Celts had discovered that the Etruscan silver which they still carried in great quantities seemed to speak the language of Umbrian merchants just as fluently as any other. Consequently supplies had never been the problem that they could easily have been with a large force moving through friendly country and unable to pillage, but the idea that they would emerge from the salt road into an unsuspecting countryside had appeared to be laughable. Roman merchants operated freely in the area, and Solemis' worries had grown by the day. Thankfully news of their coming seemed to have miraculously remained on the eastern side of the mountains. Rodolfo and Brizio had been invaluable. Able to move freely among their own people without raising any suspicion they had discovered that the Romans were expecting the force to take the main mountain pass which carried the via flaminia, past the cities of Spoletium and Nequinum, and had made their disposition accordingly.

After this first meeting at the border post, it was obvious now to Solemis that they had completely wrong-footed the Romans by taking the via salaria and his spirits rose to new heights. Free now of the confines of the pass, the rich farmlands of the Latini opened up before them as they put the mountains and the Anio behind them.

"One more?"

Solemis rubbed his face and stifled a yawn as he pondered his friend's question. Twisting in the saddle, he raised his arm as he sought to gauge the hour. The arc of the sun rested on the ledge of his hand, it was growing late.

"No, the men need rest," he laughed wearily. "*I* need a rest! Besides," he continued, "this place looks perfect."

Albiomaros hauled gently at the reins and turned the head of his mount.

"I will tell the boys. I like to be popular," he grinned.

Solemis scanned the lime washed collection of buildings in the dip before them as fifty riders detached themselves from each end of the line and galloped down into the vale. After a week of raiding, the men knew without need of any further instruction from their leader what was required, and Solemis watched as the groups passed on opposite sides of the latifundium and curved around to draw the inhabitants into their net.

Berikos and his group galloped out of the line and headed straight for the big wooden gates as they did so, and Solemis was relieved when they passed through them and out of sight. If the inhabitants could have closed the doors in time to deny them entry they would have been faced with a day's ride in order to leave the area as the occupants raised the surrounding countryside against them.

The scouts had missed this place, tucked away as it was, and they had been surprised to come upon it as they had crested the ridge. It was a warning that they were becoming tired after nearly three gruelling weeks of raiding and living off the land. They would need to stay sharp Solemis knew, or they could easily become trapped a hundred miles from the rest of the army.

His plans had worked perfectly so far. It would be a shame to die so close to the end, he thought with a snort of irony.

The transit of Umbria had been flawless. Thanks to Rodolfo and Brizio's familiarity with the land and the route of the salt road, he had been able to judge the moment when they would arrive at the Latin border to perfection. The full moon had flooded the land with its pale light for the first few days as they sought to put as much distance between themselves and the Apeninnus as quickly as possible.

That first week had passed by in a weary haze of forced rides against a backdrop of hanged estate owners and flames in the night. By the time that the moon had waned they were deep within the lands of the Romans and travelling faster than any warning of their presence. Keeping well clear of any towns, they had zigzagged randomly about the land, completely outwitting any chasing force which might be trailing them.

As the nights grew darker, Solemis had modified their tactics. Far from the mountains now, they had arrived in the deep soils of the Roman heartlands. The latifundia here were larger and the Senone chieftain knew that these were the lands owned by the elites of the great city to the North. By striking directly against the property of Rome's leading men, Solemis knew that he would cause the maximum amount of outrage and draw a correspondingly greater response. Given a further few days, he must have drawn most of the equites away from the city. He would melt away and rejoin Brennus in the North as the Romans chased his shadow.

The south-facing slope before them was filled with ordered rows of vines and they edged their mounts down between the greenery as the estate slaves dropped their tools and fled before them like a buff coloured wave.

The estate was one of the largest they had seen so far. High walls enclosed the whole, and a line of cypress trees stood sentinel along its southern edge, warding off the heat of the southern sun from the buildings and their occupants.

As the shadow of the gateway fell across Solemis he looked about the courtyard within and nodded to himself with satisfaction. The enclosure was wide and deep and would accommodate the men and their mounts with ease. Several bloodstained bodies marked the passage of Berikos and his men and the slaves which had run before them in the vineyard were huddled in a fearful group in the far corner. Shouts and screams were coming from the main building and he snorted as he imagined the scene there.

Druteos came alongside him and Solemis indicated the building with a flick of his head. Immediately his clansman gathered together fifty men and disappeared inside in support of the Aeduan's group as Solemis dismounted and stretched his weary limbs. He turned to Albiomaros and smiled at the look of contentment which passed across the big man's features as he massaged his buttocks and restored the blood flow to aching limbs and muscles.

"When you have finished, take care of the overseers and inform the cook he has lots of hungry guests." Albiomaros nodded and bustled off as Solemis handed his reins across to Rodolfo. The Umbrian had been correct when he had said that his family's wedding gift to Solemis, the horse Tantibus, would quickly adjust to a new owner. The horse was as intelligent as they had promised and Solemis had watched in wonder as the relationship between Rodolfo and the horse had subtly changed from one of master and property to one more akin to friendship.

The estate slaves were beginning to recover their composure as the realisation that they were not about to be killed out of hand by these strangers began to sink in. Several were already enthusiastically pointing out those of their number who had been appointed by the owners to positions of authority over them. Berikos had been a slave in Etruria and he had indicated that these men and women were often the most savage of all as they jealously guarded the small privileges which had been granted to them by the owners. They could never be trusted, and Solemis barely glanced their way as Albiomaros moved among them, dispatching the shrieking men and women with an expert thrust of his spear. As the last of the house slaves were herded into the group, Solemis began to address them.

"Slaves! You have your freedom if that is your wish, but understand that we cannot offer any aid other than to let you take what food and stores you will need for your journey. You all know the punishments for running from your masters but the decision is yours. All that I ask is that you remain here until we leave in the morning. Anyone who can't wait should know that I have men in the fields outside who will kill you as quickly as any Roman." He paused and swept the group with a look. Satisfied by their colouring that there were none among them from the far north, he concluded his address to them. "Get some rest and make your plans. You have much to consider."

Before the excited slaves could begin to think they suddenly turned as a group towards the villa, and Solemis knew from the looks on their faces that Berikos had arrived back with the owners. He had seen the strange look on many faces these last few weeks, a unique blend of horror, delight and incredulity as they witnessed the sudden and complete fall of the people they had thought to be untouchable only an hour before. He swung around as the Aeduan pushed them roughly into the courtyard with the butt of his lancea.

To his disappointment the paterfamilias seemed to be absent, but the middle-aged woman there was obviously too grand to be a tenant and the family resemblance of the young women at her side was clear. Despite their predicament, the matriarch clearly regarded the Celts before her with the same degree of haughty contempt that they had become familiar with over the course of the previous few weeks.

Solemis left the slaves and walked across as the closest warriors unsaddled their horses and exchanged knowing looks.

"My name is Solemis, and you are?"

For a heartbeat he thought that he saw a look of recognition flash across the woman's face but she quickly regained her composure and calmly stared into the middle distance. He gave a weary sigh. If the woman had but known, her attitude had cost more than one of her contemporaries their lives during the past few weeks. At first they had been unprepared for the arrogant demeanour of the Roman women until Berikos had come to Solemis one day and explained that the easiest way to strip them of their self confidence was to remove their sense of . To Solemis' relief it never ceased to have the desired result and, although the men and boys were always killed before they moved on, the females were left to make their own choices as to their fate. As the courtyard filled with men and horses and the big oak doors were closed behind them, Solemis indicated the Roman's stola.

"Remove your clothing."

The woman's head jerked backwards in shock, and she turned towards him at last with the now familiar look of incredulity written across her face. Solemis watched as she visibly reasserted her composure and sought to retain some control of the situation.

"My name is Licinia," she hesitated for a heartbeat, and Solemis knew that she had been about to say more but thought better of it before continuing with a familiar threat. "You are making a grave mistake, barbarian."

The last word was spat out accompanied by an undisguised sneer and Solemis stifled a yawn. It had been a long day, they were all tired and really needed to slake their thirst. He made to question her further but decided that he didn't really care enough to wait for the answer. All of the women so far had been keen to announce their family names as if it would protect them as they called down the vengeance of their menfolk on the hapless Celts, he decided that it was probably that. No doubt she was the wife of a very important man, but at that moment he didn't care who that great man might be. He shrugged as he shot Berikos and his men a look and, although their grasp of Latin was rudimentary at best, they had heard the conversation enough times since they had been in the South to follow most of it. They chuckled as he replied.

"Oh, I don't think that it is a grave mistake. You shouldn't denigrate yourself too much, you still look firm, despite your age. Let's let my men decide, they have become good judges of female Roman flesh over the past few weeks." He nodded his thanks as one of the men with Berikos handed across the first cup of wine of the night and the woman stiffened with anger at the insult. "Now, the clothing please, all of it."

A note of pleading entered her voice for the first time as she began to realise that the authority which she had enjoyed within her home throughout her adult life had simply vanished the moment that these barbarians had arrived and her expression softened.

"Not my daughters…"

Solemis looked them up and down for the first time. He estimated that the girls were about twelve and fourteen winters old and both shared the curious aquiline nose which seemed to mark out the Roman ruling classes. Hair the colour of a raven's plumage glistened and shone in the soft evening light and, although their eyes were wide with fright at the special horror which only adolescent girls could fully understand at the thought of being naked among men, Solemis had little doubt that they usually shared their mother's character as well as looks. He nodded, they could use a lesson in humility too.

"Yes, them as well. Hurry or my men here will do it for you, and they can be quite rough." He gave a weary chuckle; "barbaric even!"

As the women's composure finally crumpled along with their clothing, Solemis threw a parting command as he moved away to set the guards.

"Serve my men wine. Follow Berikos' orders and you will live."

Solemis clicked on and Tantibus shook his head and passed through the gateway. Lining the roadway Licinia hugged her daughters to her as they stood shivering in the chill morning air. Solemis thanked the woman for her hospitality as he rode past and to his surprise she met his gaze, her sense of still intact despite her nakedness. She had been the first to retain her composure, in fact he had suspected that she had rather enjoyed the attention, and he found that he respected her all the more for it.

Solemis hauled the head of his mount away to the South. A shallow valley opened up before him, its pits and hollows pooled with the mists of early morning, as the Horsetails chieftain guided Tantibus between the rows of vines and away.

Today was to be the final day of their raid. He would ride out of sight of the watching women to disguise their true destination and then swing finally north, towards the army of Brennus.

Solemis reflected on the success they had achieved over the past few weeks in Latium. Dozens of latifundia and villa rustica were now nothing more than smouldering wrecks, their dispossessed owners either dead or thrown on the mercy of friends and relatives. Slaves were either making frantic efforts to escape to their homelands or rampaging through the land as they sought to take their own form of revenge on their former masters before Roman justice finally laid them low. Surprisingly, fantastically so, they had managed to enrich themselves and sow chaos across the south without losing a single man. Solemis' deliberately irregular strikes had left any pursuers floundering in their wake as they struck out in any direction or retraced their steps almost on a whim.

He paused before glancing back at the estate buildings. The fire was taking hold now, long fronds of flame flickering within the greasy smoke, but they would be far away before help could arrive. Away to the West the early morning sun glittered on the sea like shards of ice as the mist drew a veil around the horsemen.

SIX

Lucius shifted in the saddle and took a swig from his water skin. Swilling the cool liquid around his mouth he spat out the dust and grit which had coated his throat as he replaced the stopper and hooked it back onto the horn of his saddle. Lifting his head he looked along the road to the *tabernarium* which stood hard on to the roadway. It was the perfect place to break their fast and his spirits rose a little as he anticipated the taste of the day's freshly baked bread and local olive oil. This close to the sea there may even be some fish, he mused, it had always been a favourite of his.

They had broken camp the moment that the first grey light of the pre dawn had touched the eastern hills. He was sure that this was the best time to catch the Gauls, if they were to be caught at all. Even these wild men must sleep at some time he reasoned, and although his force was far smaller than the reputed numbers of the enemy, his duty was clear.

He shook his head as he recalled the ramblings of the survivors of their attacks. Even with their honour impinged, he would have thought that they could have retained the ability to count with even a small degree of accuracy. The reports which he had collected had ranged from anywhere between eight hundred and three thousand horsemen loose in the Latium. Thankfully, unlike the distraught matrons which they had come upon, his mind was more occupied by military matters than worries about how many men had seen his arse. From the tracks and the size of the areas in which they had corralled their horses he estimated the number of Gauls to be in the region of five centuries or so.

If he ran them to ground he would shadow them and send out riders to alert all the Roman forces in the area. Aware that they had been discovered, the leader of the raiders must then abandon any more attacks and either attempt to fight or flee. If they attacked he would melt away before them and reassemble as they withdrew. Once reinforcements arrived they would strike the barbarians with overwhelming force, washing Roman swords in their blood.

His thoughts fixed firmly on his empty belly, the decurion failed to spot the approaching horsemen until one of the men called them in.

"Two riders, sir, it looks like the optio and Ferox."

Lucius looked across to the West. Two riders had crested the ridge and were cantering down towards them, the sunlight playing across the unmistakable musculature of his heavy leather *coriaceus,* the breastplate armour of which Titus was so proud. The pair came to a wide ditch and a ripple of excitement ran along the line as they watched the outriders hurl themselves across the obstacle without a pause.

"They are in a hurry. This could be it, sir."

Lucius ignored the comment and waited for them to arrive. Despite the sense of anticipation he shared with the men, he was a Roman officer and he would act accordingly. The pair reined in and the optio saluted as he caught his breath.

"There's a smudge of smoke on the far side of the valley, just beyond the next ridge."

Lucius made a fist as he began to entertain the hope that this could at last 'be it'.

"Any sign of horsemen, Titus?"

The optio shook his head.

"Just the smoke, there is not too much of it but it is thick and black." He smiled at his decurion and the men of the column shared a look as they began to instinctively check their weapons. "It is the right time of day," he volunteered. "They could have just set the fire and still be in the vicinity."

Lucius nodded his agreement.

"Well done, lads. Titus, we will do what we agreed. You take half of the men and skirt around to the North and I will take the southern route, but take care. We will only have forty men apiece so we can't afford to blunder into them. We will be no use to the republic dead. Remember," he continued, "if you see them, detach a dozen riders and send them out in pairs northwards and eastwards for reinforcements and I will scour the South and the coastal districts." He grinned, his breakfast forgotten. "Let's get going."

*

Galatus and Rodolfo pressed themselves closer to the ground as they watched the riders approach. The woman of the house, fully clothed once more, moved forward and pointed in the direction that Solemis had taken only a short while before, and the Roman in charge of the party immediately despatched pairs of horsemen from the column.

Galatus turned his head to his Umbrian companion.

"Time to leave, I think."

They shared a look and Rodolfo nodded as they began to shuffle back down the rear of the slope to the waiting mounts. Suddenly Rodolfo stiffened and threw his arm across the Celt.

"Stay still!"

The men froze as a horse snickered. It was close, and they exchanged a look as each man weighed whether their chances would be greater if they remained where they were or bolted for the horses, tantalisingly close by.

The Romans came into plain sight and they both realised at the same instant that the decision had been taken for them as they broke from cover and tore down the slope. Immediately several cries cut the air and they threw themselves into their saddles and hauled the heads of their mounts away. Galatus cried out over the sounds of snapping branches as they pushed their way clear of the copse.

"Head south, we can't afford to lead them to our men. They will have turned west by now and should be clear, we can catch them up later."

They burst from cover and Galatus led them along the gully and back up on to the hillside. The summit was thick with olive trees, the gnarled old trunks marching away in serried rows, and they urged their mounts on as the lay of the grove channelled them south. Sweeping across the opposite slope they could see that the fields ran down to the road, arrow-straight, which led to the nearby town of Ardea. The road was already growing busy as the farmers and traders moved towards the town and they saw people stopping and pointing as they galloped across the skyline.

Galatus stole a glance behind and was horrified at how close the pursuing Romans had come. Armed men were emerging from the tree line which shaded the roadway and were clearly moving across the fields ahead to bar their passage. The situation was becoming desperate and the Horsetail exchanged a look of despair with his companion as they sought a way out of the rapidly tightening net. Suddenly Galatus recognised that Rodolfo was curbing his mount as he sought to remain alongside him and the Celt felt a wave of shame that the man was needlessly risking his life on his behalf. Although he had been offered the use of one of the Umbrian war horses by his chieftain he had declined. His horse, Broc, had been with him as long as he had been a warrior and the bond had just been too tight between them. They had fought together in the forests of Celtica and he had carried him across the roof of the world to the new country without protest. He was more than a horse he was a friend and friends, Galatus knew, cannot be discarded like a worn cloak.

A small knoll, a perfect dome of grass topped by the solitary brush of a small pine, stood away to the West and Galatus choked with emotion as he recognised that the gods had provided him with the perfect place. He reached to his side and tore his dagger and scabbard from his belt, thrusting it out to the Umbrian.

"Here!"

Rodolfo looked across in surprise and they locked eyes as he realised the significance of the action. "Make sure that this gets to my son."

Rodolfo made to argue but instantly recognised that the man had made the correct decision. The stocky northern breed was hardy and could run all day, but the sheer size of the longer legged southern mounts would run him down before too long. He stuffed the blade into his tunic and gripped his new friend by the shoulder. After a final nod the men parted and Rodolfo whooped as he finally gave the horse its head and arrowed across the plain.

Galatus cantered up the rise and dismounted as he reached the summit. The position was all that he hoped that it would be and he watched as the Roman column split into two below him. As a score of them angled away to give chase to the fleeing Umbrian the remainder flowed around the hillock like the incoming tide around a rock. The Celt raised his eyes and smiled with satisfaction as he watched his friend draw further away from his pursuers with every passing moment. Already he was through the line of oncoming guards from the via ardeatina and racing up the slope opposite. He felt pride that his sacrifice had not been in vain and hoped that his clansmen would get to hear of it. He was sure that they would. The Umbrian was the best horseman that he had ever seen and the idea that the lumbering horses with their heavily armed riders would catch the fast moving stallion was laughable.

As the Romans collected at the base and shuffled into line he put his face to Broc's muzzle and breathed in the musky smell of the horse for a final time as he drew his sword.

"Wait for me in *Anwnn*, old friend. I shall be along soon and we can ride through the fields there again with our ancestors."

The horse shuddered, and it gasped in shock as the blade entered its chest and slid easily through the muscle and sinew there to cleave its great heart in two. It was perfectly judged, and Galatus held the horse's head as it fell forward and rolled onto its side. Broc shook and his legs kicked the air for a final time before the horse grew still and the man reached into the blood pulsing from its death wound and drew his hand slowly across his face. It would make the Celt appear even more fearsome to the small men who were beginning to ascend the hill towards him.

Flexing his sword arm, Galatus took up his battle stance as he began to call out his lineage and prepared to exact his death price.

Rodolfo reached the crest of the valley and curbed his mount. His pursuers were far below him and, even at this distance he could recognise from the soldiers' body language that they realised they had little chance of catching him. He was, after all, the finest horseman in the whole of Umbria and his own mount, Fulgar, lightning, had been aptly named.

He shaded his eyes against the brilliance of the morning sun and peered across the wide valley to the grassy knoll where he had left his friend. The scene sparkled with light as the silver blades rose and fell, and the Umbrian could see that the fight was drawing to its inevitable conclusion.

He could just make out the great bulk of the Celt beneath the arc of his great broadsword as it scythed his attackers like summer barley, an island of ochre and russet amid the more uniform silver and brown of his attackers.

Rodolfo reached inside his tunic and withdrew the Celt's dagger. He regarded the barbarity of the scabbard with a small smile. A chased design of intricate swirls in bronze and leather, the design was typical of his race, brash and robust but honest and true.

He glanced down at the Romans. They were drawing closer, he would have to be away or Galatus' boy would never get to hear of the magnificence of his father's death. He cast a last look across the vale. The Romans there had withdrawn a short distance, leaving behind a bloody ring of bodies to mark the limit of their advance, and men were returning from the horses with a supply of javelins.

It would make a fitting ending to his story and Rodolfo turned away and dug in his heels.

*

The usual flurry of activity was evident ahead as Numerius led the men of the turma towards the town gate. The ride down from Rome could have been pleasant had it not been for the reason for the mad dash. The town lay under a canopy of the deepest blue as the heat of the day began to come off the land and a freshening breeze blew in from the nearby Tirreno Sea.

Word had reached the city that morning that his estate had been attacked and burnt by the barbarian raiders who had been plaguing the lands of Latium for the past few weeks, and Numerius had cursed himself for placing his family in harm's way. He had never for one moment expected the Senones to act in such a brazen manner. He of all people, the man who had become almost a laughing stock among the members of the senate for the strength of his warnings about the capabilities of these people, had underestimated their reach and audacity.

To have had his own wife and daughters attacked and his property burnt around them was humiliating enough, but to be informed of the fact by one of Camillus' soldiers had heaped misery upon misery.

Thankfully the man had appeared at his *domus* before he had set out for the senate that day, otherwise his humiliation would have been complete. Gratifyingly, the men of his century had left their places of work without a thought and he had been on his way within the hour. It had been the first time that he had left the city since the attacks and Numerius had been shocked by the affect which they had had on the rural populations. Traffic on the roads had dropped almost to nothing and those who did venture abroad demanded armed escort, even in daylight. To think that this was happening, sometimes literally within sight of Rome herself, was a humiliation of the highest order.

Ahead of them the town guards had hastily arranged themselves into twin ranks lining the road at their approach, and Numerius slowed his mount as the centurion in command saluted. All the men here were loyal to the ex dictator and would count him as a political enemy of their general, but they were Romans first and foremost and he expected to be received in the manner which his rank demanded. Before he could state his business, the soldier spoke.

"Welcome to Ardea, tribune." The man glanced down momentarily, his discomfort obvious. "The men and I are sorry for the reason for your journey, sir."

Numerius blinked in surprise.

"Thank you. Would one of your men guide us to the home of the general?"

"An escort has already been arranged, sir," the man replied, "they await you through the gate."

Numerius nodded his thanks and clicked his mount on. Passing under the great archway he emerged into an open space containing the guard house and various buildings which housed the town revenue collectors and other offices of the state. A small stable stood off to one side, the covering of thatch lending it a slightly ridiculous rustic air in the otherwise terracotta tiled town. A turma of tough looking equites were mounted there and the decurion came forward and introduced himself as his men took up station at their head.

"Sextus Frontinus, legatus. I will guide you to the general's domus."

Numerius inclined his head and the officer rode to the head of the column. The tree lined road soon spilled out into a busy forum and the column negotiated their way through the throng as the inhabitants of the town stared at their exotic visitor and exchanged whispered comments. The road exited the forum alongside an ancient Greek temple and climbed slowly uphill towards the highest point in the town. The buildings grew in size and quality the further they moved from the bustling centre of Ardea and very soon the decurion and the riders of his squadron wheeled and formed themselves into twin ranks flanking a large double gate.

The gate groaned as unseen hands pulled them inwards and Numerius led his men inside. Alighting in the large courtyard within, the tribune was joined by his optio and friend, Cassius, as a dispensator, the head of the house slaves, came forward to greet him and lead him through and into the domus.

Now that the moment had arrived, Numerius was surprised to find that he felt a little anxious at the meeting. He had had little time to reflect on the events of the day since the messenger had arrived from Camillus. Although the man had been quick to assure him that his family were safe and physically unharmed he had no doubt that they would have been through a terrifying ordeal and he was desperate to meet them. He and his family were literally in the power of his political enemy, the one-time all-powerful dictator of Rome and his own gens, the Fabii, had played a large part in the prosecution for embezzlement which had led to the man's fall and exile from the city.

He had expected to be kept waiting as Camillus wrung every advantage from his temporary return to ascendency, but to his surprise the man himself appeared the moment that they had passed through the vestibulem and into the atrium.

"Tribune, welcome to my home. Please accept my sympathies for this abomination."

Numerius inclined his head.

"General, you have my heartfelt gratitude. May I see my wife?"

Camillus pursed his lips as he nodded his agreement and Numerius' experience at judging men told him that the man's concern was real. They were both successful generals and he was pleased to see that, despite their differences, Camillus appeared to be able to put them aside for the good of Rome. His regard for the man increased.

"Of course, Abrax here will lead you to them. I have set aside a wing of my home for the use of your family and yourself. Please feel free to treat it as your own home for as long as you wish." As Numerius turned to go his host added. "Perhaps we should talk later?" Numerius turned back and held his gaze as he attempted to judge the ex dictator's motives. His offer seemed genuine and Numerius nodded his acceptance. "Yes, I think that we should."

Camillus moved on to greet Cassius as Numerius was led away. Passing through the building, Numerius was led across the gardens of the peristylium towards a smaller building which appeared to be older than the rest, and he assumed that it was the remains of the domus which had originally stood on the site before Camillus had added to it in far grander style. The dispensator stood to one side and bowed as Numerius entered and crossed the small atrium. Licinia, he knew, would wait for him and greet him formally within the building. She was, after all, a Roman equestrian and would act accordingly in front of slaves and others, whatever the situation. He, and they, would expect no less. Hurrying along in his wake the man crossed to a door which led off to one side and opened it gracefully before stepping aside.

Numerius passed inside and hesitated as his eyes grew accustomed to the light. The gardens had lain directly in the full glare of the afternoon sun and, although the room was well lit, it was some moments before he could see clearly. A voice, thick with emotion came from the gloom.

"Husband."

His daughters scrambled to their feet and Cassia, the younger of his two girls, was unable to contain her surprise and relief that he had arrived there.

"Papa!"

The single word did more than any to tell Numerius of the ordeal which his family had just undergone. Cassia had begun to call him father several years before, as she had begun to grow into maturity. That she had momentarily slipped back into the terms she had used during childhood was telling. Numerius felt a knot of emotion tighten in his own throat as the pain which the word revealed threatened to overcome him. Numeria, he saw with pride, was bearing her humiliation far more stoically. At fourteen years of age she was on the cusp of womanhood and, despite the gravity of the moment, Numerius found that his thoughts briefly turned to the need to arrange a suitable husband for her as soon as order was restored and the world returned to its senses. He turned to the slaves which stood discretely nearby and snapped out a command.

"Leave us!"

They hastened from the room and closed the door with a soft thunk. Alone now, Numerius held his arms wide and the girls came forward and hugged him as he exchanged a look with Licinia. Kissing them both lightly on the top of the head he raised their chins as he attempted a reassuring smile.

"You both look well. You have survived an ordeal but you are Roman. It will make you stronger."

Licinia's voice cut in. It was gentle but would brook no argument.

"Go to your rooms now girls. We will join you when we have spoken."

They collected themselves and turned to go but Cassia suddenly turned back and hugged her father once again. She looked up at his face and Numerius saw that her expression had hardened.

"You will catch them, father." She fixed him with a stare. "Make them pay for what they did to us."

Numerius nodded and stroked her hair as she turned and followed her sister from the room. Once they were alone and the doors were closed, Licinia crumpled as she allowed herself to relax her outward show of *disciplina* for the first time since the barbarians had arrived the previous evening. Numerius held her as she nestled into his shoulder.

He clasped her to him and let the tears of relief come until she regained her composure, before leading her across to the long *kline*, the padded couch which stood along one wall. Pouring wine, he waited for his wife to describe her ordeal. In reality, he was at a loss for words. He was a Roman general, not a Greek poet. He wanted to ask her if they had suffered rape at the hands of the Celts but he realised that it would be insensitive. Thankfully his wife was strong and recovered quickly as she sipped from her cup and moved to lessen his concern.

"Don't worry, I was stripped and humiliated but not ravaged by them."

Numerius swallowed uncomfortably. Despite his initial sense of relief he noticed that Licinia had not included his daughters in the declaration and she caught his look of concern. He had commanded armies and knew what could happen when women and young girls fell into the hands of victorious soldiers. She raised a brow as she read his thoughts.

"The girls were treated the same way. They are still *virgo intacta*. I kept them close and I assure you that they would pass any examination." Numerius allowed himself a pensive smile. The latifundium was of no consequence, that would be rebuilt even grander than before once the Senones were defeated. His wife and daughters had survived capture by an enemy force with their honour intact. Although he was sure that they had had an unpleasant night, things could have been a lot worse. Licinia continued.

"Your friend, Solemis, commanded the barbarians."

Despite his attempts at showing compassion his eyebrows shot up at the information and he gasped a reply.

"Was he aware of your identity?"

She shook her head.

"No, I started to give my full name but managed to stop myself just in time. I know of the past history between you but I don't think that he would have acted any differently had he known. He certainly suspected that I was hiding my full identity from him but I don't think that he cared." To his surprise the corners of her mouth turned up into a wicked smile. "He said that I looked firm for my age," she purred. "Once I got over the shock I actually rather enjoyed being naked among so many big men." Her hand reached out to guide his wine cup to her mouth, draining it in one smooth movement. She lowered her voice, and he looked at her incredulously as the tips of her fingers ran along the inside of his thigh. "I like to think that I was not the only thing which was firm last night."

SEVEN

The night was still, the sky a bejewelled dome of jet as they ducked into the forge. Uxentio looked up from his preparations and crossed the earthen floor to greet them as his son took their belongings away for safekeeping. Soon the hut would become a place of work, of alchemy, as the body of mother earth was transformed into a thing of beauty and death. Sparks would fly and anything not safely stored away would bear the marks; if a living thing, for the remainder of their time in the world of men. The only light came from the forge itself, the glow painting the faces of those present blood red as the shadows hardened into darkness.

Ultinos, the metalworker's son, had met them in the village and led them here to the forge. Like all smithies, Uxentio's lay at the edge of the settlement. Even the slightest breeze could carry a burning ember a great distance, and Catumanda noticed that the homes nearest to them had pails of water ready to hand. The forge itself had been roofed by split stone and all brush and scrub had been scoured from the immediate area.

The village they had been led through had looked like any other she had seen. Women sat singly or huddled in small groups before their homes, combing wool, weaving, preparing food. Only the odd furtive glance in her direction giving away their interest in this strange female who had suddenly appeared in their midst. The men sat in their own groups doing as little as possible, their looks more open; as judgemental as those of their womenfolk but in different ways. Murmured comments to their friends as they reached their conclusion; yes or no?

Ultinos had described the process they were about to witness as they walked. Big and broad shouldered with a shaggy mane of blond hair tied at the nape by a thong of red leather, Catumanda had amused her own mind as he walked, and decided yes. The young man had spent the previous week in the hills, producing the charcoal which they would use to make her new moon blade, and he had described the process as they walked. As he had enthusiastically described the felling and stacking of the cypress and alder and the long nights perched upon a one legged stool her mind had drifted away. Maybe it was a no after all.

Uxentio grinned broadly and dipped his head.

"Welcome back to my forge, Olindico O Olonico." He turned to Catumanda. "A very great welcome to you Catumanda. It is always a thrill to work for any druid, but one who has visited the Sacred Isle itself," he paused and looked at her in awe. "That is a very special pleasure."

He ushered them towards the fiery hearth. The heat was intense despite the coolness of the evening and the smith's body glistened behind the thick leather apron which protected his front. He indicated several others which were hanging nearby as he hastened back to the forge itself and pumped the bellows.

"You will need to wear those if you are to come close enough to witness the birth."

Ultinos unhooked them and handed them across before he went to relieve his father at the bellows. The leather was hard, thick and stiff with age and grime, and Catumanda winced as it rubbed against her still tender flesh. The heat was already beginning to worry the weather-ravaged skin of her face and she dipped into the pouch which Ama had supplied as a parting gift and spread a thick layer of the honeyed balm across her cheeks, nose and forehead. Uxentio was already back at his forge and he peered inside and gave a grunt of satisfaction

"You are just in time, the bloom is almost ready."

He scooped up an indented clay tablet from the workbench and recrossed to Catumanda as his son slowed the action of the bellows.

"Catumanda, may I see your right hand?"

She held it forward and the smith took it in his big, meaty hand. His skin was rough and calloused but to her surprise his touch was delicate as he rolled her fingers in his own and smoothed the palm of her hand with his thumb. His left hand was mirroring the actions on the tablet and Catumanda realised that it was the mould which would produce her new weapon. The smith looked up.

"That's good work, if I say so myself," he smiled. "It's not ideal to work from a drawing, but it's only for the basic size and shape. The real work takes place after that."

He let her hand drop and replaced the mould before returning to the forge. The heat was intense and sweat was already beginning to sting their eyes as Uxentio lifted the beaker containing the molten iron from the depths of the furnace and filled the mould with one quick movement. The bloom cooled, quickly turning from a flaming orange to a dull grey and soon the smith was upending the mould and tapping out the basic blade onto his workbench. His son maintained the furnace at the correct temperature by working the bellows as Uxentio worked the blade into shape with a hammer. As soon as the metal cooled it was thrust back into the kiln until the smith judged that the colour was right to be removed and worked and reworked.

Again and again Uxentio heated and hammered at the piece, his own sweat falling in fat drops to sizzle and smoke on the metal as the blade took shape. Finally satisfied, Uxentio called across to Ultinos and the lad slid back the cover on a pan. Inside they saw that it contained a bed of charcoal, heated to a white hot glow, and the smith used his tongs to remove the blade from the forge and transfer it across.

Again he hammered at the metal, turning and working both sides until the colour dulled as embers flew in fiery arcs. Quickly he quenched the blade in a roar of steam before transferring it back to the main kiln. After half a dozen workings his hammering had lessened as he teased out the details of the weapon, and Catumanda felt a kick of excitement as she recognised the familiar features of the moon blade. The crescent was still dull and puckered, but the form was complete and she suddenly realised just how much she had missed the comforting feel of the blade against her side. Her old blade had been presented to her by her master, Abaris, in Camulodunon on the day of her initiation into the brotherhood. She had last used it to cut the ropes which bound her to the mast of the *Alexa* as it sank into the depths of the storm tossed sea, and she hoped that it had found its last resting place alongside the crew of the ship. It would be in the finest company.

Uxentio placed the piece on the bench and indicated to his son that the night's work was complete with a tired dip of his head. Ultinos covered the charcoal pan and removed the bellows from the kiln as he began to close the furnace down, and the smith slipped the heavy apron from his neck and flashed them a weary smile.

"I will need a day to file and polish the blade but you have witnessed its birth."

The man ducked outside and they replaced their own aprons onto the line of pegs and followed on. To their surprise the first glimmers of the dawn were in the East, the pink light turning the hilltops around them into beacons.

"Will you stay with me today?"

Lindo wiped the sweat from his brow and threw Catumanda a knowing look.

"That is very kind, Uxentio. I would be grateful if Philippos could rest with you until we return." Catumanda nodded in agreement as the older druid concluded mysteriously. "Catumanda has someone very important to meet."

It was midmorning when they reached the place. Scrambling up the last few feet they paused at the mouth of the cave and turned back.

"It's amazing to think that this was once a grassy plain. Men would sit where we stand now and watch the passage of the herds on which they preyed, planning the hunt as their children played about them."

Catumanda was lost in her own thoughts as she inhaled the salty air. The foot of the cliff which they had just traversed was a wide rocky platform, scoured clear of any traces of soil by the actions of the higher tides. Beyond that lay the sea, its surface whipped into peaks and troughs as the wind freshened. The next gale of the autumn was building and she watched as each gust wove a fresh pattern through the long grasses which covered the hillside.

Lindo placed his hand on her shoulder, his usual bubbly mood replaced with one of reverence.

"They buried their dead on the long shelf there. I will go and prepare for the ceremony."

Catumanda gave a brief nod and instinctively hugged the bag a little tighter. As Lindo picked his way into the dark gash which marked the entrance to the cave she levered herself up and looked about her.

The terrace sat in a natural bowl, open to the front but walled to the rear and sides by the sweep of the hillside. It would have been the perfect place to sit among ancestors, watching the seasons roll away as you shared the latest news of their descendants, and the druid felt herself smile as she recognised the thought and care which had gone into choosing the position. She could feel the spirits gathering around her and she opened her bag and began to scatter the last of the season's lavender and the tiny, grass-like orchids which had littered the sheltered valleys.

Her respects paid to the spirits of the people who had inhabited the place long ago, Catumanda retraced her steps back to the entrance to the cave.

NEMESIS

A pale glow came from within, and the druid passed through the narrow entrance and into the wider space beyond. Lindo was waiting and he smiled in welcome as he pointed the way towards a smaller passageway which led off to one side. Taking the candle she squeezed through and followed the corridor as it twisted and turned through the rock to emerge in a small round chamber. Although she had been warned what to expect by the older druid, Catumanda gasped at the beauty of the room. The domed ceiling had been stained to represent a perfect summer sky, the ball of the sun blazing at its high point. The four directions were indicated on the side walls by the same animal totems which she had been taught during her training in Albion and she greeted each in turn before clearing a sacred space in which to sit. Choosing the symbol for north, the hibernating bear, in honour of her homeland, Catumanda sat and assumed the position of power.

Soon she felt the familiar energy coursing into her body as the vitality of mother earth and father sky mixed within her and she relaxed and cleared her mind. An oak door appeared before her and she passed through to find herself in a great forest. A path lay ahead, and she followed it until it emerged into a clearing. She recognised it at once as the nemeton of the Trinobantes, its hollow bowl facing east into the rising sun, and gave an involuntary laugh as she recognised the figure who awaited her there. Squat and powerful, the shaman still wore the deerskin cloak and antlered skull of their earlier meeting, his ochre stained face thrown into sharp relief by the flames of a small hearth.

She now knew that she had met her spirit guide before, in Annwn as her body lay trapped and bleeding and she thought that she had died. The man looked up and she could see the amusement in his eyes as he gestured that she join him at the fireside.

EIGHT

The crowds cheered as the river of bronze and leather snaked its way from the forum towards the Field of Mars beneath a hedgerow of spears. Word had reached the city the previous evening that the barbarian army was already past Clusium and preparing to encamp outside the Etruscan city of Volsinia. They could be expected to reach Rome within two days if they were not intercepted and the commander of the city's army, Quintus Sulpicius Longus, had sent out the summons for the centuries to report for duty at dawn the following day.

It was a beautiful day in Latium as the early morning mists were driven from the banks of the Tiberis by the steadily rising sun, and the people were out in force as the men marched away. Food vendors had been busy since long before dawn, preparing the bread and sausage which would feed the multitude, and business had been brisk.

As the centuries paraded through the northern postern of the Carmental Gate, the people followed on, spilling out onto the field to catch a final glimpse of a husband, son or father or merely gape in awe at the martial might of their city.

Numerius swelled with pride as he stood before the men of his century and watched the last of the legions file out of the city. Despite his disappointment at not being chosen to command the army in person, he harboured few doubts that the men of Rome would crush the Gauls.

Despite the chaos caused by Solemis' raid in the South, now that the time had finally arrived to face the army of the Gauls in open battle, he found that confidence in the martial prowess of his countrymen had overridden his earlier concerns. A phalanx was only as good as the men it contained and Numerius knew that Romans would be a far tougher test for the barbarian charge than the inferior men of Etruria.

The fact that Sulpicius had chosen to lead the army through the Carmental was not lost on him. It was the very same portal which his ancestors had used on their way to Cremera almost a century before. They had been practically wiped out in the Etruscan ambush there, indeed the fight had almost caused the extinction of his gens. Numerius recognised that his commander was still seeking to belittle him but had decided to ignore the insults. They were, he decided, the actions of a man of little worth and he felt confident that others would share his conclusion.

He had dined the previous evening at the home of his father, Marcus, the pontifex maximus, at his official residence the Domus Publica. Despite the depredations of Solemis and his horsemen, Numerius had insisted that Licinia and the girls remain as guests of Camillus at his residence in Ardea. Rome was still under threat and, although he was confident in the ability of the Roman army to drive off the barbarians, he was far less confident in the abilities of their commander. A disaster, although still unlikely, was still a remote possibility with Sulpicius in command of the army. The thought of the panic which would ensue within Rome if that did happen had been enough to ensure that he take up Camillus' offer of protection for Licinia and the girls.

His father and brothers, Quintus and Caeso, had discussed the offer of an alliance between the Fabii and the house of Camillus, the Furii, which the general had made during his discussions with Numerius. The ex dictator had offered several interesting concessions which could transform the balance of power within the senate, irrespective of the performance of Sulpicius in the present war.

Numerius looked across to his commander and snorted. The man would not be looking so confident had he been privy to the discussion in Ardea.

Beyond Sulpicius the army of Rome were drawn up in their armed centuries, while to one side the senators took their places for the final religious observations before the men left for war. With the centuries and senators now outside the walls of the city, the great doors were closed and barred and the military flag which flew atop the Janiculum Hill, across the Tiberis to the South, was raised. It would remain so until the garrison returned as an indication that the city was secure.

The hubbub slowly dulled as priests led forward a great white bull. A post had been driven into the ground before General Sulpicius, and Numerius joined his brothers and the other leaders as they waited for the ritual sacrifice to begin.

Dressed in breastplates, elaborate helmets and greaves of gleaming bronze, the commanders of the army were distinguished from the ranks by the red cloaks and horsehair plumes which shifted gently in the breeze. Each man carried a short sword and dagger for close order work, their exquisite workmanship a further indication of the owner's importance and wealth.

Oblivious to its fate, the bull began to munch contentedly on a scattering of grain and oats as the priests, gleaming in their crisp white robes, secured the beast to a great bronze ring.

The pontifex maximus approached in procession as the crowd grew silent, and Numerius felt pride that the mere appearance of his father could still such a multitude. Soothsayers in the city had been busy since before dawn as the men who would fight that day handed over silver and bronze to discern their fate. Now it was the turn for the auspices of the great army as a whole to be read, and men shifted nervously as the pontifex approached. A dozen red robed acolytes moved forward to hem in the bull as Marcus turned and faced towards the Temple of Jupiter, clearly visible atop the Capitoline to the South. Raising his arms he invoked the god.

"Jupiter, *Optimus Maximus*, accept our sacrifice here this day. Send us a sign that you will hold your hands over our brave men and return them in triumph to your city."

As the Pontifex' voice rang out over the silent field, a specially chosen acolyte emerged from the Temple of Mars which stood nearby. A low murmur escaped the ranks of the citizens as they saw that the man was carrying the *hastae martiae*, the sacred spears of Mars himself. Marcus took them from him with reverence and waited for the leader of the army to approach him. To the shock and horror of the group, Sulpicius waved a hand and addressed the head priest.

"I need not trouble mighty Mars with the very little which will be required. It's positively shameful. Call on his aid if you must, but I will not trouble a great god to lead me against a horde of barbarians."

For several moments the pontifex seemed lost for words as the leaders of the Roman army exchanged horrified glances. Fortunately the group were too far from the men of the army for the words to carry and Marcus, although staggered by the arrogance of the general, attempted to retrieve the situation for them. Raising the spears he shook them vigorously and made the ritual call on the god to awaken and lead his men to victory.

"Mars Vigila! Mars Vigila!"

A roar swept the campus martius as the army echoed the invocation and Marcus returned the spears to the acolyte's safekeeping as he moved forward to the sacrificial bull. As the men in red mumbled their incantations the pontifex slipped a long blade from within his robes and slid it beneath the neck of the animal. As he did so an acolyte began to sprinkle salt onto the head of the beast and the knife was drawn through with one powerful movement. A large bronze bowl was placed quickly beneath and the lifeblood of the beast gushed out to fill it within moments.

As the men hemming the bull in moved quickly away, the animal collapsed to the ground as it struggled against its tether. The agonised thrashings of the beast quickly stilled as Marcus peered intently into the cauldron of blood. Swilling the liquid, he marked the movements within as they swirled rapidly around. Finally he held the bowl to his lips and sipped. After visibly working the blood with his tongue the pontifex moved on to the belly of the now dead bull.

The long blade flashed once more in the morning sunshine, releasing the blue ropes of the animal's gut which spilled out onto the Field of Mars in a steaming mess. Marcus knelt and, placing his hand on the great white bulk of the bull's flank he reached inside the cavity. After several moments probing he jerked the knife and retrieved the great mass of the liver, the silence on the plain becoming palpable as the climax of the divination was reached.

As the pontifex placed the organ onto a brass platter and began to read the auspices, Numerius became aware of the fact that his commanders were no longer taking any interest in the matter. Deep in conversation, the pair looked to be on the point of abandoning the ritual before its completion. The pontifex also seemed to have noticed, and Numerius knew that his father had concluded the examination far quicker than normal.

Now soaked in blood, Marcus stood and declared the results of his reading.

"The outcome will be favourable to our arms!"

The tension on the field was released in a deafening roar as Sulpicius and his deputy commander, Quintus Servius Fidenas, nodded their thanks. Sulpicius turned to his brother officers and smiled.

"Well gentlemen, the gods are on our side. Shall we chase these savages away?"

Before the men could answer the pair had turned and were making their way back to the head of the army, waving happily as the soldiers and citizens yelled their support.

The Fabii brothers clasped forearms, and they prepared to return to their own centuries as the group began to disburse. Before they too left the scene of the sacrifice, Numerius joined his brothers in walking across to their father and were shocked to see the concern on his face. Marcus let the sacrificial bowl fall and regarded his sons with unconcealed foreboding.

"Take care, the omens were very bad." He seemed to grow visibly paler as he spoke. "I never thought that I would live to see such behaviour from a servant of Rome. Sulpicius has outraged the gods and many men will pay a heavy price for the arrogance of one."

"An early break, I think."

Fidenas turned to his commander in surprise.

"Shouldn't we at least cross the Tiberis? We will want to meet the enemy as far from Rome as possible."

Sulpicius gave him a look of pity.

"We can't come upon them before this evening at the earliest. It's my guess that we won't fight them until tomorrow. Numerius says that they don't fight at night because they are afraid of the spirits." He gave a chuckle of amusement. "Apparently they believe that if they die at night they may miss the boat and be left wandering the earth for all time. With the amount of barbarians that we are going to kill, that will leave a lot of spirits wandering the land. I doubt that the locals will thank us for that. No," he continued with a breezy smile, "Fidenae is already behind us, we should eat. There is no need to tire the men unnecessarily. The further from the city we march, the further it will be to return. Also," he added airily, "I want as many citizens as possible to be able to come to see the place of my victory."

Sulpicius raised an arm and the closest messenger rode to his side.

"Tell the column that we will be taking a break in the lee of that small hill ahead. We shall cross the river after I have decided who will take which position in the phalanx."

The man made a fist and raised it to his chest in salute before wheeling his mount and cantering back along the drawn-out line of the legions. Sulpicius called across to a decurion.

"Lucius, I want the *praetorium* erected. The countryside is all very pleasant, but if we are to fight in defence of civilisation we should at least enjoy its trappings. There is no need to wallow in rusticity."

Lucius Antonius Creticus nodded. After almost a month chasing shadows in the South he was desperate to come to grips with the Gauls again. The sight of wailing children huddled beneath the bodies of their fathers and brothers and the accusing eyes of their womenfolk had been hard to take. Even when they had run a Gaul to ground the bastard had killed eight of his men before they had had to resort to javelins to take him down. He had felt humiliated, less than a man, and his sword arm ached to take revenge.

"Shall I order the men to prepare a marching camp, legatus?"

The commander laughed aloud.

"Good grief no! We shall only tarry there for an hour or two. Tell the men to eat, and their centurions to report to me."

The Fabii were riding immediately to the rear of the commanders and they exchanged a look. Numerius urged his horse forward and spoke for them.

"We shall return to our centuries."

Sulpicius glanced across with a smirk.

"As you wish. But," he added as the smile fell from his features, "I really think that you should call me commander, Numerius; Protocol and all that."

Numerius gave a curt nod and managed to spit out the formality to Sulpicius' amusement. The brothers wheeled their mounts out of line and walked them back along the column. Caeso was the first to speak.

"Bastard! Tell me," he continued as they rode out of earshot, "who is beginning to grow concerned?"

They shared a look and Numerius grimaced, his brother had always been a master of understatement. Although he was a fearsome soldier, Caeso had a sharp sense of humour and could generally be relied upon to see the best in any situation. If he shared Numerius' own growing doubts at this early stage of the campaign things really were getting bad. Quintus cut in.

"Let's wait until the briefing takes place, we can air our views there. The Gauls are still a day away, we still have plenty of time to instil discipline and a sense of just how dangerous these Gauls can be into the army."

Numerius nodded his agreement.

"You are right. This stop could be just the opportunity we need to shake the army up."

*

The Roman column came to a halt less than a hundred paces away and Solemis instinctively pressed himself closer to the ground, shifting the tall grass before him aside with his fingertips. Satisfied that he remained concealed, he opened the small pigskin bag and began to count off the twigs.

They had been sent by Brennus to establish if the army of Rome had left their city. If it had, they were to return as soon as possible with an estimate of their composition and numbers. Leaving the camp soon after dawn, the Horsetails had moved south along the cassian way until midmorning. Soon after they had spotted the telltale dust cloud made by the approaching Romans hanging in the near distance.

Solemis had asked Camulos to provide him with a suitable vantage point, and the war god had provided him with the perfect place almost immediately.

The plain was wide here, and the road shadowed the sluggish brown waters of the River Tiberis as it meandered and made a turn to the south-west. The floodplain was girded by a small wood and hard against it snaked a long, grassy hillock. Leaving his clansmen with the horses in a small glade, he had stolen forward and taken up position on the rear of the mound just as the first Roman horsemen had cantered into view.

He had intended to count the columns as they passed his position, before doubling back to Brennus. Grouped together in neat blocks of eighty, the enemy numbers were easy to estimate with a high degree of accuracy. Each stick which he deposited represented the formation which he knew was called a century. A quick tally of the equites and Brennus would have all the information that he needed to plan his attack.

Suddenly, with the column fanning out to a halt before him, his plans lay in tatters. He had noticed the Fabii brothers leave the head of the column before the halt was called and he wondered that they had not been placed in command. The eldest, Numerius, seemed to be the most experienced among them and he had noticed how his brothers always deferred to his judgement. He had broken the law of nations when he had led the intervention by the Roman delegation outside Clevsin and Caturix, Aia's brother, had watched the man strike down their father, Crixos, the clan chieftain of the Crow.

He would be sure to seek out his new brother-in-law and inform him that the Fabii were present when he returned to the army.

The Roman leaders, resplendent in brilliantly polished armour and horsehair plumage, were gathering near the head of the valley and Solemis cast a look back along the road as he sought to judge the rate at which the rest of the army would come up. A quick attack now would decapitate the enemy, and his thoughts swirled at the possibility. The quick glance was enough to tell him that the opportunity would have been already lost before he could return with his clansmen. The Romans were already sweeping around their leaders as they began to set up camp and Solemis gave a shrug. He would have to live a little longer after all!

The sun was overhead now, its torrid heat beating directly down upon his back as Solemis judged that his survey was complete, and he drew the cord of the bag closed with his teeth as he prepared to leave. As he started to move a movement caught his eye and he froze. A Roman had passed twenty paces from his position and halted at the tree line. Solemis cursed as the man lifted his tunic and fumbled beneath before he began to urinate into the scrubby underwood.

Solemis pressed his face further down into the rough tangle of grasses on the lee of the hill as he waited for the man to finish. To his dismay, dozens of Romans began emulating their companion all along the tree line and Solemis' heart beat faster as he considered what to do. If he remained where he was he was bound to be discovered sooner or later. The Romans were obviously settling in while they ate, before moving forward again. He knew from experience that the first and last thing which all men did on a day march would be to take a piss. The Romans marched in column, unlike the unordered ranks of the Celtic army, and it was not possible for them to drop out at a whim. He realised that his situation had suddenly become desperate.

A soldier passed close by and pushed his way deeper into the trees and Solemis knew that as soon as he turned and squatted he would be seen and the alarm raised. He moved his hand carefully to the grip of his sword as he prepared to cut his way to freedom. Surprise would be on his side for the first few yards, but after that, he knew, his chances of escape would be slight. The tree line was now full of Romans in varying states of undress, and his muscles tensed as he prepared to burst from cover. He risked turning his head slightly to bring the Roman into his field of vision and he caught his breath as the man lowered himself and regarded him with a look of puzzlement. Suddenly his mouth fell open as he prepared to call out, but an instant later his features disappeared as a hand smothered his face and pulled him sharply backwards. Solemis just caught the flash of silver as a blade rose and fell and then all was still once more.

Taking a deep breath, Solemis took the only action which he could if he was to stand a chance of escape. Despite the fact that he would be the only man wearing trews in the entire clearing, he knew that he had no option other than to stand and calmly walk away. He thanked the gods that he had worn his red checked cloak that day despite the fierce heat. He had noticed that the senior Romans tended to wear a similar shade and it could only help. It had been a gift from Aia and he always wore it for luck when battle seemed imminent. Today he would find out if he had been mistaken.

Solemis rose and walked as calmly as he could towards the safety of the trees. Without daring to look to left or right, he waited for the cry of alarm as each step brought him closer to safety until, with an ease which astonished him, he passed from the harsh light of the field into the welcoming embrace of the shadows.

As he began to breathe more easily the bulk of Albiomaros emerged from behind a trunk, his features split with a grin.

"Nice stroll?"

Solemis stifled a laugh as the tension of the moment was released. They were far from clear and could still be discovered at any moment. His friend indicated a nearby bush and Solemis could just make out a pair of feet protruding from the base.

"Give me a hand with Titus, here. If we can dump him further away, they may think that he has just changed his mind about taking on the savages after all and run for it."

Solemis nodded.

"Push the bloodied leaf mould further into the thicket. It's the best we can do."

Solemis helped Albiomaros to hoist the dead Roman onto his shoulders and then scooped the worst of the bloody leafage into the hollow of a tree. A quick last scan of the area told him that they had done the best that they could to hide the killing and, snatching up the bag containing the tallies, the young chieftain followed on.

NINE

The outriders exchanged looks of concern as their cheerful greetings were ignored by the Horsetails who thundered past without a glance. Barely a mile behind them, the army of the Senones, twenty-thousand strong, were coming on fast as they sought to close the distance to the city which had treated them with such disdain.

Solemis reined in as he reached the column as they rested in the shade of the tree lined road, and he allowed a small smile to crease his features as he contrasted the demeanour of the two armies. The Celts had squatted where they came to a halt on the roadway, still set in their clans and ready for action at a moments notice.

Brennus himself sat in the roadway at their head as he chewed the same food and shared his wine with even the youngest, downy cheeked clansmen. The tribal chieftain saw Solemis approach and rose to his feet, brushing the road dust from the seat of his trews as he did so. The small group with him stood also as they noticed the look on Solemis' face and they listened in as he breathlessly reported his findings to Brennus.

"They are only five miles ahead of us."

Brennus looked shocked.

"Five miles? We have seen no scouts. Is it an ambush or are they behind prepared positions?"

Solemis shook his head as he reached out for his chieftain's amphora. Swilling the wine he spat the road dust from his mouth onto the verge.

"Neither; they are taking a leisurely meal. The commander has pitched a magnificent tent while the men of the army are wandering about the plain or laying about, talking in groups." Solemis gripped his chieftain's sleeve as the light of vengeance burned in his eyes. "We have them, Brennus. They have no idea that we are so near!"

Brennus made a fist and grinned. Turning back he raised his arm and called back along the column.

"Chieftains!"

The army rose to its feet with a clatter as the men hurried forward. The sense of urgency had been obvious from the war leader's tone, and dozens of men turned aside to empty their bladders where they stood as the prospect of battle suddenly loomed large. Brennus paced the road impatiently as the last of the leaders rode up and dismounted. The army of the Senones covered almost two miles of the via cassia, and Solemis looked on with pride as the warriors instinctively checked their weapons and adjusted armour as they waited for instructions. Brennus began as the last chieftains to arrive hastened across.

"The Romans are in disorder only five miles ahead of us." He turned to Solemis who had been counting out the sticks from his bag.

"How many are there, Solemis?"

He finished counting the tallies and tossed them aside.

"Two legions…that's six thousand spear men, plus maybe two thousand light skirmishers."

Brennus' face lit up.

"Equites?"

Solemis smiled and shook his head.

"Only fifty or so; unless they are following on I would say that they must still be in the South, searching for raiders."

The chieftains laughed. Solemis' attacks in the Latium had succeeded beyond their wildest dreams. Not only were the Romans blundering blindly forward but they would be fighting a battle with badly depleted numbers. Brennus' expression became serious as he pumped Solemis for information.

"Describe the place where they are, quickly now."

The good humour died away and the expressions on the faces of the chieftains hardened as they caught the mood. Their war leader was coming to a decision and they listened intently.

"The Tiberis meanders there between two sets of hills. The Romans are encamped on the left bank as we look at it which carries the road, this road. It is," Solemis paused and pulled a face as he estimated the width of the plain, "roughly one mile wide there, it varies due to the winding nature of the river. The road keeps to the rising ground, away from the floodplain and hugs the side of a wood. A small, steep sided brook emerges from the hills close to their position and runs alongside the road for about a mile before it enters the Tiberis. A long, low hillock stands hard on to the wood there. It is not tree covered like the other hills, they may use it as a vantage point to threaten our flank if we cannot deny it to them. It's where I hid as I watched them arrive."

Brennus looked at him earnestly as he spat out a question.

"Yes, but you said that they were eating. I need to know what they had."

Solemis gaped in confusion before Brennus' face creased into a broad smile. The other chieftains laughed as their war leader clapped Solemis on the shoulder.

"A jest, Solemis; we could not have asked for a more detailed description of their numbers and disposition, well done."

Brennus hugged the bemused Horsetail affectionately to him and turned to the group. The chieftains were clearly buoyed up by their leader's confidence and good humour and they strained like wolfhounds at the leash.

"You all know the place which has been assigned to your clan in the battle line. The men are fed and rested. We keep to the road and jog the five miles to this place." He turned to Solemis and laid a hand on his shoulder. "The Horsetails will lead us and halt their mounts as the enemy come into sight." Looking back he continued. "That will be the sign for the clans to deploy from the roadway into the battle line. Don't stop, just fan out from the road, carnyx to the fore, and charge on my signal. We can hit these bastards before they know we are coming and roll over them." He paused and scanned the group, the excitement of the moment reflected in his eyes. "Any questions, make them quick ones."

Caturix spoke.

"Are there any obstacles in our path, Solemis? Settlements or bridges which might slow us down?"

Brennus looked across and raised his brow.

"It's a good question."

Solemis smiled and shook his head.

"Nothing, it's a clear road all the way to the enemy camp."

Brennus quickly scanned the group.

"Is that it? Good," he concluded. "Let's get going!"

As the chieftains wished each other luck and began to hurry back to their clans, Solemis called across to his friend.

"Big brother!"

Caturix turned back as the other chieftains pushed past, grinning widely despite the urgency of the moment. He had begun to call Solemis little brother on the journey across the Alps. Crixos had paired the two as he sought confirmation that the young Senone was a suitable suitor for his only daughter and it had been Solemis' first indication that he might be successful.

"The Fabii are with the army; I saw them."

Caturix' features broke into a wolfish smile and he gave one, curt nod, before he hurried back to his clan. Today he would take the blood price.

*

The valley of the Tiberis sweltered under a cobalt sky as the heat of the day pressed down on the Roman officers. The praetorium was airless, and Sulpicius wondered if it would be better to abandon it altogether and hold the briefing in the open air after all. After a moment turning the idea over in his mind he decided against the move. He had had the chairs lined up in a neat row now and he would savour the moment as he presided over them. It was worth the discomfort.

He neither possessed, nor particularly aspired to, the natural aura of military command which some of the other men present seemed to exude almost effortlessly. He was not a military man, but it had always been the duty of every free citizen, great or small, to serve in the army when called upon. The politician in him recognised the value of a great victory to his further advancement, and the barbarians had happened along at just the right time.

He would have preferred if the other cities of Latium had supplied their own contingents to the army as had been agreed under the terms of Cassius' treaty. After all it had only been in effect for six years, but he could understand their reluctance. They had suffered under the depredations of the Celts over the course of the last few weeks, and Rome had sent her equites to support them as the terms of the treaty dictated. They had yet to return when word had reached the city that the barbarians were coming against them, and although the more timid among his colleagues had advised him to await their return, time was against them, the barbarians were moving too quickly. Still, he reflected, it would make his removal of the threat all the more impressive.

He glanced up as the Fabii entered the tent to take the last of the places and greeted them with a vacuous smile. Numerius stifled a yawn as his commander began his address.

"Thank you, gentlemen. Now that we have all arrived I shall outline our plan of attack. As you all know I expect to make contact with the barbarian army sometime this evening. We shall of course construct a marching camp and... "

Numerius watched as a crane fly bounced repeatedly against the canvas ceiling in an effort to escape and allowed himself a surreptitious smile as the general droned on in his irritating way.

I know how you feel, little one!

To face the man across the floor of the senate house was bad enough but to receive a lecture in the field was more than he could be expected to bear. Quintus was always attentive, he would let him know the salient points later.

As the last to arrive, the brothers had taken the only places available, and Numerius was near enough to the entrance to the command tent to be the first officer to notice the sound. At first he thought that he had heard the melancholy lowing of a cow as it was slaughtered to provide meat for the men, but the sound seemed to rise and fall and show no sign of coming to the customary abrupt end. As his mind began to concentrate on the mysterious sound, another added itself to the rising din. Ignoring the others, who seemed to be blissfully unaware of the commotion outside, he left his seat and peeled back the tent flap. He was dimly aware that Sulpicius had stopped speaking and his brother, Quintus, came to his side and gripped his arm, startling him. They exchanged a look of horror as they reached the same conclusion.

"They are here!"

*

Solemis peered into the heat haze as he slowed his mount to a walk. The sun was high overhead now and the heat seemed to radiate back from the valley sides as it narrowed to a choke point. It would have been the ideal place for the Romans to draw up their army and he thanked Camulos that they had not taken the opportunity. He had missed the small detail on his mad dash north and he hoped that the other chieftains would be too caught up in their battle fervour to notice.

Once through the gap he was back on familiar territory and his heart leapt as he saw the end of the long hillock appear away to his left hand side. The poor visibility had caused him to practically run onto the Roman positions and he halted Tantibus and waited for the rest of his clan to draw up alongside him.

They were within a mile of the enemy and still they had not responded. No guards had been posted and not even a solitary horseman had scouted the road ahead. It could only be the work of the gods, and Solemis promised that he would repay their generosity with gold and weapons once the victory was theirs.

Albiomaros came up and threw him a lopsided grin, the owl face above his helm glinting in the sunlight as he hefted his shield and kissed the blade of his spear for luck. Solemis raised his head proudly and called down the line as the thunderous rumble made by thousands of heavily armed men filled the bowl. Without glancing back he knew that the army had reached them and was deploying in his wake. Within moments the carnyx players would walk proud of the line and fill the valley with their mournful notes. He was determined that the war horn of the Horsetails should be the very first to shake the Romans from their slumbers.

"Cotos, I believe that we promised them that our battle swine would return when the Bel Fires had burned and the snows had retreated." He looked sidelong and grinned. "Shall we keep our promise?" Cotos nodded proudly and walked his mount forward a dozen steps. As he spat to clear his mouth and raised the great boar headed horn to his lips, Solemis saw that the haze had lifted to reveal the enemy still at rest, the tips of their spears points of light as they rested, sheaf-like, on the plain.

The mournful howl rose into the sultry air and Solemis watched as heads were turned their way for the first time. Within moments a blast of noise came from the army to his rear and Solemis felt the hairs on the back of his neck rise as the clans beat their shields and called their challenges.

A group of druids emerged from the centre of the line pushing a captive before them. Distinctive in their brown clothing and shaved brows, the leading man thrust a spear into the captive's belly as his companions slashed at him with their crescent shaped hand blades. The prisoner fell to the ground and the druids watched as he writhed before them in agony. Close by, Brennus' face looked pensive as he waited for the gods to give their blessings to his plan but within moments the chief druid stood and announced that the omens were good and a great roar of joy erupted from the Senone ranks. Brennus beamed and raised his spear in salute as Solemis watched his chieftain mount up and canter along the length of the shield wall.

*

Numerius turned and called across the upturned faces of his brother officers as the sound of the Gaulish battle line rolled down upon them.

"Sulpicius..." He paused as he recalled the man's sneering comment from earlier that day. "Commander; the Gauls have apparently decided not to wait until we have eaten. What are your orders?"

He watched as the man stood, frozen in indecision, and shook his head in dismay.

"I will assemble the men into their formations while you decide where you would like to position them."

He hastened off as the sound of the barbarian army rose and fell away to his right. The men seemed transfixed by the sound and the majority stood and stared into the haze in disbelief. Numerius called out and they turned to him instinctively.

"Gather into your centuries in battle order, *rorarii* to the rear."

As men began to come alive to the danger, he spotted a burly centurion calmly indicating where the front row of the phalanx should draw up into its battle array. It was a well chosen spot given the limitations of the field and Numerius trotted across.

"Centurion; what do they call you?"

Despite the desperation of their situation the man saluted and pulled a small smile. Numerius instinctively knew that he was a man who could be relied upon. Every army possessed a smattering of such individuals who seemed to grow happier the bleaker the situation became. He had been lucky enough to have more than his fair share in the army which he had commanded when the

Volscian City of Anxur had fallen to him and he knew their worth.

"Quintus Caedicius, tribune, although the men have several other names for me."

Numerius snorted as the men ran in all directions around them.

"Yes, I am sure that they do." He glanced back at the praetorium as the other officers began to emerge and disperse to their centuries. There was still no sign of either Sulpicius or Fidenas so he turned back to the centurion.

"Caedicius. Hold the centre until General Sulpicius arrives. I will send the centuries to you here and I want you to get them into line as quickly as you can."

Everywhere men were snatching up lances and javelins as they organised themselves into their centuries and rushed to the front line. Sulpicius finally emerged from the praetorium and walked calmly across. Impending catastrophe or not, it was beneath a patrician's to panic, and Numerius found that he had finally discovered a quality in his commander of which he approved.

"Thank you, Numerius. I shall take over now."

He glanced back at the Gauls who were now clearly in view at the point where the Allia Brook emerged from behind the curious long hill.

"A quick private briefing, as it would appear that you could not wait like the others."

The officers had shepherded the main phalanx into position now, and a quick glance told Numerius that the few equites which remained with them in the North were beginning to gain the crest of the hillock on the right. Sulpicius continued.

"I will lead this legion with the second legion to my right under the command of Quintus Servius Fidenas. A small reserve will join the equites and a number of the rorarii on the hill to our right. The centuries under the command of the Fabii will anchor the left wing against the Tiberis with the remainder of the skirmishers."

Numerius realised that the brothers were being kept as far away from the scene of any potential glory but he was experienced enough in warfare to know that this was no time to argue. He nodded and turned away just as his optio hurried across.

"Cassius, move the men across to the left." He shot the man a wry smile. "We have been given the honour of defending the ducks and reed beds."

Numerius cast an experienced eye over the ground on which he was to fight as he jogged across. Years of spring flooding had levelled the plain there and although the ground was dry and firm, numerous small runnels crisscrossed the part nearest the riverbank. Although the heat of summer had long since removed any water from them, the stinking channels would prove treacherous in the unlikely event of an advance. Packed closely together, the men in the phalanx would find it impossible to keep formation as the ground suddenly fell away beneath them.

To the rear, the river curled back upon itself in a wide meander and Numerius grimaced. If the centre gave way, they would have little chance of retreat. It was, he decided grimly, pretty much the worst position which he had ever been given to hold, a veritable death trap.

Cassius had already chivvied the century into position when he arrived and further across he saw that his brothers, Caeso and Quintus, stood ready at the centre of their own.

As he gained his century he saw that the goddess Fortuna had at least favoured him with a small smile that day by placing the century commanded by Quintus Caedicius immediately to his right, and he acknowledged the grizzled veteran with a nod and a smile as he passed.

The line now reached from the edge of the wood, across the mile wide plain to the riverbank itself, but Numerius saw at a glance that it was stretched painfully thin. Solemis' attacks in the south had not only stripped the Roman army of the vast majority of its horsemen, but caused their Latin allies to retain their forces to guard their home cities. It had practically halved the number of men available for the defence of Rome which, added to Sulpicius' failure to scout ahead of the army, was threatening them with the catastrophe of which he had always warned. Threadbare or not, there was no excuse for the lack of scouting by the remaining equites. At the very least it would have provided the army with the chance to pick its ground, narrowing its front. Numerius sent a word of prayer to mighty Mars, the thunderer.

Great Mars. Forgive the arrogance of Quintus Sulpicius Longus on the field which bears your name, the Sulpicii were always thus. Send a thunderbolt to aid your devoted followers and I will sacrifice this chieftain of the Gauls, Brennus, at your temple."

The army of Rome was finally set, and the great lances of the phalanx lowered as one to deny passage to the horde. It was not a moment too soon as, half a mile distant, the wail of the Gaulish war horns and the ferocious din of the warriors redoubled as their first attack of the day went in.

TEN

As the Romans scattered across the plain and fell into line before him, Solemis wheeled Tantibus and trotted towards the army. Mounted, Brennus was riding the length of the Senone war line as he pointed out men from their fellows, praising their past deeds and lineage. A mighty roar followed the passage of the chieftain and Solemis reined in and watched the display with pride.

On the dusty plain below him the druids had completed their work, and the unfortunate captive had already set out for the realm of Aita, Etruscan god of the underworld. The young Horsetail gave an involuntary shiver as the druids discussed the secrets which the ceremony had revealed to them. Like all warriors, he respected and feared the power of the seers but preferred to place his trust in muscle and skill for the dance of death which was to come.

In the line opposite throats were parched from the rapid march, and the men passed around skins of water, wine or their own cervezia as the noise rose to new levels.

Brennus turned back at the riverbank and, spotting Solemis, galloped across, the great battle raven which capped his helm beating its wings in time to the horse's hoof fall. He indicated the hillock with his head.

"Solemis, I don't like the look of that position. I can see the horsemen, but what are they hiding? They could be screening any number of men on the far side of the hill. If that is the case they will outflank us as soon as we launch an attack."

Solemis looked across as he began to fasten the straps of his helm. It had been a pleasure to remove his headgear as he rode to battle. The heat on the plain was intense and sweat began to trickle down his neck almost immediately. Even the handle of his sword was almost too hot to grasp. Following Brennus' gaze over to the hilltop, he began to grow concerned for the first time that day as he watched the distant Romans forming up on the ridge.

"Shall I take the Horsetails and drive them off?" He unstopped his own water skin and took a swig as Brennus studied the Roman line.

"It's a shame that we couldn't have just hit them as we arrived, but the run in this heat really sapped the men's strength." He shrugged. "No matter; if they have less than ten thousand men in total as you say, that line will be stretched as tight as a virgin, especially if they have taken men to mount a flanking attack." He nodded as he came to his decision. "Yes, take your Horsetails and Caturix' Crow and drive them off. If you can, get in behind the phalanx on the plain and roll them up." He glanced back at the roistering multitude behind him and smiled. "I don't think that they would wait for the champions to issue their challenges today, the run has already warmed them up nicely! I will wait until I see you gain the ridge line and launch the main attack."

Brennus dismounted and picked the sweat soaked trews from his legs with a grimace of discomfort. Retrieving his shield and lancea, he slapped the horse on the rump and watched as it trotted away. As he prepared to take up the position of honour at the centre of the battle hedge he threw his young friend a last smile.

"If you beat me to *Anwnn*, save me a place at the benches."

Solemis pulled a wry smile and shook his head.

"I can't go yet. I promised the Romans that I would return." He indicated the roadside with a flick of his head. "According to that stone, I still have eleven miles to go!"

*

Lucius Antonius Creticus crested the shallow rise and curbed his mount. Even the small hillock offered a commanding view of the table smooth flood plain below and he drew an involuntary gasp as he looked out across the heads of both armies.

It was plain from his vantage point that only the intervention of a god could save the day and Sulpicius had, of course, already done his best to anger them. There were rumours among the men that he had taken the auspices sent by Jupiter with less than the reverence that the father of the gods would expect. To then refuse to invoke the spirit of Mars by leaving the old pontifex to shake the sacred spears on his behalf was breathtaking, both in its arrogance and stupidity. To compound the feeling of dread, the sudden arrival of the Gauls had left no time to offer a sacrifice for victory, much less a taking of the auspices for the battle to come.

Behind him the first of the rorarii were labouring to the top of the hill. Drawn from the middling class of the citizenry, they carried no armour save a small round shield and the dubious protection offered by a cap of wolf skin. Most, he noticed with relief, seemed to have provided themselves with a sword and a small dagger but he harboured no illusions as to their effectiveness if the northern giants reached his position.

He could see that the depth of the phalanx had been reduced, from eight to five in the centre where the main Gaulish blow could be expected to fall, tapering down to a truly horrifying three ranks at the extreme flanks. He knew that his commanders had had no choice if they were to present the barbarians with a continuous front, and he cursed the actions of the Gaulish raiders which had kept so many of their men in the South.

His gaze wandered over to the animated ranks of the enemy and he suddenly craned forward in his saddle and shielded his eyes against the glare of the sun. His heart leapt as he realised the identity of the horseman there, and he gripped the sleeve of his optio as he pointed him out.

"Titus! It's him!"

Titus leaned into his saddle horn and nodded sagely.

"Yes, I believe it is!" He gave a sidelong look. "Who, exactly?"

Despite the tension of the moment, the decurion found that he was laughing.

"Titus, if you were not about to die, I would be seriously concerned that you may one day produce offspring."

He watched as one of the horsemen dismounted and crossed to take position at the centre of the army of Gauls while the other cantered across the field, his men funnelling in his wake.

"The horseman...there; it must be the man Solemis, the man who led the raiders in the South."

Titus looked unconvinced as Lucius explained.

"He wears a conical bronze helm with a horsehair plume just as his victims described and all of his men carry spears topped by horsehair, it must be them. They have obviously doubled back and rejoined the army for the main assault." The decurion found that, despite his hatred for the man and the results of his raid, he felt a grudging respect for the Gaul. His actions had drawn away the Roman equites and denuded the army of almost half of its potential strength.

"This could be our chance old friend. If the opportunity presents itself, I promise you that I will kill the man."

*

The Horses tossed and snorted as the Horsetails swept across in front of the army. Refreshed, the Senone clans were now a roistering wall of noise as spears were beaten against shields and challenges called across the plain. The carnyx players still stood forward of the line, and a rising wail filled the air as Solemis halted before the Crow clan. Caturix, their chieftain came across and Solemis leaned forward and shouted above the din.

"Brennus wants us to clear that hill and outflank them if we can before the main attack goes in." He pulled a grin at his friend. "Lead the attack with the Crow, we are here to take revenge for the slaying of Crixos after all. We will follow you."

Caturix' face shone with pride. It was the greatest honour to be the first to close with the enemy and he gripped Solemis' forearm in an unspoken gesture of gratitude before turning away and calling his men back to their mounts. Solemis wheeled Tantibus and rode into the press of his own men as they waited for the Crow to mount up.

"The Crow will lead us. We are to clear the hill on the left and then swing behind the main Roman army and cause as much havoc there as we can." He looked about the eager faces of his clansmen as they clustered around him. Albiomaros looked fearsome in his owl fronted helm and the others, toughened by years of fighting and a month in the saddle, looked no less formidable. They had only rejoined the army a few days previously and the smell of smoke and grime hung about them still.

Caturix came up and he adjusted the strap of his helm a final time as his men began to collect around him. Hefting his shield and spear he exchanged a final grin with his brother-in-law and urged his mount forward with his knees. His clansmen whooped and followed on as Cotos sounded the Horsetail war horn in salute.

As the last of the Crow passed him, Solemis pulled his own shield into his left side and brandished his lancea. His war cry, *'Horsetails!'* was taken up by his clan and he kicked Tantibus towards the incline.

After a very few paces Solemis sawed at the reins, guiding Tantibus to one side as the dust rose to cloak the riders, and galloped on. The direction of the Senone attack was obvious now and, as he watched, the skirmishers came forward onto the brow of the hill and hefted their javelins. A quick estimate told him that there were several hundred men facing them, and Solemis felt a sharp pang of guilt as he recognised that the blow would fall heaviest on the Crow, now approaching the incline.

Cotos, at his side, braced himself against the horns of his saddle and blew a rising note as they swept onto the long arm of rising land. A glint of silver ahead told him that the Romans had released the first wave of javelins and he instinctively raised his shield and hunched over as the wicked projectiles fell among them. The howl from the Horsetail carnyx ended abruptly and Solemis was half aware that Cotos had fallen away from his side. Tantibus, trained in the ways of war by the expert hand of Rodolfo, barely broke stride as he picked his way through the dust and chaos of fallen men and horses.

Despite the din of war which engulfed him, a throaty roar at his elbow made Solemis start and he felt a sense of reassurance as he recognised that the voice belonged to Albiomaros.

A second fall of javelins rained down among them, but despite the mayhem all around, Solemis sensed that the assault had been far more ragged. Either Caturix was among them or close enough that they had been forced to retire behind the equites, only the bravest remaining for one last volley before they too scrambled for safety.

Discounting the aerial threat, Solemis lowered his shield and raised his lancea as the line of enemy horsemen came into view. The Roman right had already descended into a scrum of maddened horses and desperately hacking riders. Solemis noted that the skirmishers were returning and attempting to duck and weave beneath the Crow mounts, using their short swords and daggers to stab up at the riders or into the sides of the horses. He watched as

Ferox, one of Caturix' leading warriors, was unhorsed by the tactic and he cried out a warning as they approached their own opponents.

"Draw swords and look out for skirmishers!"

He picked out a Roman horseman who had left it late to raise his shield and launched his lancea at the man. The spear flew true and the Roman slumped forward as it punched home. Solemis recognised the decurion in charge of the men by the plume on his helm and watched as he raised his own sword and called the charge as they breasted the slope. It was a good tactic but it had confirmed to Solemis that the Romans were relatively few in number. Reluctant to leave the safety of the high ground, the decurion had waited until the climb had sapped the power of their charge. If he had had the numbers, he would have used the slope to his advantage, adding weight to their charge in an attempt to sweep them aside before they could threaten his position.

Solemis gripped Tantibus' flanks with his knees and braced himself as the view ahead was swallowed by an avalanche of horses and men. A heartbeat later they came together with a bone jarring crash.

Solemis held tight to the reins as Tantibus was momentarily pushed back and a Roman spear glanced from his shield to pass harmlessly along his side. The horse was strong and recovered quickly, forcing itself forward into the ranks of the enemy and Solemis slashed out to his right as an *equite* was pushed against him by the crush. He caught a glimpse of the terrible beak on the front of Albiomaros' helm for an instant before a body was pushed between them. Too close to bring the sword blade into play, Solemis twisted his wrist and sent the heavy pommel crashing into the man's face as he pushed his way through. His opponent fell away, opening up a gap between Solemis and the next Roman and he quickly hacked down into the man's shoulder as the brawl began to open up.

After the first shock of impact, the fight had dissolved into tangled knots of stabbing, slashing madmen, and the young chieftain knew that it was a dangerous moment. The skirmishers would seize their chance to return and attack the Celtic horsemen while their attention was on the life and death struggle with their opposite numbers.

Solemis quickly looked about him, the fight miraculously melting away as the Crow charge carried the main fight to the South. The way was open to him for a dash at the summit but the charge would be premature. Hundreds of spear men stood ready there, and although thankfully it would appear that they had already discharged their supply of javelins, the sight of hundreds of sword blades in the hands of the desperate looking men was enough to discourage any thoughts of a lone attack.

Solemis quickly looked across the ridge line as he sought to see how well the fight was going. The Crow seemed to have drawn most of the opposition across to the right and the fighting there was still heavy. Albiomaros had been drawn across there and he watched as the big man's sword blade rose and fell as he chopped a path through the Roman riders.

Without the great beast head of Cotos' carnyx to mark his position, only the horsehair plume on his helm would mark him as the clan chieftain and, heavily engaged, his clansmen had momentarily lost sight of their leader.

Before he could decide where to re-enter the fray the decision was taken from him.

Lucius glanced across and, despite the pall of dust which hung in the air, Solemis could see that the decurion knew him as the enemy leader. Expertly detaching himself from the fight, the Roman urged his mount into a gallop as he came on, his face contorted into a snarl as his sword swung in great arcs above him.

Solemis tugged at the reins and urged Tantibus forward as the Roman closed. Foregoing the protection of his shield he guided his mount to the left at it cantered across the gradient of the slope. The move would take him above the decurion, and he hoped that the added weight which the advantage would lend to his sword stroke would more than compensate for his lack of protection. It would also help him to guard against any sudden rush downhill from the Roman skirmishers, and the world seemed to narrow to encompass the two men as they came together.

Solemis raised his sword and brought it down in a raking blow. To his horror the blade bit deeply into the rim of Lucius' shield and he watched, helpless, as the decurion twisted his grip and wrenched the sword from his grasp. Tossing them away down the hillside, Lucius grinned in triumph as he sawed savagely at his reins and turned back towards the unarmed Celt.

Solemis risked a glance back towards the fighting. Several of his men had now realised that he had become detached from the main fight and he could see that they were desperately attempting to disengage from their opponents and come to his aid. He could also see that they would arrive too late and his mind raced. As the Roman raised his sword to administer the killing stroke, Solemis threw his body back along the spine of his horse. The blade hissed inches above his outstretched body, and Solemis rolled from the back of his mount in one slick movement.

Lucius cursed and hauled back on the reins as the Roman rorarii on the crest above roared their encouragement. Solemis skipped and ducked as he sought to keep Tantibus between himself and the Roman while he desperately searched the ground for a discarded weapon. Several javelins from the earlier onslaught had fallen short and Solemis grabbed at Tantibus' bridle as he guided the horse across to them. The war horse seemed to understand that his master needed help, and he pushed his way between the men as Solemis made a dive for the javelin and rolled back onto his feet.

Lucius lashed out at the horse with the flat of his sword as he forced his own mount through. A quick glance told the Roman that several Celts had extricated themselves from the fight and were desperately trying to come to the chieftain's aid, but they would fail.

A momentary flash of burned buildings, hanging bodies and wailing women came into his mind as he stared down at the man responsible. The memory flooded him with anger and his sword came crashing down to sever the metal point from the javelin. The fight was won, and he allowed himself a small smile of triumph as he brought his blade back across to knock the flimsy shaft of the javelin to one side. He knew in his heart that this was the man who had inflicted so much destruction on the people of his city, but he grudgingly recognised the man's courage as he finally seemed to accept his fate, standing proudly as he awaited his god to ferry him below.

Steeling himself for the end, Solemis watched in disbelief as Tantibus turned back and bared his teeth. Rodolfo had tried to describe the ferocity which made an expertly trained war horse such a thing of fear on the battlefields of the southern lands, but this would be the first time that the Horsetail would witness the savagery for himself.

As Lucius raised his sword again to take his prize, Tantibus reared and kicked the air with his forelegs. Before the man realised that he was in any danger, a hoof crashed down into his skull, spraying blood and bone in a crimson arc as the decurion was thrown from the saddle. As Solemis looked on in amazement, the horse curled its lip back into a snarl and nipped the Roman's horse in an effort to reach the body of its rider. As the horse bolted, Tantibus reared and fell, again and again, pummelling the body of the Roman until it was little more than a bloody smear on the hillside.

As his horse bucked and wheeled in anger, Solemis attempted to push the scene from his mind. The fight was still to be won and although the horse had saved his life, as he had been trained to do, Solemis was accustomed to the violence of battle. The gods were forever dreaming up ways in which warriors could lose their lives for their entertainment; death by horse was far from the most bizarre end he had witnessed. Gathering up the Roman's shield and sword he walked across and remounted as Berikos and Druteos finally arrived and circled him, protectively.

Solemis patted Tantibus on the neck as he shared a grin with his men. Berikos was still staring, wide eyed, at his war horse and Solemis laughed.

"Extra oats for someone tonight!"

Albiomaros had managed to disengage himself from the fight and he led half a dozen men across. Before he could come to a halt, Solemis had made his decision and he drove Tantibus up the incline towards the now silent ranks of Romans. Their joy of victory had been replaced by sudden and horrific defeat and the confidence of the skirmishers had drained away in an instant. It was the perfect opportunity and Solemis called his men on as he bore down on the Roman line.

As he reached the crest of the hill he could see that the rear ranks, the natural gathering place of the weaker and less able, were already streaming away into the safety of the trees. A robust assault here would keep them running all the way back to the city, and the young chieftain yelled his war cries as he plunged into their ranks. Still shield less, a well coordinated Roman attack would have brought him down but he hacked madly to left and right as the demoralised men shrank back before him. Within moments the others were up with him and they screamed in fury as they drove a wedge into the enemy line. Suddenly they broke, and the Horsetails chased the fleeing Romans into the wood, hewing scores of them down before they could reach the safety of its shadows.

Solemis curbed Tantibus at the base of the slope and hauled on his reins as he looked back up at the fighting. Large numbers of men at the rear of the main position had watched the fate of their flank and Solemis knew that a quick push there could decide the fight. Gathering his men around him he blinked the stinging sweat from his eyes and pointed with his sword as he called out to them.

"Hit them again. Hard!"

Cantering across the back slope of the hill, he watched with savage delight as hundreds of the Roman skirmishers there began to stream towards the wood, casting aside their weapons in their haste to reach safety. As Solemis reached the brow he could see the familiar sight of Caturix' helm less than fifty yards away as it swept to left and right in time with the scything arc of his blade. The hill was almost theirs, a final push and it would fall.

ELEVEN

They were less than a day away from the castro when the riders appeared on the low ridge line to the South. Philippos' young eyes had been the first to pick them out against the browns and greens of the grassland which the locals called the meseta and the carter, Caciro, had cursed the delay caused by the broken wheel as he scourged the oxen. Catumanda twisted on the bench and looked back at the horsemen.

"Who are they?"

Caciro turned his head and spat into the dust of the roadway before replying.

"Lusitani; it is best that you ignore them and hope that they have better things to amuse themselves with. The boy can keep an eye on them for us."

He moved his head to the side and called over the rumble of wheels.

"Philippos, just watch them and let us know if they look to be heading this way."

The Greek rested his back against the side panel of the wagon and settled down as if unconcerned by the sudden appearance of the armed party, and Catumanda smiled at the boy's composure. The druid moved a hand inside her tunic and ran her fingertips across the handle of her new moon blade. She had not yet had the opportunity to use the blade in anger and she found that, to her surprise, she was hoping that the riders *would* attack.

They had been travelling east now for almost two weeks. Lindo had escorted them back to the smithy where Uxentio had proudly presented the finished blade to a delighted Catumanda before the druid had arranged their onward passage by boat. The same River Dubro which emptied into the sea at Cale cut through the uplands of the interior, almost to the great hill fort at Numantia. Sheer sided, the watercourse had led them unerringly towards the Greek trading city which was their ultimate goal.

Emporion lay on the north-eastern coast of Iberia and Lindo had assured his fellow druid that she would find a ship there to take the young boy home to the Greek settlements on Sikelia. Transferring to the cart as the river grew ever narrower and wilder as it neared its source, the pair had been delayed by a broken wheel. Now it would seem that the gods were to provide one more delay before they reached the safety of the castro. Philippos called out from the bed of the cart as the oxen laboured on.

"They are coming down off the ridge and moving towards us."

With all his hopes dashed, Caciro drew back his arm to whip the lumbering oxen on. Catumanda touched his arm, causing him to pause in mid action. She raised her voice as he did so and leaned in to him.

"How far is it to the castro?"

Caciro looked confused for a heartbeat but finally answered.

"Six...seven miles; why?"

She glanced across his shoulder at the oncoming horsemen. The whites of their faces were already visible, they would be upon them in no time.

"It is senseless to run and we can't outdistance them anyway. Keep to a steady pace and tell me what you know about them."

Caciro hesitated. Everything told him to delay the confrontation for as long as possible but the wisdom of the druid's words were undeniable. He lowered his arm, pursing his lips nervously.

"They will be young warriors led by a war chief, elected from among their number. They roam the land like a pack of wolves with no settled home. Some of the tribes speak our tongue but those further south," he spat in disgust, "babble away in gibberish, and they are practically feral. They are bound to this leader by a code of honour which they call *devotio*. It is the most important thing to them, it is far more important than their own lives that they uphold this. Whatever you do," he glanced down to the place where he knew Catumanda kept her moon blade hidden, "do not kill the chieftain unless you intend to kill them all. They will be honour bound to kill you, even if it means their total destruction."

Philippos' head appeared as he thrust it between them.

"They are splitting up. Three of them are going on ahead while the others are still coming straight for us." He threw Catamanda an impish smile. "Are you going to kill them all?"

She pushed his head back and stifled a grin. Despite their numbers she was confident that she could if the need arose and she was proud of the boy's confidence in her.

The three outriders came into view and swept around in an arc to cut them off. A brace of hoopoe clattered into the air before them, their distinctive orange crests flashing in the late afternoon sun as they beat the air with panicked strokes of their great wings.

Catumanda glanced behind. There were four further Lusitani and they split up into pairs as she watched, taking up positions a little way off each corner of the tailgate. Each man, she could see, wore circlets of leather thonging around his head, and she relaxed a little. She knew that this was where the warriors of Iberia stored their slings and the fact that they were still slung gave her hope that there was discipline among them. The accuracy of the Iberian slingers was well known and she was well aware that they could have stood off and picked them off with ease if they had wished to do so.

Ahead, the three others had gained the road and taken up position to halt their progress, and Catumanda watched as Caciro hauled at the reins and brought the great beasts to a halt twenty paces before them.

The riders walked their mounts towards them and Catumanda studied them as they came. For an irregular war band the men were dressed remarkably similar. These were obviously more than a band of cut throats. Each man wore a war shirt made of small bronze plates over a short, fringed, tunic and knee high leather riding boots. Arm rings in silver and gold encircled their upper arms and each warrior wore a bowl type helmet in bronze. The man who was obviously their leader wore an iron helm, tall and crested, and Catumanda saw from the typically Celtic swirls which decorated its cheek pieces that it alone must have been a spoil of war. Although armed with a long spear known as a *falarica*, she saw that each man also carried a single edged sword, the *falcata,* suspended from a baldric and a small round buckler type shield known as a *caetra,* suspended from his saddle horn.

Catumanda watched the other riders move up out of the corner of her eye as the leader addressed Caciro.

"What is in the wagon?"

Caciro cleared his throat.

"Salt from the coast, mainly. Plus a few barrels of wind dried or salted fish."

The Lusitanian nodded and spoke to one of his men in what she assumed must be this language called 'gibberish' and Catumanda felt the carter sag a little beside her. Turning back he addressed her, directly.

"You are a druid, yes?"

She glanced at her distinctive holed staff which was resting casually against her shoulder and pulled a mocking smile.

"You are very observant; for a bandit."

Catumanda felt Caciro stiffen at her side but their priorities were different. He was hoping to get away from the situation with his life, if possible with a little of his valuable goods. She, on the other hand was spoiling for a confrontation. She felt as if she had abandoned any control over her destiny the moment that she had set foot on the *Alexa*, back on the foreshore at Isarno. It was an unfamiliar and unpleasant feeling and she had resolved it was one which would end here, now. The Lusitanian snorted softly at the insult and smiled. She could see why he was the leader of the band; level headed and calm. He spoke again to his companion in the language of his people and the man urged his horse forward with a slight pressure of his knees.

"We will each fill a bag with salt and share a barrel of fish between us," he paused to emphasise the menace which backed up the words, "with your permission."

Catumanda felt the sense of relief which emanated from the man at her side that he would escape the meeting with the heavily armed band with so little loss. He eagerly accepted.

"Yes! Yes! Take as much as you need."

As the horseman drew level with her the druid moved her staff across to block his path.

"No."

The man checked his horse and looked back at his leader for instructions. Catumanda felt the carter deflate like a pricked water skin at her side as the Lusitanian hardened his face. In truth, the druid recognised that the man had asked for as little from Caciro's stock as he dare without losing the respect of his men. She had no doubt that it was out of regard for her and her relationship with the gods, but the challenge had now been made, and a death must inevitably follow. The Lusitanian made one last attempt at avoiding bloodshed and Catumanda, to her surprise, found herself beginning to sympathise with his position. She steeled herself to finish what she had begun as he addressed her again.

"I believe that the goods belong to the man sat beside you. He seems quite willing to make a gift of the items to us."

She fixed him with a stare.
"No."

NEMESIS

The man snapped a command and the horseman at her side clicked his tongue to move his horse forward. Instantly, Catumanda swung the staff back and around. As it swept through the arc she let the shaft slide through her hands until she gripped the stave at its base. A blur of movement, the staff whispered through the air and struck the warrior on the rear of his helm with a mighty crack. Taken unawares the raider shot forward to strike his face on the neck of his mount before slipping from the saddle, slumping to the roadway in a pall of dust.

A deep throated cry rent the air as his companions hefted their falerica, and Catumanda raised her voice to cry above the hubbub.

"The goods are available." She waited as the chieftain held his arm out to placate his men. "At a price."

The chieftain glowered at her but waited for her to continue. They both knew that Catumanda was solely responsible for the stand off and she could sense his anger.

"I want to fight one of you."

She felt Caciro poke her in the side but ignored him. She knew which warrior opposite would answer the challenge and it was not the chieftain. He looked far too canny.

As the leader translated, the Lusitani shared bemused looks at the unexpected demand. One of their number however brightened immediately, and Catumanda watched as a black toothed grin cut a line in his beard. The face above the beard was puffy, still bearing the pock marked scars of some childhood disease and framed by lank hair the colour of crow wings. An angry scar ran vertically across one eye, the pale unseeing orb adding to the sense of menace as the man accepted the challenge and slipped from his mount.

Catumanda handed her staff to Philippos and hopped down from the wagon, drawing her new moon blade as she did so. Her opponent emerged from behind his horse, rolling his shoulders and jabbing with his spear as he loosed muscles and joints stiffened by a day in the saddle. As Catumanda went through her own stretches and practice sweeps the Lusitani chieftain called across to his man.

"Falcata…"

The man glanced across and shrugged, confident of victory over the strange looking girl before him. By the time that he had returned from swapping the weapon, Catamanda was prepared. Dropping into a crouch, her body swayed from side to side as she rolled on the balls of her feet, fixing her eyes on the man like a snake about to strike.

Surprised at her prowess, her opponent circled warily as he began to swing the curved blade in short circular movements. Suddenly he snapped forward, amusement dancing in his eye as he made the girl jump back. A rumble of laughter came from his mounted brothers as the warrior made Catumanda dance away from a series of feints, and she watched as confidence returned to his movements. Little more than a hand-held knife, the moon blade had none of the reach of the Lusitanian's sword and the warrior drove the druid back with a series of slashing attacks. The other raiders were shouting now, egging on their man as his superiority became obvious and the girl ducked and swayed away from his powerful strikes.

Forced backwards by the strength of the assault she heard Philippos yell in dismay as her foot slipped on a loose rock and she was thrown off-balance. Her opponent seized his chance to end the fight, stabbing forward with the hooked point of his blade at the Celt's unprotected chest. Catumanda's old master, the druid Abaris of the Trinobantes, had hailed her as his finest pupil with the blade and she proved it now. Already planning her counter move as she fell, Catumanda waited until she saw that the man had overreached himself and spun across the dusty ground. Springing to her feet, she brought her own blade up in an arc to slash through the exposed tendons of her attacker's forearm. As the *falcata* fell from nerveless fingers and the man gasped in shock and surprise, Catumanda pirouetted past, sweeping her blade back down to lay open the knotted muscles of his thigh from groin to knee in a spray of blood.

The shouts and calls from the watching Lusitani trailed away as Catumanda turned back to her opponent; the sun glittered on cold steel as she slashed again. The man's eye went wide in horror as the red line of a smile opened at his throat, his beard matted in a sheet of blood.

In desperation, he clasped his hand in a futile attempt to staunch the flow as his legs folded beneath him and he sank to his knees, pitching forward to land on the dusty track with a grunt.

Catumanda stooped to clean her moon blade on her victim's cloak as blood pulsed out to make a gory mash on the road beneath.

She nodded to herself with satisfaction as she examined her weapon. Lindo had been right, Uxentio was indeed a fine smith. The weight, the balance, there was god-cunning in the blade.

Straightening, she slipped it back inside her tunic and arched her back, exhaling with pleasure as she looked back at the Lusitani leader and smiled beatifically.

"The items are still for sale. My friend will tell you the price."

TWELVE

Away to his right, on the far side of the field, Numerius watched as the mounted horsemen of the Senones galloped up the slope under a pall of dust. He had anticipated that the heat of the day would prove too much for the pale northerners, but their rapid march south and the undiminished vigour of their attack had quashed any such hopes. He owned a slave from the far north who lolled around like a girl when the heat of the summer was fully on the city. Numerius gave a short snort of irony. He had always suspected that the man was a shirker.

The Roman army had looked on as the Celtic priests, men Numerius knew to be called druids, had sacrificed what looked to be an Etruscan noble. The killing had soon been over, and the animated roar from the army facing them had told the Romans that the omens, as far as they were concerned, had been bad. Despite the gravity of the moment, Numerius had pulled a wry smile. He had been on dozens of campaigns, and he had yet to find the omens declared unfavourable once the armies were in sight of one another. He had wondered idly what the results would be should such a thing ever occur. Would the Celts have turned around and walked away? It seemed likely, and he had determined to talk to his father, the pontifex maximus, about it should he ever see the man again.

Numerius' mind came back to the present, and he saw that the riders had weathered the storm of javelins and were gaining the summit of the hillock as fighting spread along its length. The rorarii disappeared from view, and flashes of sunlight glinted from polished metal like broken ice as the rival horsemen met in a clash of steel.

Away to his front, the sound from the Gaulish battle front ebbed away like a receding wave and the Romans looked back as one. Clearly the eerie silence presaged something terrible, and moments later their fears were confirmed as a rising crescendo of noise rose to fill the valley. Spears clattered, and the howl made by tens of thousands of barbarian warriors rose to new heights as the haunting wail of the carnyx blared forth. Suddenly one man, an enormous chieftain, glorious in a raven capped battle helm, broke into a sprint, his huge sword raised high.

Numerius looked across the heads of the three ranks which were all that remained of his century. Over one-third of his men had been stripped from him to reinforce the centre and replaced by a handful of rorarii. Despite the desperate fighting which would ensue, he hoped that the Gauls would attack on a wide front. Even thickened by the men from the flanks, he doubted that even the soldiers of Rome could withstand a concentrated blow by the northern giants.

The Celtic charge spread across the plain and came on like a tidal bore, unstoppable, and Numerius called across the heads of his men.

"Remember your training. Stand together and hold your ground."

The men before him hunched into their shields and braced themselves as the Gauls began to emerge from the heat haze, solidifying with frightening speed into thousands of charging figures led by naked giants. As they came on, the Gauls reached the area of dry ditches which mazed the riverbank. The runnels were clearly visible to the leading barbarians and they vaulted them with ease, but those following close behind stumbled and fell as the ground unexpectedly disappeared from beneath them. It was enough to draw the sting from the charge, and although the thunderous crash from his right told Numerius that the main strength of the Gauls had struck the line, pitifully few had managed to reach his own position.

If their opponents were lacking in numbers and clothing they lacked nothing in bravery, and they threw themselves upon the lances of the phalanx as they reached the line. Despite the heroics displayed by the leading Gauls the line held firm, and Numerius thrust forward overarm with his own lance as the snarling face of a warrior came within range. The man, his features contorted by hate, angrily knocked the blade aside with his head and forced his way deeper into the crush, punching with the pommel of his sword or thrusting his head at any who came within reach. Constricted in the phalanx, the Romans were unable to lower their arms to ward off the blows from the barbarian who twisted and squirmed as he came closer to the tribune. He had obviously marked Numerius as the leader of the group by the quality of his armour and he was clearly prepared to trade his life for the Roman's.

Numerius dropped his lance and drew his short stabbing sword as he prepared to face the onslaught. The man was almost upon him, and the Roman could now see that he was one of the warriors who fought naked in the front rank of the army. True to his warrior code and huge in stature, the man wore a golden torc around his neck of exquisite design. A conical helm of bronze largely hid a shock of reddish hair, beneath which piercing blue eyes and a bristling red moustache marked the man as one of the Gaulish nobles.

Numerius raised his shield and moved forward. The action brought him face to face with the Gaul and the Roman whipped the heavy bronze rim of his shield smartly up to strike his opponent squarely on the chin. It was a blow which would have stunned a horse, but the Gaul hardly seemed to notice as he attempted to bring his great blade into play. Now the press of bodies acted to Numerius' advantage, as he had intended. He had witnessed the fighting outside Clusium the previous summer and he knew that the Celtic blades were at their best in open order fighting. Pushing in closer he worked his blade forward. As the men on either side pushed sideways to pin the warrior's arms, Numerius felt his blade slide effortlessly into flesh. A momentary look of shock flashed across the face of the Gaul, quickly replaced by one of anger as the man struggled to bring his own great blade into play while his strength yet held. Numerius pushed the blade in up to the hilt and twisted it as he sought to bring the man down but, to his amazement, his desperation only seemed to make his opponent stronger. Aware that he was nearing his end, the giant looked to take down as many Romans as he could while his strength lasted. Swinging his great blade in an arc he chopped to left and right. Packed tightly within the confines of the phalanx, the Romans were unable to take any avoiding action and the blade bit into exposed necks and shoulders, slicing through bone and muscle before emerging and continuing its grisly journey.

The Gaul was cutting a wide swathe through their ranks and, in desperation, Numerius managed to work his own blade free and stab again. This time he took greater care with his aim and the blade slid into the barbarian's abdomen with ease. The Roman twisted his grip and, stepping in, used all the power of his shoulder muscles to drive the blade up and into the warrior's chest. The Gaul gasped as his heart burst and the strength finally left his great arms. With a final look of defiance he fell to his knees among the bodies of his victims before toppling forward.

The barbarians were striking all along the line now and men struggled to push back as the naked champions cut deep inroads wherever they hit. Another of the Gauls, his body covered in a mass of chaotic swirls and patterns, began to cut his way through the phalanx towards him and Numerius realised with horror that his sword was still embedded in the chest of the first man. He risked a look down and saw that the Gaul had died face down in the grass, trapping Numerius' sword beneath his great bulk. The tip of his blade, slick with gore, pointed mockingly from the back of the man and Numerius knew that he would never have the time to roll the Gaul over and retrieve it before this new killer arrived. As Romans tumbled before his great blade like summer wheat, Numerius suddenly remembered the knife at his side. Driven by desperation now, he snatched it from its scabbard and leapt upon his attacker. Taken by surprise the Gaul hesitated for a heartbeat, but it was enough. Numerius plunged the dagger into the man's neck, sawing the blade back and forth as a great gout of blood pumped out from the severed artery to cover them both. Enraged now and determined to sell his life as dearly as possible, the Roman tribune stabbed and stabbed again at the Gaul until he lay dead at his feet.

Gulping down great lungfuls of air, Numerius wiped the stickiness from his hand as his mind and body recovered from the fight. The men around him were looking at the dead Gaul in shock and he shouted at them above the din.

"Look to the front and close up." He called across the heads of those around him. "Front rank, keep it tight!"

It was not a moment too soon. The main body of the Gauls had crossed the worst of the ditches and reformed into a ragged line. With a great cry they burst forward and, moments later, hit the phalanx with a deafening crash. As the Romans braced and shoved back, Numerius risked a glance across the field to see how the rest of the army was faring under the onslaught and gaped in horror.

Unimpeded on the smoother surface of the floodplain, the barbarian charge had been far more concentrated. Led again by their naked champions, the bull-like men had smashed into the front ranks with unstoppable force and the whole position had given way. Men were already streaming away from the rear of the phalanx, casting aside their armour and weapons in a bid to hasten their escape.

A hole had been punched into the Roman line and the men closest to it were already beginning to waver as they fought their own personal battles between the conflicting demands of honour and self preservation. On the far side of the field the horrified Roman could make out the Gallic horsemen streaming down the sides of the hillock as they prepared to harry the panic-stricken Romans from the field.

Numerius looked back to the front as his mind struggled to cope with the scale of the disaster. Expecting the victorious Gauls to be massing for a final, devastating assault, he blinked in surprise as he watched the enemy expertly disengage and begin to trot across to join their tribesmen at the breach. He needed to see the extent of the rout as he desperately sought a way out of the debacle for himself and the men of his century. His horse was a short distance to the rear and he made to move across before he realised the effect that it would have on the men under his command. One look was enough to tell him that their courage hung by a thread. They would look to him to extricate them from the ongoing nightmare, and to see their leader mount his horse for whatever reason, would cause them to throw down their weapons and follow their fellow citizens south. He turned to the men at his side.

"Here, help me with these."

As the men in the phalanx warily watched the Gauls streaming across their front, Numerius began to drag the body of the second dead warrior across to the first.

"Drape him across the first one. I need to see what is happening."

A soldier reached beneath the corpse and worked Numerius' sword free, wiping the worst of the blood and viscera from the blade and handle before handing it back to him with a grim smile. The tribune nodded his thanks and replaced it in its scabbard, snapping it home as his spirits began to rise once more. As the immediate danger passed he realised just how close they had come to being overrun themselves. The collapse of the Roman centre had been a disaster for the army as a whole, but it had saved the men on the flanks from complete annihilation.

Numerius rested his hands on the shoulders of two of his men as he levered himself up onto the back of the corpse. His optio had edged across and he looked up at his leader.

"What can you see, tribune?"

Numerius shook his head in wonder at the sight which met his eyes, a sight he thought never to witness. It was nothing other than the total and absolute destruction of the army of Rome. The breach, already large, had widened as the Roman army simply melted away. He had witnessed the Tiberis swollen by the spring rains break its banks as a boy, and the sight which met him now resembled the picture which his mind had retained from that day. The Gauls were gushing through on a rapidly widening front as the men at the flanks pulled themselves in a desperate effort to defend themselves. Away to the right thousands of his fellow citizens were following the road back to Rome, a mere dozen or so miles away, discarding their weapons and armour as they ran, while at their head Numerius saw to his disgust the mounted figures of Sulpicius and his officers. He glanced down at the expectant faces but found that the words refused to come. As Cassius and the men exchanged looks of fear, Numerius shook his head and lowered his gaze.

*

The last of the Roman equites formed into two small knots of riders and prepared for the end. Abandoned by the rorarii, they had fought with spirit and determination until superior numbers had overwhelmed them. As the men of the Horsetails and Crow closed in for the kill, Solemis guided Tantibus across to the place where he had lain only that morning and shook his head on wonder. The grass was still flattened, the perfect outline of his shape still easily visible, and he knew that he should have died there. So much had happened during the few short hours which had passed since he had witnessed the arrival of the Roman army. The gods had aided his escape and he would keep his promise to them when the time for sacrifices and offerings arrived at the end of the day.

Suddenly his reverie was shattered as Caturix arrived in a flurry of excitement, driving his horse to Solemis' side and exclaiming in awe.

"They're breaking!"

As their clansmen drove the last of the Roman skirmishers from the heights, Solemis gripped his friend's arm and whooped with joy. The first of the champions had barely got among the phalanx and already the Romans had collapsed spectacularly.

Solemis watched as Brennus, surrounded by the men of his *cantref,* drove deeply into the enemy position, and cried out again with excitement.

"You're right!"

He shot Caturix a look, and the Crow leader could see the excitement shining in his eyes.

"Let's get down there and hit them before they can rally."

Caturix was older by a few years, and he placed a hand on his brother-in-law's arm as his greater maturity recognised the moment.

"Wait for our clansmen to reform, there will still be enough for us to do." The Crow chieftain shook his head slowly and a small smile played about his lips as he watched the Romans streaming away from the fight. "You remember when we had just taken the pass up into the Alpes from Lugdunon?"

Solemis looked at his friend and laughed.

"Yes, what of it?"

"And that Allobroge war leader," he paused as he racked his memory but the name escaped him. Solemis let him suffer for a short while but eventually came to his aid with a chuckle.

"Ullio."

Caturix laughed at the memory as he continued to marvel at the men of his tribe pursuing the defeated Romans along the valley floor.

"Ullio, that was it. Ullio took us to the edge of the pass and showed us all the wonderful sights which lay spread out below us and said, *'remember this moment always. You see your world through the eyes of the gods'.*"

Solemis snorted and cuffed him playfully.

"What are you going on about? The Romans are defeated and we have to help chase the arrogant bastards from the field."

The Horsetail leaned across and dug his friend in the ribs.

"You are not turning into a woman are you? Any unusual bleeding? Strange mood swings?"

Caturix grew serious and indicated the plain below with his head.

"Take a moment before we are swallowed once again by the mayhem; fix the scene in your memory. One day, when you sit around the hearth and a bard tells of Brennus' great victory against the Romans, you will bounce your grandchild on your knee as the cold winds howl outside and you will be back here again."

THIRTEEN

The Roman, a military tribune of the city, stepped down from the improvised mound, his ashen features already betraying his thoughts to the crowd of men. Suddenly he became aware of the fearful faces which crowded in, and his sense of *disciplina* reasserted itself. He pulled the rictus of a grin.

"The whole centre has given way. We are on our own."

As jaws gaped in disbelief, he moved quickly to assert his authority. The natural reaction of his men now would be to discard their own weapons and flee, but he had already seen that the time for flight had passed. He hauled himself back upon the bodies of the dead barbarians heaped at his feet and called across the heads of his soldiers.

"The only hope that we have of surviving this day is to keep our discipline and formation intact." He jerked his head to the South as the men exchanged fearful glances. "The Tiberis takes a large bite into the plain at our rear and the barbarian army are already beyond it, there is no way through." He looked across and was pleased to see that the men under the command of the centurion,

Caedicius, were already in the process of turning their flank to face the Gauls. Caedicius' men, added to the centuries of his brothers to his left, still gave him a sizeable force to work with, and the first flickers of hope kindled within him. He called out to his optio.

"Cassius, wheel the men so that they have their backs to the river. I need to discuss the situation with the other commanders."

Numerius hopped back to the ground and made his way through the phalanx. Ahead of him Caedicius was already busy checking the strength of his disposition, his back turned contemptuously to the Gauls, some of whom were little more than a dozen paces away. The big man was striding along the front of the phalanx, grasping the great lances and testing the resolve of the men holding them with vigorous shakes. Numerius smiled as he came close enough to hear the comments which accompanied them.

"Marcus, keep it tight…Cato, don't think that I have forgotten the invite to your wedding. If you are brave enough to want to spend every night with Albina, these barbarians should be easy meat!"

Numerius could see nervous smiles began to appear among the men of Caedicius' century, and he sent a prayer of thanks to Mars that the man had fallen under his command. He called out as he came up.

"Caedicius, a word if I may?"

The centurion turned and nodded. Calling to his optio to complete the inspection, he came across and saluted as Numerius looked out beyond the men of his century. They still had a little time remaining before the inevitable return of the Gauls. Although the vast majority of their army were still in pursuit of the retreating Romans, several hundred remained on the plain before them, dispatching the wounded and collecting the arms of the Roman dead. They appeared to be acting on the instructions of a number of druids, and Numerius felt a shiver of fear for the first time that day at the consequences of falling alive into the hands of the priests. Horrific tales had reached Rome the previous autumn of the aftermath to the fighting outside Clusium. Tales of trees festooned with Etruscan dead and burning giants filled with the terrified survivors of the battle had swept Rome and, although he knew that they were likely to be wild exaggerations, he was determined not to discover for himself just how much truth the stories contained. Caedicius broke into his thoughts and Numerius snorted at the man's laconic description of their situation.

"A nasty business, tribune."

He nodded his agreement.

"It is, as you say, a very nasty business. If we are to survive the return of the barbarian army we need to pull our position back against the river."

Caedicius made a face. He obviously felt less than overwhelmed by the plan and waited for permission to speak. Numerius nodded his assent.

"Feel free to make any suggestions, centurion. That is why you are here."

"I was thinking, sir. While the way is clear, it might be a good idea to make for the woods over there. A well drilled phalanx could cross the plain in no time. Once we were hidden we could double back to the city or link up with other survivors. There must be hundreds of men scattered between here and Rome."

A familiar voice carried to him.

"It's a good suggestion, brother."

Numerius turned to see that Quintus and Caeso had come across from their positions, further down the line. Quintus continued.

"It could be our only chance. We have just been down to look at the river; it's wide, deep and fast flowing. Some of the men would get across but many wouldn't."

Numerius sighed and shook his head.

"I think that we will have to accept those losses. The abandoned city of Veii stands only a few miles to the West. If we can reach there, we can hold out for as long as we have food. The Gauls won't follow us anyway, they will march on Rome, surely, now that the city lies undefended."

Caedicius remained unconvinced.

"Maybe the Gauls aren't interested in the city."

The Fabii shot him a look of incomprehension and Caedicius shifted uncomfortably. He was after all merely a centurion, while each of the men before him had been elected tribune by the citizens of Rome. Suddenly, Numerius caught the man's meaning. "You mean us?" He blew out his cheeks as he thought on the centurion's words. Finally he nodded. "I agree, we must be high on their list of priorities. However, that makes your plan even less likely to succeed, Caedicius. If we start to move the men across the plain and the Gauls return in force, we will be stranded in the open."

Caeso agreed.

"Even if we did make it to the wood we would have to abandon our lances. They would be more of a hindrance among the trees, and it would leave a good number of the men barely armed at all."

Numerius looked from one man to the next.

"Are we all agreed then? We make an attempt to reach Veii."

Quintus nodded.

"It is five or six miles to the nearest crossing of the Tiberis at Fidenae. Even if they were thinking of cutting off our retreat, which I very much doubt, they would need to ride as far back again to block our route. They don't know the lie of the land like we do, as far as they know there may be no crossing point at all. They are enjoying themselves chasing a defeated enemy, but they have left their priests here so they must intend to return soon. We have no choice."

Numerius loosened his helm and wiped his brow. The day was still hot and he hoped that the sultry heat of the valley would sap the Gauls strength. For once their great size would work against them.

"Let's get back to our centuries, as soon as we can start crossing the better. Find out who the best swimmers are and use them on the perimeter. If the Gauls do try to interfere they will need to swim for their lives at the end."

They dispersed and hurried back to their men as the first sounds of the returning Gauls carried across the field. Numerius looked across and was gratified to see that the heat of the day seemed to have drawn some of the vigour from their movements. No longer a seething mass, the warriors were drifting back in weary groups, the twin exertions of the initial jog to the battlefield and the harrying of the defeated Roman army beneath the unrelenting sun at last beginning to exact a price. It was clear that they had overtaken the wagons containing the supplies for the army, and the amphorae had naturally been among the first items plundered. It could only help, and for the first time since he had sat in the praetorium and listened to the wail of the approaching war horns, Numerius began to hope.

*

"Fabii?" The terrified man could barely tear his gaze from the blade of the sword as he racked his memory. He knew that his life depended on the right answer but he simply didn't know. As he reached the decision to give any plausible answer, his time ran out. The Roman opened his mouth to let out a cry of protest but the blade crashed down, snuffing out the sound along with his life.

Caturix moved across to the next in line.

"Fabii?"

The Roman gestured with his hands and gabbled in Latin and the sword shot forward to take him in the throat. The victim's eyes went wide with shock and horror as he fell to the dusty ground, a curtain of blood already cascading from his neck. Solemis reached forward and stroked Tantibus' neck as the horse pawed the ground. No horse, war trained or not, really enjoyed the smell of blood.

"I should be a little slower with your blade if I were you big brother," he chuckled. " The last one got as far as saying, '*Yes, I know. They are...*' before you decided to remove half of his neck!"

Caturix threw an answer without looking back.

"He should have been quicker then!"

The violent deaths had had the desired effect, and the next man in line was volunteering an answer before the question had left Caturix' lips.

"Fabii, flumen!"

The chieftain of the Crow glared as the desperate Roman flattened his hand and made a waving motion as he pointed to the West. The man repeated the gesture as his half dozen companions echoed the actions.

"Flumen! Flumen!"

Caturix turned to Solemis and screwed up his face.

"What are they on about?"

Solemis echoed his friend's confusion.

"River; they keep saying river."

He raised himself in his saddle and peered across to the Tiberis. They had ridden four or five miles from the site of the battle and the valley had narrowed considerably as the hills came down to form another choke point. Shimmering in the heat haze, a mile or so ahead, sat the town which the stone mile markers told them was called Fidenae. Caturix was still confused.

"Why are they saying river? Can you see anything over there?"

Solemis shook his head. The pale yellow hills baked under the Etruscan sun and the smell of pine drifted across the valley. Suddenly his expression came alive as he realised what the men were telling them.

"The river! The Fabii must have been cut off back at the river when Brennus' attack broke through the centre!"

Caturix thought for a moment and nodded.

"There was a large group there. I saw them as we galloped down the hill."

NEMESIS

The Romans pulled nervous smiles and hoped that they had said enough as the Gaul spat and cursed in frustration.

"Shit!"

Suddenly the Gaul exploded in anger, lashing out with his broadsword as the captives made pathetic attempts to protect themselves with their hands and arms. It was soon all over, and Caturix stood panting over a pitiful heap of bloodied torsos and severed limbs.

"When you are finished, it might be an idea to get back to the battlefield before the men you really want to kill get away."

Solemis turned to Albiomaros.

"Genos, take the Horsetails and find Brennus. Tell him that we think that we have found the Fabii."

He held the reins of the Crow chieftain's horse out for him as the man wiped splashes of blood from his face. Flies were already settling on the fresh corpses as Caturix mounted and pointed its head back to the North. He shook his head in disgust.

"What a shitty country; sometimes I would give anything to be back in a cool forest of oak and elm."

Solemis looked wistful as he moved to his side, the clans trotting back across the grass towards the road.

"Or fishing for pike or trout beneath the shade of a willow."

He glanced across as they hauled on their reins and headed back.

"Why did you kill them all?"

Caturix shrugged.

"They should have kept their mouths shut. Nobody likes a coward."

Numerius was elated. The retreat across the Tiberis was going far better than he could have hoped, and still the Gauls were ignoring them. After several of the first men to enter the water had promptly drowned, despite removing their armour, Caedicius had come up with the idea of using the horses to ferry men back and forth. They had brought twenty of the best mounts inside the perimeter rather than leave them to the Gauls and they had quickly proven their worth. Three men could clutch each side of the saddle as the horse ferried them across the river, and very soon half the men were across without a single mishap.

The men in the phalanx looked on anxiously as the Gauls returned from the chase in greater and greater numbers. Already large parties of them had come across to taunt them and display their collection of severed Roman heads; dozens had come forward to issue challenges for individual combat between the opposing forces. Numerius had forbidden such duels. Victory for either side would only inflame the barbarians and they were close to achieving their aim. He snorted with delight as he watched the Gauls cavorting about the field, drunk on a heady mixture of victory and wine. He knew that if the men opposite knew just how few Romans remained behind the front ranks of the phalanx they could overwhelm the perimeter in a heartbeat. It was, in reality, a hollow nut; one smart crack would shatter it.

Caedicius moved to his side and spoke casually so as not to mark him out as a commander to any watching Gauls.

"That's it. There are only the men of the phalanx left on this side of the river."

Numerius kept his eyes on the enemy as he replied. This would be the hardest part of all.

"Start to withdraw the rear rank from the flanks inwards, but make sure that they don't shorten the line. Try to make it look like they are being relieved if you can. We can't afford to let them see how weak we really are."

The centurion sniffed and walked casually away and Numerius had to suppress a small smile at the man's demeanour. Fortuna really had smiled upon him when she placed the man's century next to his own. Numerius turned and left the line, walking across to the riverbank to witness the evacuation for himself. His brother, Caeso, was already there and he came to stand at his side.

"Not long now."

Caeso glanced across.

"I shall wait until we are safe behind the walls of Veii before I celebrate, if you don't mind."

Numerius patted his brother on the shoulder and smiled reassuringly.

"Nonsense. Even if the Gauls decided to mount an attack now we could just make a break for the river and leave them gaping at the bank. It would take them time to form their battle line, and by the time that they were ready we would be away. That's the reason why I kept the strongest swimmers back until last."

Suddenly, a worried looking soldier appeared at his elbow and Numerius threw him a questioning look.

"Spit it out, man."

"The centurion's compliments, sir. But the barbarian horsemen are in sight. They appear to be galloping this way."

The Fabii exchanged a look which said that all their hopes had come to nought. Both men knew that even if they abandoned the position and took to the river, it would be a small matter for the Gauls to ford the Tiberis and chase them down as they had the men in the main army. Numerius' heart sank, and he was about to round on the inanely smiling soldier who had brought him the news when the man spoke again.

"Centurion Caedicius respectfully asks that you order the withdrawal the moment that they have finished seeding the ground with *tribulus,* sir."

*

The Crow thundered north as they chased down the men who had taken the life of their chieftain and brought war upon themselves. The valley of the Tiberis was strewn with Roman dead and the horses were forced to weave around the largest concentrations, slowing their progress as crows and vultures rose in clouds or waddled away with a bad natured cry. High above, more of the giant birds were soaring in great circles on the sultry air as they decided which part of the field held out the greatest prospect of a rare feast.

The sun was lower in the West now and the worst of the heat was beginning to come off the land as the battlefield came into sight and Solemis held Tantibus back as he let Caturix forge ahead with the charge.

The river looped away to the West and the plain broadened before them as they left the road and followed its course. Away to their right, the field was beginning to take on a sense of order as the druids directed the growing number of warriors to strip the dead and pile their weapons in preparation for the later rituals. Such a great victory at so small a cost could only be the work of the gods, and they would need to be honoured before the army could move on the city.

Suddenly the stranded flank of the Roman army came into view, a hedgerow of spears and lances anchored tightly against the riverbank a mile away, and Caturix edged the column to the left as he prepared to lead his clansmen straight into the attack. As the Roman phalanx grew closer, Solemis watched as hundreds of tiny objects sailed through the air to pepper the ground directly in the path of their charge. Tantibus had seen them too and, to Solemis' astonishment, he immediately hauled himself out of line and slowed to a canter.

Bemused, Solemis could only watch helplessly as the Crow swept past in a veil of dust, brandishing their swords and spears and screaming their war cries. Moments later, as the horsemen prepared to unleash their first volley of missiles, the leading horses suddenly collapsed in screaming heaps, throwing their riders and bringing down those behind them. Solemis watched in horror as Caturix tumbled through the air to land within feet of the Roman spear men and he caught his breath as he watched one of the Romans hesitate as he debated whether to leave the safety of the phalanx to dispatch the fallen rider or not. The delay had been enough to save the life of his friend as a shouted order cut the air and the

Roman soldiers suddenly broke and fled to the rear like a flock of startled birds.

As the Romans disappeared over the lip of the riverbank, Solemis managed to persuade Tantibus to edge warily forward towards the chaotic tangle of horses and men which was until a short time ago a terrifying charge.

His horse halted once again at the edge of a deep swathe of dark grey objects. Liberally scattered in an arc surrounding the now empty Roman position, the vicious looking spikes were as effective as they were simple. Dismounting, he reached down and plucked one of the small metal objects from the ground, turning it over in his hand as he examined it closely. It seemed to be made of three sharp metal objects which were designed in such a way that whichever way they fell, one of the spikes would always be pointing upwards. It was a new weapon to him, though clearly not to his horse, and he cursed himself that he had not brought his own clansmen along with him. The Umbrians, Rodolfo and Brizio, would have known immediately what the objects had been the moment that they had witnessed the Romans hurl them into the path of the assault. What's more, the majority of his clan now rode trained war horses similar to Tantibus, they too would in all likelihood have pulled up rather than blunder straight into the trap.

Despite the spectacular defeat of the Crow attack most of the warriors were already back on their feet, looking about themselves in bemusement. Solemis was relieved to see Caturix rise again clutching his shoulder and grimacing with what he knew would be an odd mixture of pain, frustration and embarrassment. Looking around the warriors, Solemis could see that several arms had been broken as they fell but, although many of the horses still writhed in pain, they appeared to have got off lightly.

Solemis raised his head and squinted into the setting sun, watching as the last of the Romans pulled themselves up the far bank of the Tiberis. With a last cheeky wave at their frustrated enemies, the final few set off at a jog towards the city which stood in the middle distance. There was no chance now that they could be overtaken. He tossed the spiked object aside and cursed softly. The Fabii had eluded them once again.

FOURTEEN

She pulled her shift closer and stared out across the rooftops. From her elevated position above the castro she could see for miles into the Iberian countryside as the sun crept into the eastern sky and the town slowly came back to life. The night had been cold on the mesa, and the russet tiles which capped the roofs everywhere glistened under a thin lick of frost.

They had reached the hilltop castro of the Arevaci two days before. Catumanda had marvelled at the defences as Caciro had turned off the road and taken the causeway which led to the fort. Perched atop a hill, sheer to three sides, the castro of Numantia glowered across the surrounding valley, dominating the area for miles around. Girded by water, the only approach lay to the north-east, the steady slope which carried the road rising in a series of switchbacks to the outer defences. Several ditches and banks cut the rising land, each topped by a stout palisade and reinforced at regular intervals by rounded towers of stone. Once through these, any assailant would find themselves in an area which Catumanda recognised as a 'killing ground'. A further wide ditch stood before the walls of what they knew as an 'oppidum' at home. The walls of the castro stood beyond this, stone faced to a height of twenty feet, capped by a timber palisade. Further twin towers, again massively built in stone, guarded the entry itself and afforded the defenders a commanding view of any approaching attackers and the druid shivered despite the warmth of the day as she had imagined the carnage that spears, arrows and slingshot could wreak in the confined space.

A brace of ravens had soared above the town on the sultry air, and she had chuckled to herself. No army, however mighty, would ever supply their chicks with carrion faced by such defences. They would have to fend for themselves.

Catumanda closed her eyes and turned her face to the sun, sighing with contentment as the warmth of the returning orb seeped into chilled muscles.

The gods had sent her a dream last night but she no longer feared them and, although she was beginning to suspect that she would never return to Albion, she felt an acceptance of her fate. Unable to sleep after the new revelations, she had thrown open the shutters and sat under the stars as she committed every aspect of the vision to her memory.

For the first time, she had been shown the fire-mountain in greater detail. It lay behind a wide bay the arms of which reached out to sea, gathering seafarers into their embrace. The far shore was dotted with settlements, white painted houses, red roofs of clay for the wealthy, yellow straw for the poorer people. Suddenly she was in a town and standing before a fine home. White walled, an oak door stood before her and she had wondered whether this was another visit to the Otherworld. A tree, its trunk twisted and gnarled by great age grew through the wall and she was in no doubt that the roots had broken the soil long before the foundations of any house. Pushing on the door it opened easily, revealing a line of bronze shields hovering magically in the air before the building. One by one the shields came towards her, revealing a series of repeating designs as they came on and disappeared over her shoulder. She had awoken as the last of them faded away, stealing to the window seat to reflect on the latest revelation on her great journey to the southern lands.

A cock crowed somewhere in the town and was answered by another as Catumanda came back to the present and ran her eyes back across the buildings below. Women were beginning to appear at their rear doors, shaking out ash as fires were relit to prepare the morning meal and provide hot water for washing clothes and bodies. A cart rumbled past in the alleyway below and a man moved behind a wattle screen, lowering his trews as he sat to ease himself.

It was time for her to move, they had a long day ahead of them. The druid rose, twisting and stretching away the tensions of the night as she cast a glance at Philippos and was a little surprised to see that the boy was still asleep. As faithful as any hound, the young Greek was usually the first to wake, bustling off to provide her with her first food or drink of the day. She smiled, lovingly. Their journey together was reaching its end. Soon they would part, never to see one another again. Her spirit guide had revealed to her something of the future which awaited the boy and she was glad. The fates had smiled on him.

Caciro halted at the head of the valley and threw his arms wide in a dramatic pose.

"The valley of the Iber!"

Ahead of them the vale stretched into the distance to a sawtooth of distant peaks. The highest of them were capped with white; it was a reminder to the druid that the year was drawing rapidly on. Very soon the last ships would leave the Greek trading city which was her immediate goal for their settlements across the southern sea. She simply had to be on one of them, the dreams were insistent. At her side the helpful carter was still describing the terrain before them.

"The mountains on the horizon are known as the Perines, they separate the lands of Iberia from those of Celtica." He rambled on as the wagon started its descent down the dusty road, Philippos bouncing around in the back as he listened in on the tale. "The mountains are named after the daughter of a Celtic chieftain who lived in the area long ago. The Greeks have a god called Heracles who had killed his wife and sons. He had to perform twelve tasks which they called 'labours' in order to win absolution for his deed from their chief god, Zeus, and win the gift of immortality." Caciro stole a glance at the druid and chuckled happily. Bringing the gods into his tale had brought her rapt attention as he knew that it would, and he kept her waiting as he used his goad to ease the mule around a large depression in the road surface. She dug him in the ribs playfully and he laughed aloud as the corners of her mouth lifted into a knowing smile.

"Go on."

He lay his goad back across his lap and pulled a face.
"Where was I?"

A voice chirped from the back and Catumanda turned, tousling the boy's dark, curly locks as Philippos craned forward to listen. Heracles was, after all, one of the gods of his people.

"You were about to describe one of the labours of Heracles, the one where he steals the cattle of Geryon."

Catumanda raised her brow in surprise.

"You have never mentioned that you know the tales of the gods!"

Philippos threw a nonchalant shrug.

"All Greeks of good family are educated. I am trained in music, literature, art and mathematics."

The druid and carter exchanged a look of astonishment.

"Anything else?"

"I liked astronomy and debating. When I reached seven years my family arranged for me to be sent to a 'good school' in Syracuse, on Sikelia," he spat.

Catumanda was beginning to understand why the gods had chosen the boy as her companion. She reached out and pulled him to her, giving the surprised boy a hug and planting a kiss on the top of his head before she finished his sentence for him.

"Where you ran away and joined the crew of the *Alexa*." She let him go and he settled back against the rolled up awnings which would provide their shelter that evening as she continued. "I too was sent away from my family when I was very young, to walk the path of the oak." Philippos cocked his head and narrowed his eyes. The boy possessed an enquiring mind and she felt a sudden guiltiness that she had been so preoccupied with her own journey that she had neglected the fact that others too had a journey to take, that the gods may have a use for them also.

"The path of oak is what we usually refer to as druidry. The word for our brotherhood is very old and is made of two parts, *Dru*, which means oak, and *wid* which is the old word for knowledge, a knower or seer you might say. I was lucky, I was able to return to my home settlement and right the wrongs which were occurring there. I think that the gods have thrown us together for a reason, Philippos."

Caciro cleared his throat and sniffed indignantly.

"Don't you want to hear my story then?"

Philippos jumped up with a grin.

"Yes, I have never heard the tale told by a barb..."

His voice trailed away in embarrassment as the Celts shared a look of amusement. They had both had plenty of dealings with Greeks and were well aware of their innate sense of superiority. Caciro chuckled as the cart rolled on.

"Very well. I will wait until the end before I spit you over the fire and eat you. Now where was I?" He raised a finger in a dramatic pose. "Ah yes! The noble, civilised Heracles, driven mad by the goddess Hera, killed his own wife and their six sons. To atone for the wicked deed he visited the oracle Pythoness who told him that he must serve his enemy, King Eurystheus. This king set Heracles a number of tasks, the 'labours', at the end of which he would be granted immortality by Zeus."

Caciro called back across his shoulder and Catumanda turned and laughed with delight at the young Greek's astonished expression. A barbarian carter was reeling off a story of the gods as if they were his own and Catumanda recognised that he was being taught a valuable lesson.

Just because a man was born to humble parents and plied the roads to support his family, it did not necessarily follow that he was coarse, vulgar or uneducated.

"Am I going too quickly for you?"

Catumanda shared a smile with Caciro as Philippos averted his eyes, embarrassed.

"One of these labours, as you rightly say, the stealing of the cattle of Geryon, took place in those mountains. The gallant Greek stayed with a chieftain called Bebryx and as payment for his host's generosity, our scion of civilisation raped his daughter Pyrene before he left. As a result, the girl gave birth to a serpent," he grimaced, "which was probably not the child she had always dreamt of, and runs away to the wooded slopes of those mountains opposite, where wild animals discover her and tear her to pieces. Our hero," he continued with a wry smile as Philippos shifted uncomfortably, "on returning with his stolen cattle, finds the pieces of the poor girl and, overcome with grief, lays her sad remains to rest and cries out her name, *Pyrene! Pyrene!* Impressed by the manliness of his voice and the depth of his remorse, the animals, plants and the very hills, rivers and mountains return the cry, *Pyrene! Pyrene!*" Caciro paused to sink a long draught from his water skin and handed it across to the grateful druid as he prepared to end his tale. Catumanda took a swig and passed it to a chaste Philippos with a sympathetic smile as Caciro continued his tale. "Heracles, as he drove off the cattle," he paused again as he teased the boy mercilessly, "which did I mention were stolen? Asked the mountains to preserve the name in the girl's memory, so you see," he concluded with a sly wink to Catumanda, "despite what we mere mortals might think, the meeting with the civilised Greek, *had* in fact been a blessing for the poor barbarian girl who now had a whole mountain range named in her honour!"

He turned to the boy and smiled disarmingly.

"Did I miss anything out?"

The winds had been favourable and the city hove into view as they rounded the last of what seemed like several hundred headlands. The owner of the ship turned and flashed her a gap-toothed smile, calling the name in case she had been in any doubt.

"Emporion, druid!"

It was Catumanda's first glimpse of a Greek town and she had to admit to herself that the impression which it gave was favourable. The town nestled at the head of a series of small bays girded by low rocky headlands, the largest of which jutted out into the sea like the horns of an enormous bull. Sailing past the smaller bays which seemed to be the domain of fishing vessels, the Iberian captain waited until the town came up on the beam before striking his sail and taking the way of the ship. The crew were a buzz of activity as the sail was stowed and oars run out as the helmsman worked the big steering oar and guided her into the harbour.

Catumanda ran her eyes over the town as they approached. Philippos, at her side, could barely conceal his excitement at the nearness of his own people and he had promised to introduce her to the delights of Greek food as soon as they were ashore.

It had taken only two more days after they had reached the mouth of the River Iber and hired a ship to carry them north. The first night they had slept on a beach under the stars, and the simple meal of roasted fish and fresh bread had sparked memories of the last meal on the shores of the Reaping with Attis and Dorros. The muted grey skies of her homeland had seemed further away than ever and the druid had felt an unexpected sorrow, despite the beauty of her surroundings and the good-natured jollity of the Iberian crew, as she began to realise that she would never see the like again.

The coaster swept into the bay as the crewmen laboured at their oars and Catumanda hung from the prow as she studied the waterfront. It was growing late in the year and she saw to her consternation that her worst fears appeared to have been realised. A sandy beach ran up to a low stone wall, beyond which clustered the white fronted warehouses and official buildings common to all ports in the South. A dozen or so ships had been hauled onto the strand and all were in the process of being refurbished after a hard summer plying the trade routes of the southern sea. The majority had been rolled onto one side as workmen set about careening, removing the crustaceans and other sea life which attached themselves to the hull of the vessels, prior to beginning the never ending task of caulking seams and repairing damage which had been delayed until the end of the trading season.

The town was settling in for its winter slumber, the time when Poseidon thrashed the surface and Notus, the bringer of storms, made sea travel too dangerous and unpredictable. Catumanda resigned herself to the fact that she may be forced to overwinter in the town with a heavy sigh. She had left it too late.

"Where bound?"

She whirled around as she realised the importance of the hail, and her heart leapt at the sight which met her. A large trading vessel, its great stern post arched forward, scorpion-like, wallowed on the lee as the crew stowed their oars and shook out the great woollen sail. The *kubernetes* released the handle of the big *pedalia* and cupped his hands as he replied.

"Neapolis..."

As the Iberian turned to her and wrinkled his brow in question, Catumanda felt a frenzied tug at her sleeve. Glancing down she saw that Philippos' eyes were wide with excitement.

"Neapolis is my city!"

As the Iberian impatiently waited for her decision, she quickly answered the boy.

"Philippos I will get you home, I promise you, but first I need to go to Syracuse."

Philippos looked confused.

"Why?"

"Because I promised Hektor on the *Alexa* that I would do something for him."

The Iberian captain called across as Catumanda's mind raced. This was likely to be the last ship to leave Emporion this year. She had a moment to make the decision whether to take passage on her or attempt to travel on by road but the druid still had no idea where Neapolis was, it could be at the other end of the southern sea. Philippos was tugging at her tunic again and she snapped at him.

"What?"

"So why do you want to go to Syracuse?"

She shook her head in frustration and grabbed her crane skin bag and staff. There was no time for a calculated decision. Leaping a thwart, she scrambled across to the Greek trader and threw herself bodily over the rail just as the stern posts of the ships began to glide past one another. A cry went up as she landed in a heap, and she turned to see a crewman snatch Philippos from the air as he bounced from the rail and tumbled back towards the water, heaving the lad aboard and bundling him onto the deck.

Catumanda squinted up at the startled helmsman and smiled what she hoped was her most innocent smile.

"Neapolis will be fine."

The pirates had saved them. The crew of the Greek ship had found it difficult to hide their dismay when they discovered that, not only were they to test the benevolence of the sea gods by making such a late run, they were to do so with a woman on board. Every Greek who had ever put to sea knew that they invited *katastrophe* upon themselves by doing such a thing, but she had managed to stop them throwing her overboard by promising to pay them handsomely when they arrived in Neapolis. The fact that she had no idea where the port was and did not know a soul there even if she had, she would have to deal with when they arrived safely.

The first few days at sea had gone well. *Ksiphias, Swordfish,* was a well-found ship and, although the winds were unseasonally light, the sun pulsed from an azure sky and the men had sung happily as they bent their backs to the oars.

Philippos of course had been keen to show his compatriots all the skills he had picked up on the *Alexa,* and this had been their undoing. By chance, one of the crew asked the boy why he had left his last ship if he had had such a happy time there, to which he had replied truthfully, as any boy of good family would, that Poseidon had taken her and her crew into the depths, he and Catumanda being the sole survivors. In the uproar which followed the revelation, Philippos had managed to give the crew the slip and Catumanda had drawn her moon blade and retreated to the bows as the terrified crew armed themselves and prepared to toss them overboard.

As the situation began to look grim for the pair of travellers, a cry of alarm from the kubernetes at the stern caused the men to back away and Catumanda seized her chance. She cupped her hands to her mouth and cried the length of the ship.

"I can help you to escape. I have power."

The helmsman, Alexandros, called her to him with a sharp jerk of his head as the crew flew back to their oars like frightened mice. The druid hastened to the steering platform and looked out. A small island lay off the beam and a long, low ship had emerged from cover there and was racing to head them off. The day was calm, without a whisper of wind and Catumanda could see immediately that the *Ksiphias* had no chance of escape against the sleek rowboat. She could see that the kubernetes knew so too, and she recognised that the gods had turned her situation completely around; she was their only chance.

"Put the helm over and head south. I need you to give me as long as you can before they come up."

Jumping down from the platform she reached into a wooden pen and pulled out a kid by the scruff of its neck. The goat kicked and squirmed as the druid hurried back to the bows and drew her moon blade. As the crew exchanged fearful glances, Catumanda held the kid bodily over the side and mumbled an incantation to Manannan. Her blade flashed and the animal cried its last, its kicks growing more feeble as its lifeblood ran in torrents into the blue waters below. Catumanda let the limp body fall with a splash as, turning back to the kubernetes, she giggled at his expression.

Despite the desperation of their situation, the crew turned and looked across to the south, following the outstretched arm of their helmsman, his mouth a perfect circle of disbelief.

As she wiped the sacrificial blood from her hands onto the legs of her trews, the druid called down the ship.

"That will not save us if we cannot reach it. I suggest that you bend your backs to the oars."

FIFTEEN

He found Brennus among the ruins of the town. As members of his clan quenched their thirst and celebrated the great victory, Albiomaros led Solemis through the broken gates of Fidenae and into the main forum. The big man explained that the town had been a thriving Etruscan settlement until, a few years previously, it had been sacked by the Romans along with its nearby neighbour, Veii. The men of both cities had been slaughtered and the boys and females taken into slavery. Solemis nodded gravely as he listened. The power of Rome was spreading like a dark stain throughout the lands. They must be stopped before they reached the lands of the Senones.

A cry of recognition cut the air and he grinned as he made his way across to the small, smoke blackened building.

"Congratulations on your victory, Brennus the Great!"

The great man threw back his head and laughed as he slid off of the edge of the table and opened his arms in welcome.

"Solemis, what a day!"

The warriors gathered in the open space paused from their drinking, smiling happily as the chieftains embraced. It *had* been a great day. Brennus took a pace back and cocked a brow.

"Caturix?"

"Bruised and embarrassed, but alive."

The corner of Solemis' mouth turned up into a wry smile as a memory of the last of the Romans to cross the Tiberis flashed into his mind. The only Senone with an uninjured horse within a mile, he had been forced to look on helplessly as the Fabii and the last men under their command had formed themselves into an ordered column and carried their arms to the safety of the very same city of Veii, so recently the object of their hatred.

There had been a moment when he had been recognised by one of the brothers, Quintus he thought, and the man had called Numerius across. The Roman had stared long and hard at him before turning to walk away, and Solemis had wondered at the intensity of the man's hostility towards him. It seemed to have become more personal, more than the result of the humiliation which they had just inflicted on the army of Rome. Maybe he had suffered personally during his raids in the South. Solemis hoped so. The Roman had killed Crixos after all, it would be some measure of vengeance for the deed. Brennus flashed a grin as he broke into his thoughts.

"That's all of my chieftains alive then; that's all the greatness I need from the day."

He threw an arm around Solemis and guided him towards several wagons which had been pulled clear of their hiding places. A knot of warriors had gathered there as word had spread about the goods which they carried, and hungry men tore at loaves and cheeses as they swapped stories of the rout.

"Roman supplies," Brennus explained with a wave of his hand. "Their drivers seemed anxious that we have them, so I let them go." He pointed out a wagon which had been set aside from the others. It was piled high with amphorae and casks of food, and the warriors set to guard it smiled happily as they approached.

"I kept this wagon load for you and your boys. Take as much as you want, and rest awhile."

Solemis sighed, weariness and resignation mixing in equal measure.

"Awhile?"

The strange sound grew as they rode slowly southwards until it came to resemble the buzzing of a great hive. As the mile markers counted down to two, Solemis led the Horsetails clear of the low hills and out onto the plain. Halting Tantibus, he shifted in his saddle and looked once again on the walls of the great city. Low in the West, the sun was an indistinct ball of flame as he waited for his clansmen to draw alongside him and, despite the euphoria of victory, Solemis felt as weary as he had ever been in his life. He squirmed again and grimaced as he attempted to find a comfortable way to sit. Albiomaros chuckled as he came up.

"I know how you feel. How long have we been in the saddle today?"

Solemis threw him a pained look. They had left the army just as dawn had crept into the eastern sky, galloping south to scout the way ahead, and he shook his head in wonder as the images of the day flashed through his memory. The arrival of the Roman army and his narrow escape. The frantic dash to the battlefield and the fight on the ridge. The hectic chase to intercept the Fabii before they could slip through the net; the failure of the Crow attack.

The gods; Was it still the same day?

He rested his hand on his friend's shoulder and pulled a tired smile as he answered truthfully.

"Too long, genos."

Several of the clan had accompanied them to Rome the previous autumn to demand compensation and justice for the death of Crixos, but for most of his clansmen it was their first glimpse of the fabled city and Solemis paused as they took in the grandeur of the place. Albiomaros raised his hand to shield his eyes from the glare of the sun.

"It looks different without the crowds. The last time we were here the roads were full of wagons, horses and people." Solemis let his gaze drift absent-mindedly along the walls of Servian and suddenly sat bolt upright in his saddle.

"And the gates were closed!"

His big friend looked at him incredulously as he guessed what his chieftain was contemplating.

"You *are* joking, right?"

Solemis laughed and urged Tantibus forward as his startled clansmen whipped their own mounts and funnelled in his wake. As the hills receded and the River Tiberis began its great arc to the West, the place which they knew to be called the Field of Mars opened up before them. Barely a mile stood between the Horsetails and the open gates of the city and, although the idea that it may be a trap flashed through his mind, Solemis quickly discounted it. The Romans were leaderless, and he knew that the opportunity to seize the gate could be fleeting.

Hurtling past the porticoed mausolea which lined the roadway, the horsemen instinctively scanned the city walls for archers but they were as deserted as the field, and Solemis checked Tantibus as they entered the shadow cast by the great defences.

The Celts hunched behind their shields and hefted their lancea as the sound of their hoof beats echoed back, the rhythmic clatter unnaturally loud in the silence which seemed to hang over the deserted entrance. Beyond the great opening, Solemis could make out an open space, cast into deep shadow by the steep hill to the West. Further in, a wide thoroughfare lined by a collection of buildings of varying sizes and designs skirted the hill before cutting sharply to the right and disappearing from view.

Reassured that the area was not thronging with vengeful Romans, Solemis whooped with joy and drove Tantibus through the portal and into the city. As the rest of his clan hastened in his wake and spread out into a defensive screen, Solemis quickly scanned the clearing for signs of opposition.

A large stables lay off to the right, adjoining a double storied building which obviously housed the city guards, although both buildings appeared to be empty. Across the square, the shuttered windows of shops and a tabernarium faced towards the gateway, jostling with each other to be the first to relieve weary travellers of a small part of their wealth. To the left of the gateway itself, a small shrine waited patiently to endow travellers with the protection of its resident goddess for a small donation or sacrifice. Satisfied that there would be no immediate opposition, Solemis dismounted and began to plan their defence.

"Berikos, take half a dozen men and make sure that the northern tower is clear, then cross the walkway and check out the southern. We don't want any arrows to take us in the back as we work." He turned to Albiomaros. "Genos, pull down the stables and form a barrier around the gateway," he paused and snorted. "Not too close though, we may get singed." As the clan champion narrowed his eyes at the remark and opened his mouth to question it, Solemis ignored him and continued. "Make it chest height if you can, with a platform running along the inner wall for us to stand on." It was obviously important and, his query forgotten, Albiomaros hastened away to do his chieftain's bidding.

Their Umbrian allies made to follow but Solemis called them across. The brothers exchanged a look as Solemis indicated that they step to one side. As his clansmen scattered about their tasks, Solemis gripped the men by the shoulder. "Rodolfo…Brizio, I need you two to ride to Brennus and tell him what has happened here. Tell him that we control this gate, and to get as many men as he can up to us as soon as possible." Both men made to protest, but Solemis held up a hand and his look was enough to cut them short. "The Romans may be asleep at the moment but they will soon wake up when they realise that we are here. If we hold this gate, the city falls." He fixed them with an earnest stare as a small smile of affection curled at his lips. "You two are the finest riders among us, you are our best hope." He indicated the horses with a jerk of his head. "Take our mounts with you. If it comes to a fight, they will be ideal targets for the attackers. I have just witnessed the effect that wounded horses can have on a formation and I don't want to risk that happening in such a small space. Besides," he concluded grimly, "I am going to set a fire and they will be terrified. We will either lead our army into the city or we shall die here in the gateway, either way wounded and terror-stricken horses will be of little use."

The brothers nodded that they understood the finality of his decision and turned to go. As they gathered the horses together and mounted, the Horsetail warriors exchanged knowing looks as they continued to construct the barrier. The Umbrians clattered out through the gates and the sound of horses was replaced by that of the panicked city once again, adding urgency to their labours.

Tempted as he was to investigate the chaos which must be ensuing further within the great metropolis, Solemis knew that to split his meagre force would only invite their annihilation. A city this size would contain only the gods knew how many inhabitants, and many of those would have lost loved ones that day. Only a prepared defensive position could have any hope of withstanding an attack until the rest of the army arrived.

Albiomaros deposited a heavy beam with a crash which resounded around the open space and Solemis indicated that he follow him across to the great gates.

"Come and help me fire these. Even if we are overrun, the city will fall to Brennus without gates to close against him."

Great drifts of thatch from the stable roof lay scattered about the square and the pair gathered it in armfuls and stacked it against the open doors. Heaped chest high beneath the archway, the tinder dry stalks caught immediately and they danced back as the flames took hold. Albiomaros cocked his head and chuckled happily as the tongues of flame roared upwards to lick hungrily at the base of the timber walkway above.

"Shall we get Berikos and the boys down, or do you plan to roast them?"

Solemis cursed as he remembered the men he had sent to check for archers or other guards. As choking black smoke billowed into the warm evening air, he hastily called the men back down as the remainder of their clansmen laughed and called. It was not a moment too soon. Within moments the great gates and wooden walkways were a seething mass of flames.

*

He could smell the smoke in the air before he could see the city, and his body sagged a little more with the weight of guilt it shouldered. It had been his attack on the Gaul chieftain which had brought the ire of the barbarians down upon them all. Although he felt no sense of responsibility for the conduct of the army that day, the initial spark which had lit the fires of war had undoubtedly been struck by him.

Breaking free of the western hills, Numerius paused his mount and stared out across the valley of the Tiberis towards Rome. One of the western gates was burning but, to his surprise, there was no sign of the Gauls. Ahead of him, the tribune was shocked to see people abandoning the city, streaming across the Pons Sublicius and passing from sight beyond the hill of the Janiculum.

Numerius cocked his head and listened but there was no sign of an approaching army. He well knew by now the haunting sound of the war horns which the Gauls called carnyx and the guttural cries of their warriors, but no sound reached him of their imminent approach and he glanced up at the capitol and thanked mighty Jupiter for the delay.

Away to the North, a vast moving mass marked the point at which the armies had clashed as vultures circled in the rising currents of air. The heat was finally coming off of the day as the sun sank beyond the western hills in a brawl of reds and the tribune frowned as he thought back on the humiliation they had suffered.

The men had jogged the few miles from the Tiberis to Veii without further mishap. Numerius had led a screen of equites, sweeping around the rear of the column in case of interception by the powerful Gaulish horse warriors but none had appeared. The tactical acumen shown by the centurion, Caedicius, had been impressive. The deployment of the *tribulus* had been a masterstroke to which he very likely owed his life and Numerius, as a military tribune, had felt confident enough in the man's abilities to appoint him as commander of the Roman forces at Veii.

As the men had set to work repairing the fortifications damaged during Camillus' siege and storm of the city a few years previously, he had discussed their situation with his brothers. It had been agreed that Quintus and Caeso would each take half of the remaining equites and search for parties of Romans who had become detached from the army in the rout. None of them were aware of how many Romans had managed to retreat to their home city, and those left wandering the countryside would be easy pickings for the vast number of Gauls in the area. Defensible, unknown to the Gauls and only a few miles from Rome herself, Veii offered the ideal gathering point for the scattered troops.

The road arced away across the plain and Numerius was soon riding alongside the river, the great walls of the city themselves lining its far bank. The heights of the Janiculum rose before him and, slowing his horse to a trot, he approached the mass of humanity as they spilled out from the bridge. He was pleased to see that a troop of soldiers had been stationed at the junction, it indicated that law and order still held within the city despite the disaster which had overtaken them all, and he curbed his horse as he came up to them.

A weary looking spear man turned his way and Numerius, despite his own weariness and the gravity of the situation, smiled inwardly as the man started at his sudden appearance. The soldier clenched his fist and saluted as Numerius leaned forward in the saddle.

"What is happening here?"

The soldier looked nonplussed and blurted a reply.

"The people are fleeing to Caere, sir."

It was Numerius' turn to look bemused. Things must have been even worse than he thought if the entire city was being evacuated.

"Is this by order of the senate? Where is the army?"

The soldier narrowed his eyes but the tribune cut short any doubts which he might entertain that he was completely in the dark about events that day.

"Don't say that they were defeated. I know, I was there."

The soldier pulled himself upright.

"I am aware of that, tribune; the Fabii have never shirked a battle."

The reply drew the sting from Numerius' temper and he nodded his appreciation for the man's remark. A cry from the road caused him to look across. A cart wheel had injured a child and the carter and the boy's parents were about to come to blows. Numerius sighed.

"You had best get back. I will find out the situation soon enough."

As the man waded into the dispute, Numerius forced his horse onto the bridge. Carts and Wagons had largely blocked the span, but he forced his way through, the presence of armed troops at each end of the span and his obvious high rank seeing him safely across.

It was a short distance from the bridge to the city gate and Numerius was gratified to see that more troops had been placed at this strategic location. They used their spear shafts to push the multitude aside as he approached and soon he was back within the walls of the city. Steering his horse to one side, Numerius sat and marvelled at the sight before him.

The population of Rome was abandoning her in their thousands. Every class of citizen was represented in the throng, from the poor who came with little more than the clothes on their backs to those who seemed to be attempting to carry away the entire contents of their *domus* with them, either in hired wagons or pushed along in hand carts by the ubiquitous slaves. Here and there, bundles of belongings lay abandoned by those who had given up trying to save it all, those who had realised that there would simply be no place for all the belongings in

Rome, even if they did manage to manhandle them all the way to Caere.

With a shake of his head, Numerius steered his horse away from the river of people and in the direction of the *forum boarium*. The familiar hills of the Palatine and the Capitoline, capped by their temples and fine houses, stood like twin sentinels before him, guarding the entrance to the *forum Romanum* which lay beyond.

To his surprise, the *boarium* was filled with livestock and he paused once again as the scale of the disaster which had struck the city suddenly threatened to overwhelm him. It had been that very morning that they had collected in the forum and marched out onto the field of Mars to be reviewed by the members of the senate and cheered by their fellow citizens. As they marched away, the city had returned to the business of the day, confident in the ability of their men to see off this barbarian rabble. Cattle had been brought into the meat market here and slaves would have been sent down to buy supplies for the victory feast. All had been well until early afternoon when the first of the army had burst back into the city to spread the terrible news of their defeat, and from that moment nothing would ever be the same again.

He looked down as the sound of a man politely clearing his throat cut through his thoughts, and the slave bowed respectfully before returning his gaze with a confidence unusual in one of his position. He was a giant of a man, his long black hair tied into a knot which sat at one side of his head and, although he wore the finger ring of plain iron which confirmed his lowly status, the slave was finely dressed and well armed. Numerius was intrigued as to who would own such a man and gave permission for him to speak with a curt nod.

"My mistress sends her greetings and asks if you are the tribune, Numerius Fabius Ambustus, sir?"

Numerius looked beyond the slave and saw that several fine litters had removed themselves from the throng and sat waiting for the man's return. A wagon had pulled over before them and a number of similarly dressed slaves and spear men stood guard around it, forcing the citizens to give the whole a wide berth as they moved towards the gate. He nodded.

"I am. And your mistress is?"

"The Virgo Maxima, tribune; she asks if she might speak with you?"

Numerius was stunned. The litters obviously contained the Vestal Virgins. If the sacred women were fleeing the city things must be even worse than he feared; this really was a full scale evacuation. He dismounted and handed his reins to the slave as he walked across. The curtain on the leading litter was pulled aside and the figure of the high priestess emerged and greeted him with a thin smile.

"Numerius, I am sorry that we must meet for the first time this way. I have just left your father, the pontifex maximus, and I thought that you would like to know that he has decided to remain in the city."

To the Virgo Maxima's evident surprise, Numerius found himself smiling.

"I would have expected nothing less."

He glanced across to the wagon. An ornate bronze cauldron was securely lashed to a supporting framework and attended by a young woman whose sacred vestments he had failed to notice at first. Guarded by four burly soldiers, each sat facing away from the cauldron with their weapons drawn, she was obviously one of the Vestals, her hair kept permanently braided in the Roman bridal fashion. Numerius' face dropped.

"Is that...?"

The Virgo Maxima nodded.

"The Eternal Flame, yes; we are transporting the goddess Vesta to Caere in her hearth fire. As long as the eternal flame endures, Rome will live."

The priestess touched his sleeve lightly causing him to jump. There were severe penalties for touching so exalted a person as the Virgo Maxima and he had never thought to do so. The gods seemed angry enough without adding further insult. She smiled at his reaction.

"You are not allowed to touch me. I can touch whoever I want!"

He returned the smile, but her face had hardened as she led him aside.

"Your father fears that he will not see you again so I will explain his concerns. He is afraid that you will blame yourself for the present calamity, but he assures you that any blame lies with him alone. His hubris angered the gods when he sent his sons to Clusium and they are taking their revenge on the city. Nemesis, the daughter of justice, appeared before him and demanded that he forfeit his life."

SIXTEEN

Bent forward, the shadowy figure paused by each man as he scooped a handful of the greasy powder from the pot. Rubbing their hands together, each warrior worked the mixture briskly into his face until they appeared to fade into the shadows. Druteos leaned forward and whispered to his clansman.

"Don't forget your torc."

The warrior smeared the remainder across the body and terminals of the necklet and smiled, his teeth suddenly appearing as a shocking line of white from the gloom.

"Satisfied?"

Druteos, his face and neck already blackened, flashed a smile in return and moved on.

Solemis, as chieftain, crouched at the head of the line and he nodded his thanks as he repeated the process. Tense, they watched the doorway opposite for the signal to go as they gripped their weapons and propped their shields reluctantly against the barricade. Although they would soon be needed if all went well, the boards were just too big to carry through the restricted space ahead. Leaving the garishly painted boards in full view of the

Roman defenders would hopefully lull them into a false sense of security; only madmen would attack so many armed men without their shields.

The fire at their back had long since burnt itself out as night finally drew a veil on what had been a tumultuous day for Celt and Roman alike. The great doors to the city, desiccated by the heat of the summer, had flared and torched immediately. Within the hour the flames had weakened the great timbers and posts to such an extent that they had crashed outwards in a welter of sparks, bringing a portion of the walls tumbling in their wake.

The rear of their position was now horribly exposed, and they had waited anxiously for the thunderous noise which would accompany the arrival of Brennus and the army but, despite their expectations, it had never come. As the darkness deepened, Solemis had ordered the line of their defences extended to meet the walls of the buildings which lined the square, and a final bulwark looped around to incorporate the travellers' shrine.

Finally, just as they were beginning to think that the city must be abandoned, disorganised groups of defenders, emboldened by the darkness and the fact that they were not after all about to be overrun by the barbarian army, had begun to creep forward. Word had evidently been passed back into the city of the paltry size of the enemy force at the gate and soon the numbers had swelled to fill the far side of the square and the roadway beyond.

Although heavily outnumbered, it was obvious to Solemis that the men opposing him were little more than the rabble of the mob. There was no sense of leadership or the fabled Roman *disciplina* among them and he quickly came to the conclusion that if they could cross the square without losing any men to the javelins and bows in evidence, the Horsetails would sweep them away.

The line of shops and drinking dens at their back would prove the ideal route. Solemis had dispatched Albiomaros across and he had reported that, although the walls which divided one property from the next were built of mortared stone, those on the upper floors were of wattle and lime plaster, much like those of their own roundhouses. He had eagerly seized the opportunity to outflank the mob, and Albiomaros had led Vortrix and Galba into the building to cut a path from one building to the next as their clansmen waited impatiently for the signal which would unleash their fury against their tormentors.

The signal was not long in coming and they rose from the shadows and hurried across to the doorway. Vortrix smiled as his chieftain came up and motioned that he follow on with a jerk of his head. The Horsetail disappeared up a steep wooden staircase and ducked through into a side room on the upper floor. By the time that Solemis had reached the opening all that was visible of the warrior was the seat of his trews as it melted into the gloom of the next room in the chain. Bent forward, they hurried through room after room, painfully aware that they were gambling everything on one attack. If the men opposite discovered that they had left their defences they could easily block both ends of the terrace and fire the buildings; it would be a grisly and ignoble end.

Solemis finally spilled out into the last room in the series to be greeted by the smiling face of his champion. Albiomaros thrust a cup into his hand.

"Drink up!"

The wine was good and, glancing around, Solemis realised that they must be in a storeroom above the tabernarium as Galba handed cups of wine to the others as they came through.

Albiomaros had turned back to the far wall and raised the blade of his lancea. Solemis could see that a rectangle of plaster had been carefully removed from the final wall, exposing the wattle beneath, and he gave a small nod of recognition at his big friend's preparation. Hopefully the room on the far side was clear of the enemy but if not, the wall would appear no different to anyone in the room beyond until the moment that the tips of the heavy spears punched through.

Albiomaros placed the blade of his lancea between the stalks of wattle and nodded to Vortrix who followed his action. Tensed, Solemis crouched and gripped his spear in sweaty hands. The long strands of his horsehair plume tumbled forward to obscure his view just as the pair began to frantically saw at the wattle and he flicked it away with an angry toss of his head. The bindings, as dry as the bones of a corpse after their years encased in the moisture-sucking lime plaster, shattered under the assault and within moments the pair of warriors jumped back. It was the signal and Solemis, clan chieftain, launched himself forward at the head of his men.

A heartbeat later he had burst through the flimsy barrier in a cloud of dust and he quickly swept the room with his gaze. A woman screamed and before he had time to think he had leapt across to plunge his lancea into her gaping mouth. As her eyes widened in shock and terror he let go of the shaft of the spear and whipped his knife from its scabbard. The man on top of her, his back to them, had only just begun to react and as his head turned Solemis gripped his hair and opened his throat, pushing his head forward into the sacking which lay beneath the couple to stifle any sounds. Satisfied that the pair were no longer a threat, he raised himself and worked his spear free as he looked about the room. His clan were all through, twenty men with blackened faces, the whites of their eyes *daimonic* in the murkiness of the chamber as they strained to hear any reaction from below.

The sound of footsteps caused them to exchange worried glances and they moved back as one to either side of the doorway. Solemis drifted back into the murk as the shadow of a man appeared on the wall of the staircase and began to climb.

"I take it that scream means that you are finished?" The voice sounded light-hearted as its owner climbed unknowingly to his death. "You'll appreciate some of this wine while you wait for me!" A figure appeared in the doorway holding a small amphora, and Solemis watched in detachment as the Roman died before he even realised that he had been in any danger.

Albiomaros slipped behind him and covered his mouth with a massive hand as several other shadowy figures moved quickly forward to plunge their spear blades into the man's chest again and again.

Berikos had the presence of mind to leap forward and snatch the amphora away from the Roman's dying grasp, and the pale line of a smile split his darkened face as he raised it to him in the Celtic toast for health, "*slantu!*" The men smiled at the irony as Berikos moved the body away from the doorway and Solemis glanced at it as he came across. Dark blood mixed with the air from his lacerated lungs was bubbling out through dozens of holes in the victim's chest and, although he was sure that the man would never move again, he added his own spear thrust into the chest of the man for luck. The Horsetails who had been crowded out of the frenzied attack came across to wet their own spears in the bloody mash, and Solemis moved to the head of the staircase and turned back as his clansmen bunched behind him.

Reaching up, he wiped the grime from Albiomaros' silver owl-faced helm and spoke softly to the eager faces which crowded around them. "Our clan champion is leading the attack today." He smiled as a look of pride crossed his friend's face before taking in the faces of his clansmen one by one. "Let's show this rabble what real warriors fight like!" They touched spears and shared a look of determination as Albiomaros rolled his shoulders and kissed the bloodied blade of his lancea as he moved through the doorway.

Solemis followed on closely, watching as a man staggered from a side doorway to collide with the wall opposite. His heart leapt at the sight. If the mob had had access to the supplies in the tabernarium the whole time that they had been in the square it could only aid their attack. The bulk of the man blocked the passageway and Solemis watched as Albiomaros thrust his spear deep into his flank and heaved him aside. The big blade slipped in easily and the Horsetail champion hesitated for a heartbeat as he attempted to tug the shaft free but the heavy set man had twisted and slumped to one side, trapping it against the wall, and he quickly abandoned the attempt before the attack lost momentum.

Pounding towards the open doorway at the end of the short passageway, Albiomaros waited until he burst out into the open before drawing his great broadsword with an extravagant sweep of his arm. It was the perfect action and Solemis emerged moments later to be confronted by a swathe of startled faces as his friend roared his battle cry and swung his blade in great sweeping arcs.

Solemis felt the joy of battle surge through him as he saw that they had achieved complete surprise. The crowd shrank back under the onslaught, tumbling over one another in their panicked efforts to escape the death dealing giant as Albiomaros scythed into their ranks, the embodiment of Camulos himself.

The retreating mob had opened up a space between themselves and the emerging Horsetails and Solemis dropped his lancea and drew his own sword as he came on. The loss of Albiomaros' spear in the tabernarium and his decision to abandon it for his sword had had a devastating affect on the Romans. By opening a gap between them it had provided the space which they needed to swing their great blades and they took advantage of the opportunity to cut great arcs through the packed ranks.

The light cast by the quartered moon cast a silvered glow over the multitude as the brands which had lit the scene were extinguished along with their owners. Solemis took a pace back and surveyed the scene as the crowd continued to fall away before their attack, and he cried out as his men came up alongside him.

"Keep them moving! Push them out of the square!"

Albiomaros led several men in a sweeping attack to Solemis' right as they slashed at the disorganised mob.

They were still heavily outnumbered and they all knew that the key to victory was to chase the enemy from the area, not engage in a fight to the death with a cornered foe. If the Romans were given the opportunity to think they could still overwhelm the Gauls by sheer force of numbers.

The crush which had formed at the exit to the square had forced several men to turn and face their attackers and Solemis instinctively knew that these men were the most dangerous. More than a few carried spears and, shield less, the Horsetails would be particularly vulnerable if they could galvanize themselves to mount an organised defence.

Solemis' gaze alighted on one particular Roman and he moved back into the fray. Clad in a magnificent breast plate of muscled bronze the man, although helmetless, was probably one of the men who had been at the battle that day who had discarded the item in the rout. The shame of that defeat was writ large on his features and Solemis knew that he would be a tough opponent. He screamed a challenge as he approached but the man braced and stood firm, his eyes fixed on the silvered arc of the broadsword. Solemis brought the blade sweeping across, feinting at the last moment to take off the Roman's thigh, but the soldier was experienced and he read the move perfectly as he flicked the butt of his spear shaft up to scoop the strike away. Momentarily off balance, Solemis tried to slip aside but his foot brushed against one of the many bodies which already littered the ground. To his horror be began to fall, and he twisted his shoulder and dragged his sword clear as he tumbled to the ground. Experience told him that the blade of his opponent's spear would be swinging back around to finish him off as he lay defenceless, and he was rolling away the moment that he felt the solid ground beneath him. A heartbeat later the blade sparked as it struck the stone road surface a finger width from his face. Rolling away and back to his feet in one fluid movement, Solemis skipped back to dodge the follow-up strike. As they began to circle one another warily, Solemis saw that the soldier's small victory had encouraged those around him. It was the very thing that he feared and he knew that the man had to die, quickly, if the attack was not to lose momentum.

A small salient was forming in the line opposite as those nearby moved towards the spear man for protection and Solemis yelled with anger and frustration as he launched himself at the man once again. Trusting to the strength in his wrist, he grasped the shaft of his opponent's spear in his left hand and thrust it aside as he swung his sword with his right. Taken by surprise, the Roman managed to twist his upper body away as the blade crashed down to glance off the polished bronze of his armour. The movement had been enough to save the man's life, but the strike had been good, and although Solemis was encouraged by the look of pain which swept across the spear man's features he knew that time was running out for them. Increasing numbers of Roman soldiers were forcing their way through the mob and a tight knot of spear wielding men was beginning to coalesce around his opponent.

The number of bodies which lay strewn about were beginning to slow their attack to a crawl as the Horsetail warriors attempted to push the enemy away through sheer force of violence. Solemis suddenly felt a sting of pain in his calf and, looking down he saw one of the earlier wounded had reached up to thrust a knife into his calf. He hobbled back and took the top of the Roman's head off with a contemptuous swing of his sword as he risked a glance to either side.

On his right hand side, Albiomaros was still swinging his broadsword in great arcs, the blade a blur of silver in the moonlight. Hacking through the men opposite, the terrified Romans fell away before him in disarray. Solemis looked across to the left and let out an involuntary gasp at the sight which met his eyes. The left wing of their attack was moments away from being turned as a strong counter-attack threatened to envelope his men there. Well-armed men were emerging from the doorway which they had themselves exited only a short time before and the cause of the disaster was as obvious as it had been unavoidable. The ground floor room in the tabernarium had been taken over by a group of soldiers as they took advantage of the missing owner to help themselves to the unguarded wine supplies. Now they had come to their wits and were spilling out of the same doorway which the Horsetails had used only a short time before to hit their rear and flank. As he watched, Vortrix was surrounded and overwhelmed, the Romans gathering over his body to gleefully stab down as he fell.

It was clear that the plan was unravelling, fast. It was time to retreat. Solemis took several paces back and called out above the din.

"Horsetails! Back! Back to the rampart!"

The dead and dying now hindered the Romans as Solemis anxiously called out to his clansmen to disengage. He watched as Druteos on the right acknowledged his call with a stern nod, moving forward to stab a Roman with his spear as he attempted to pass the command to a battle-crazed Albiomaros.

As his clansmen began to back towards him the Romans moved forward, the light of victory flashing in their eyes. It was barely fifty paces to the safety of their defences, and Solemis choked down the feeling of humiliation as he ordered the retreat. On the point of being overrun, he knew that he had no choice if he was to save at least some of the men of his clan and keep the way open for Brennus when he arrived, but he burned with shame as he growled the command.

"Ready. Get back behind our defences when I say so." He watched as the Roman advance faltered as it crossed a line of bloodied bodies and cried out.

"Now!"

Solemis braced himself for one last attack as the men turned and ran, determined to fulfil a chieftain's duty to his people and be the last to leave the fight.

"You take those on the left, and I'll take this side, genos. Let's see how many we can take with us."

Without looking Solemis could sense the man grinning, and he felt a wave of emotion threaten to overcome him as the thought that he expected them to die side by side in the streets of Rome passed through his mind. He shook his head as he replied, and Albiomaros laughed as he heard his childhood name for the first time in years.

"Our story cannot end here, Acco. We still have to meet Catumanda in the grey forest."

As the Romans picked their way through the last of the corpses Albiomaros laughed again as he launched himself into a counter-attack, bellowing the name of his people in far off Albion.

"Trinobantes!"

Taken by surprise, the Romans fell back in disarray as Albiomaros cut a bloody path through the spear men. Solemis glanced across towards the tabernarium, hoping to see the remainder of his clansmen either retreating towards the barricade or coming across to lend them support, but he saw only Romans there now and his heart sank as he realised that they must have been wiped out. Determined to avenge the men who had trusted their lives to him and fought to the end, Solemis screamed his own war cry and vaulted into the breach made by his friend. Several fresh bodies lay at his feet as he landed, the blood pulsing from them to add to the sticky mixture underfoot, and Solemis swept his own war blade in great arcs as the Romans stabbed and probed in reply.

The first wash of light, the iron grey birth of the new day, picked out the temple of Jupiter high on the Capitoline as their sword blades hacked to left and right. Suddenly, petals of flame appeared among the upper levels of the buildings through which they had passed what seemed like hours before. Solemis knew that the Roman attack must have reached the barrier and he smiled grimly at the realisation that their druid friend was wrong after all, maybe the grey forest had been *Anwnn,* the underworld.

As the flames suddenly flared into life, the crimson light flickered across the features of the men who crowded in on them, their faces contorted by hate as they rallied and fought back harder. Working together as they probed for any weakness in his defence, Solemis' muscles screamed as exhaustion threatened to overcome him. He had been riding and fighting for a full day and night and he knew now that the end was very close. A face flashed before him and he brought his elbow crashing up, feeling the man's nose crumple under the blow as he forced his way to Albiomaros' side. The big man shot him a characteristic wink and Solemis felt a sense of peace wash over him as he moved to stand back to back with his blood genos and they prepared to die together after all, regardless of Catumanda's dream.

Despite the press of men all around them, Solemis noticed that the light had changed from grey to pink as it moved relentlessly down the Capitoline towards them, and he felt glad to have made it to the full light of day.

Spears darted in as they parried together, twisting this way and that as they dodged the deadly points. It was only a matter of time and eventually one broke through their defence to pierce Solemis' mail shirt. A last-gasp twist caused the blade to pass along his side and the point of Solemis' sword flicked out to take the spear man in the throat.

A heartbeat later his mind seemed to explode in a lightning flecked storm of pain as a heavy object collided with the back of his helm with sickening force and, despite his efforts to remain on his feet and conscious, he felt himself slipping away into a dark abyss. The Stygian depths felt warm and welcoming and he struggled against the desire to slip further in as he forced his eyes open for what must be the final time among mortal men.

A foot planted itself before his face and, although coherent thought was almost beyond him now, he recognised the boot of Albiomaros as his friend stood protectively over the body of his chieftain.

His genos was singing the battle song of the Trinobantes as he hewed at their foe, and Solemis felt a wave of love for the man, his greatest friend.

As he slipped away, his befuddled mind became aware that the carnyx were calling him to the place of his ancestors. Cotos lay dead on the battlefield to the North, alongside his beloved war pig, and he recognised that his clansman was guiding him to the great hall of their people as the darkness finally took him.

SEVENTEEN

Alexandros raised his chin and whispered into Catumanda's ear.

"Is it just a narrow bank?"

The druid shrugged and leaned into him as she scanned the gloom for fire arrows.

"I don't know. It's not my fog, I just asked Manannan for his help."

A flicker of light, indistinct at first but quickly growing in intensity, arced through the mist to land with a hiss only feet away from the *Ksiphias* as the men not employed at the oars or helm scanned the sky for more. They were not long in coming and the following one whickered out of the greyness to land with a thud on the deck. Catumanda quickly doused the flames and refilled her pail from the sea. Hauling on the horsehair rope, she was ready and waiting as the next arrow passed overhead and disappeared back into the murk, its comet-like tail searing a distinct trail through the moisture laden air.

The haar had risen from the surface like the silvered pelt of an old wolf, its flanks moving like bellows as it panted from the chase. Seizing their chance, the Greeks had gritted their teeth and rowed through the burning protests made by shoulder and arm muscles and before the attackers could close they had been swallowed by the haze. Alexandros muttered under his breath.

"I could steer a complete circle and resume our original course."

Sound carried a long way in such stillness and all speech had been banned. Even the long oars had been hauled in as soon as they were concealed, the sailors removing their chiton and wrapping them around the blades to deaden the sounds of rowing. Catumanda knew that the kubernetes was really asking for her advice and leaned in again.

"What if they are still holding their position at the edge of the fog, loosing arrows into it to see if they strike us. We would steer straight back into them."

Alexandros chewed at his lip and blinked away the condensation from his lashes. The day was warm for the time of year and the moisture laden air was thick and clinging. All of them wore a mantle of fine droplets as they watched anxiously for any signs that the pirates were following them.

Another arrow arrived from the haze, falling alongside the hull of the *Ksiphias* where it was extinguished in a fizz of steam. Alexandros looked perplexed.

"They are falling too close. Soon one will lodge in a hard to reach place and they will mark our position before we can extinguish it. They must be able to guess where we are, but how?" He cast about the ship but the crew were quiet and the oars made barely a sound as they stroked the glassy surface of the sea. Suddenly he had it and he handed the steering oar to her as he lowered himself to the main deck and padded towards the mast. Philippos was there and Catumanda watched as he bent to whisper to the boy. Despite the sad fate of the *Alexa* and her crew, the boy had impressed the hardy sailors with his seamanship in the time he had been on board. His wiry frame and youthful vigour had been put to good use aloft and he listened intently as Alexandros gave him instructions.

He nodded that he understood, and a heartbeat later he had scurried up the mast and been swallowed by the fog. It seemed only moments before he reappeared, dropping back to the deck without a sound. Alexandros stooped to listen to the boy's report and gave a stern nod that he understood. Tearing his own chiton over his head he signalled to one of the rowers who scrambled across and dipped into a chest which stood at the base of the mast.

Catumanda caught Philippos' eye and beckoned him across as the Greek sailors began to work furiously.

"What did you see?"

The boy cocked his head and whispered.

"Everything! This fog only covers the bottom half of our mast, the rest is in clear air. From the top you can see the other boat standing off and firing arrows at us. If they move into the fog they will lose sight of us so they try to set us alight first. They have no mast so they cannot send a man aloft."

A soft thud came from amidships and she looked back to see that Alexandros had folded his work shirt and placed it against the bracket which held the mast. The other member of the crew was taking careful aim, ready to strike the shirt again. Philippos saw her narrow her eyes and explained.

"There is a wooden pin which passes through the mast-step and secures the mast in place. Once it is removed, the mast can be lowered and we can make our escape."

They both started as a meaty clunk echoed through the ship, and Catumanda looked back to see that the pair had obviously decided that the need for speed was now more important than silence. The mallet struck again, Alexandros working the peg free with a twisting motion. As the mast came down, willing hands grabbed at it and laid it carefully onto the cross trees, the moisture sodden sail hanging, curtain-like, between them.

The fire arrows arrived in a flurry as the pirates quickly realised that their ruse had been discovered, and Alexandros hurried back to the take the pedalia from the relieved druid. Pulling it to his chest he called out, all need for silence now gone.

"Put your backs into it, boys. Let's put some distance between us!"

The arrows were pattering all around the ship now as the *Ksiphias* pulled away. Another thunked into the hull near the waterline and Catumanda was about to douse it when a gentle wave careened along the strake to smother it. The ship was moving quickly now, and Catumanda watched as the kubernetes worked the blade to zigzag south. The fall of arrows was growing ragged as the pirates groped blindly for their prey and soon they stopped completely.

Alexandros raised his chin and sniffed the air like a dog tracking a scent, and a smile spread across his features as he called down the deck.

"Get the mast back up and work the braces." He threw Catumanda a grin. "Let's ride this wind away from here!"

At first she thought that it was a cloud. Her mind went back to the brooding peaks of Ordovicia, each capped by its own bonnet of greyness, as she and Rufos had followed the course of the River Sabrinna to lower, gentler lands. Philippos was riding the masthead as he craned forward, eager to catch the first glimpse of his home city, and Alexandros tossed in an observation as he followed her gaze.

"Vesbios, druid!"

Catumanda glanced across.

"The mountain which overlooks the bay is called Vesbios in my language." He chuckled as he worked the pedalia and guided the ship eastwards. "It means 'hurler of violence'. Hopefully you will not discover how violent the god can be!"

Catumanda felt a kick of excitement as she realised that the darkening cloud above the mountain was coming from within. Her head shot back just as the crew heaved on the braces and brought the great woollen sail around, hiding it from view. The druid raced along the deck and stood at the prow as the great bay which contained the Greek City of Neapolis opened up before them. The *Ksiphias* cleared the lee of a large island and tears of emotion welled as the mountain which she now knew to be called Vesbios came clearly into view. The slopes and fire-capped dome had haunted her sleep for as long as she could remember, and the druid drank in its lines as the slap of the waves on the bows sounded in her ears.

Philippos appeared at her side and he pointed out Neapolis at the head of the bay as the bows of the ship began to turn, and within the hour they were docking alongside a busy jetty.

It was the first time that she had stepped ashore in one of the great cities of the South, and Catumanda marvelled at the bustle and sense of chaos which reigned there.

She retraced her steps to the steering platform and came to Alexandros as he supervised the docking of his ship. He sensed her presence and looked up with a gleam in his eye.

"There is no payment due, and no need for thanks, druid," he said. "Were it not for you and your god, we would all be slaves or lying on the bottom." Twisting his mouth into a rictus he drew his thumb across his throat as he made a tearing sound. He smiled. "To live to see our families again is all the payment which we require."

Alexandros looked back to the dockside, waving and grinning as the mooring ropes were secured. A boarding ladder was thrown across and Catumanda laughed as a mob of small boys and girls, the hair on their heads uniformly dark and curly, raced across to hurl themselves into the arms of their fathers. The women, more constrained by their ankle length clothing followed them across and soon the reunion was in full flow. Alexandros saw her surprise and explained.

"Each ship is reported by watchers on the shore as it rounds the headland and word is passed to the families of the crew." He smiled as he went forward to greet his own family. "May your gods bring you health and happiness, Catumanda."

Catumanda collected her crane skin bag and staff and stole from the ship as discretely as possible, Philippos scrambling along in her wake. Standing on the quayside,

Catumanda was struck by the diversity of the people who worked the area. Clearly ships from all around the southern sea called at the city on a regular basis and Philippos was able to explain their origins as they walked. The cosmopolitan nature of the waterfront was also helping her to blend in and she was thankful for it after the rigours of her journey. Not only did she appear to be the only one dressed in trews, her shaven scalp, braided red hair and oak staff, marked her out as unmistakably barbarian.

As Catumanda weaved her way through the multitude, she suddenly realised that Philippos had left her side. Casting around, anxious not to lose her only guide among the heaving mass of humanity, she was relieved to hear a familiar whistle carry from a side passageway and she shook her head, smiling as she caught sight of the boy's amused face peering around the corner. Forcing her way through the crush, Catumanda found herself standing in a stone laid passageway which led away in a gentle incline. Too narrow for carts, the alley was bordered by twin gulleys which obviously served to channel rainwater and any waste water from the small homes which marched their way up the hill. Philippos caught her sleeve and guided her across.

"Keep to the centre as much as you can," he said with a look of distaste. "Far more than rainwater finds its way to the harbour along those channels."

Lines had been stretched across the passageway and clothes were drying in the warmth of the afternoon sun as Philippos ducked and weaved along. He obviously knew his way around, and Catumanda called after him as she struggled to keep pace.

"Is it far to your home?"

The boy stopped and waited for her, a smile playing upon his lips.

"We are not going to my home. You said that you needed to go to Hektor's"

Catumanda drew up in confusion.

"But Hektor's family live on Sikelia."

Philippos laughed.

"Did he tell you that?"

Catumanda realised that, no, he never had. The boy laughed again at her puzzled expression.

"I tried to tell you outside Emporion, but you would not listen so I waited until we got here."

"But Hesperos told me that the *Alexa* sailed from Syracuse. I just assumed..."

Her voice trailed away as Philippos suddenly placed a finger to his lips.

He came across and lowered his voice as a woman came from a doorway to rest in the sun. The house was small and, Catumanda could see through the opening, sparsely furnished. Her clothes were old and worn, but both home and clothing were clean as was the boy who toddled at her feet.

The druid shared a look with Philippos and he gave a small nod of confirmation. Now the time had finally arrived, Catumanda felt like she wanted to walk on by. The woman's life looked hard enough without hearing the news which she would bring, but Catumanda steeled herself as she remembered the last look which she had shared with Hektor as he had been swallowed by the depths, and the promise which she had made to the seaman.

Taking a deep breath she walked across, the woman gaping in astonishment as she was suddenly confronted by a hulking barbarian on her own doorstep. The druid pulled a sympathetic smile and pulled up a chair.

"Hello, Aikaterine. My name is Catumanda." She reached forward to tousle the dark locks of the bairn as he sailed his small wooden ship through a dusty sea. "And this young man must be Thestor."

Catumanda blew out her cheeks and held up a hand.

"No, really I am quite full. Thank you."

Another plate of stuffed vine leaves was pushed before her nevertheless, and she smiled weakly as the family fussed over the son which they had thought lost to them. She glanced about her surroundings and sighed with contentment as she surreptitiously massaged her aching belly. The food was delicious, if a little spicy, and her insides were beginning to growl. She knew that there was enough wind in there to propel a good size ship half way back to Iberia and the effort it was taking to contain it was taking up all of her attention. She had to find a place where she could release the pressure, and soon, or she might just spoil the boy's homecoming.

Her druid clothing had been taken away for wash and repair and, even if the loose fitting garment which she had been supplied with felt strange and unfamiliar, there was no doubting the fact that it had made the difference.

She managed to catch the eye of Philippos' mother and winced as she patted her stomach. The woman understood immediately and pointed out a passageway with a knowing nod and a flick of her eyes. Catumanda smiled her thanks and left the celebrations behind her as she passed into the cool of the marble paved home. Small wooden shutters lined the right hand wall which had been opened to allow the plants which filled the outside space to add their delicate fragrance to the home. Light slanted in, and the druid could see that the facing wall contained several further doors. The room which she needed was at the far end of the corridor and she made her way quickly there.

She had recognised the house of course before Philippos had led her with great excitement to the heavy oak door. Now, finally inside the building from her dream, the sense of anticipation within her mounted as she left the communal bench and returned to the passageway. Rounding the corner she caught a glimpse of a sight even more incongruous than herself in the civilised surroundings, as a stocky figure in a deerskin cloak and antlered headpiece flashed her a grin before disappearing into a side room.

Catumanda stole across and, pushing the door ajar, grinned like a fool.

There was no sign of her spirit guide, but the reason for his visitation stood propped against the far wall, gleaming dully in the half light. The objects, she could see now, were not shields but large tablets of bronze, each one the height of a man's forearm. Divided into a number of vertical columns marked by figures representing suns and moons, Catumanda could see immediately that it was a method of measuring the passing of time and the seasons. Immersed in attempting to understand the complexities of the tablets she jumped as a voice spoke at her shoulder.

"I see that you have found them. What do you think?"

Catumanda swung around and began to blurt out an apology, but the old man held up a hand to silence her and she was shocked to see tears brimming in his eyes.

"Druid, you have no idea how long I have been waiting for this day to arrive."

Philippos' grandfather held his arms wide and smiled warmly.

"May I hug you without being diced by your moon blade? I am aware of your rules about such things."

Bemused, Catumanda held out her arms and the old man embraced her lightly. Stepping back he indicated that the druid take a seat beside to him on a bench there.

"My name is Demokritos and the gods have sent me shadowy visions of you for nearly seventy years. My old friend Abaris told me in Massalia many years ago that his gods would send a messenger to me one day to learn of my calendar." He began a chuckle which developed into a spluttering wheeze as he added; "he didn't say that it would be an attractive young woman though!"

Despite her familiarity with the workings of the gods, Catumanda was staggered.

"Abaris was my old master in Albion. He took me from my family when I was little more than a bairn and taught me the ways of the brotherhood. When did you know him in Massalia?"

Demokritos chuckled again and laughter danced behind his rheumy eyes.

"Let's just say that we were both young men."

He shifted on the bench and suddenly grew serious again.

"Let's begin, you have much to learn and very little time." He turned to the tablets and added, mysteriously.

"We will both be setting out on a long journey tomorrow, but we will meet again soon."

Catumanda faced the tablets and ran her eyes across the figures and images which had been delicately worked into the face of the bronze. She could sense the old man's pride in his voice as he spoke again.

"Tell me what you see."

The druid's eyes flicked across the waxy surface as she studied the markings.

"I am familiar with most of this but I have never seen it in written form before. It is a means of measuring the passing of time using the sun and the moon."

Demokritos nodded.

"I call it a *lunisolar kalendae*. Go on."

"Each column represents one year, divided into twelve months. Each month is split again into a dark and light period corresponding to the waxing and waning of the moon, as shown by these symbols." She pointed out the various images of the moon as she spoke. "The month starts with the full moon and the first, dark half of the month is fixed at fifteen days as the moon wanes. The light side of the month alternates between fourteen and fifteen days in length." She glanced at him for confirmation and he nodded sagely as he confirmed her thoughts.

"It is as you say, but that will lead us to a year containing only three hundred and fifty-four or five days."

Catumanda ran her finger across the smooth surface of the tablet and pointed to the third column.

"That is why you have repeated this month every two and a half years. It will bring the..." She squinted as she tried to recall the word he had used to describe the tablets.

Her mind was a whirl of numbers and figures but finally she had it and he jumped as she almost shouted it out with glee. *"Lunisolar kalendae!"*

They shared a laugh as Catumanda reeled off the facts contained on the tablets to the astonishment of the old mathematician.

"The years are divided into dark and light halves, beginning with the start of the dark months of the year with the first full moon at Samhaine. You have used the rising of the star marked here to fix the point in time. That star must be Antares. That means," she continued as the astonished old man gawped beside her, "that the other festivals are also fixed by the stars. Look, here," she pointed, "is Aldebaran in the constellation of Taurus next to the mark for Beltaine. It's all quite simple."

A strangled wheeze came from beside her and Catumanda looked at Demokritos in alarm as she worried that the old Greek was choking, but the wheeze became a rolling laugh as he pulled a scroll down from a shelf. Shaking his head in amusement he mumbled to himself.

"The work of a lifetime! It's all quite simple she says!"

Dabbing away tears on the back of his hand, Demokritos unrolled the yellowish sheet and smoothed it out on the table before them.

"This we call *biblos*, it is made from a plant known as *papuros*. The gods have sent you here, Catumanda, to take this knowledge back to your people in the North. Copy my work in a form which will incorporate your own beliefs and festivals in a way which will be easy for other druids," he smiled warmly as he paused, "perhaps not as astute as yourself, will find easy to understand."

Catumanda looked up in surprise.

"There is no need. I understand the kalendae completely."

Demokritos placed his hands, the backs of his aged skin almost indistinguishable from the biblos beside them, onto the bench and levered himself up. He bent low and kissed the young woman tenderly on the crown of her head, allowing it to linger for a moment before moving off to the door. He turned back and she let out an involuntary gasp at the great age of the man as he stood, a hunched silhouette surrounded by a corona of sunlight from the window opposite.

"Let me tell you a truth of the gods, before I return to my family."

EIGHTEEN

The forum resembled the body of a gigantic, multi coloured squid, its tentacles frantic citizens as they made their way through from the surrounding *viae*, heading for the dome of the Janiculum and the road to Caere beyond. Numerius guided his horse to one side and dismounted as he mentally sifted the tasks he wished to accomplish before the arrival of the Gauls into some sort of order. Armed men were in evidence once more, and a sense of order prevailed among the groups despite the chaos which had gripped the city. As he made the decision that he would cross the forum to the Senate house to seek his father, a familiar voice hailed him.

"Numerius! Just got back?"

He turned to see the grinning face of his cousin, Gaius Fabius Dorso, and he smiled for what felt like the first time since he had left his brothers, outside Veii. His cousin was irrepressible, it would take far more than the rout of the army of Rome and the impending destruction of the great city to dampen his spirits. He reached out and they gripped forearms in the Roman greeting.

"Gaius, you don't know how good it is to see you."

They stood side by side, watching as the flow of humanity swept past the massive stone columns which ringed the space, the faces of the great men and gods inscrutable as they regarded the chaos below. Gaius sniffed.

"A shitty day."

Numerius snorted and nodded.

"The shittiest day ever I would say. How long have you been here?"

Gaius indicated a turma of equites which were waiting patiently for him near the foot of the Capitoline.

"We were called back from the South last evening and reached the city around midday. We had been out hunting those bloody raiders in the hills around Tiburum but we never got close, it was like chasing fog." He suddenly averted his eyes and lowered his voice. "I heard about Licinia and the girls. I am very sorry." Numerius shook his head. "There is no need, cousin. Save your pity for those who suffered far greater injury. They were humiliated and we lost property, but none of them were despoiled in any way. I have that to thank this Solemis for, at least. They are Roman women, what does not kill them will make them stronger." He raised a brow. "Your family?" Gaius looked at him with amazement. "They are on the Capitoline of course, with the others." It was Numerius' turn to look surprised and his cousin grew apologetic. "I am sorry, you really have just got back, haven't you! I will explain what I know and you can decide what you want to do." He looked across to his men and indicated that he would be along shortly. Numerius noticed that the men's expressions were tense, they were obviously keen to be away.

As Gaius opened his mouth to speak, the ominous rumble of falling masonry carried down to the forum from the North and a great groan of fear rose from the crowd. To his surprise Numerius saw a flicker of fear pass across Gaius' features before his cousin reasserted his control and glanced in the direction of the sound.

"That can only have been the Colline Gate coming down. Nobody in our imbecilic army thought to close the door behind them in their rush to save their own skin and the first barbarian scouts seized it and fired the gates earlier." Numerius looked horrified but his cousin shook his head. "It is of no consequence. The city has been given up for lost. The decision has been taken that all men of patrician rank and fighting age are to retire to the Capitoline and fortify it to withstand a siege." Numerius cocked a brow.

" Women and children?"

"Only patrician women of child bearing age and their offspring."

"Plebs?"

Gaius shook his head sadly.

"There is no room for the whole city on the hill. Every extra body is another mouth to feed. This is a siege, Numerius, even the older members of the patrician class are to be left to their fate."

He nodded across to his men. "We are one of the groups who are having a final sweep for supplies before the walls and pathways are sealed."

Numerius looked aghast as the desperation of their situation became clear. The city was still full of people and he looked back to the forum as the sound of fighting carried to them. The crash made by the collapsing gate had changed a fearful but relatively disciplined population into a panicked herd. If the collapsing wall heralded the arrival of the barbarian army they could be expected to descend upon the forum in a matter of minutes.

A woman screamed as a thickset man was stabbed and pulled from his horse. Mounting the beast, the killer had only advanced a few paces before he too was dragged from its back and replaced by another, equally desperate to escape. The scene began to repeat itself throughout the forum as order began to break down and Gaius took Numerius by the sleeve.

"Come, cousin, it's started. We need to reach safety."

He shook his head.

"I came here to see my father. Do you know if he is at the Senate house or the Temple?"

Screams and crashes drew their attention across to the place where the crowd were exiting the forum. The roadway narrowed as it cut between the twin hills of the Capitoline and the Aventine and the panicked mob had begun to overturn carts and wagons in their haste to escape. The pathways which led up to the heights of the Capitol were nearby, and Gaius could see that his men were growing increasingly impatient to scale them before they were sealed. He reached out and grasped Numerius by the forearm and fixed him with an earnest stare.

"Most of the paterfamilias have decided to dress in their finest and meet the Gauls before their homes. I would look for your father at the *Domus Publicus.*"

Numerius watched as Gaius crossed to his men and wondered if they would meet again. He had to admit to himself that the plan to fortify the Capitoline was sound. Not only would the Temple of Jupiter be saved from desecration but the presence of an army within the bounds of the city would be important psychologically. Unless the hill was taken, neither the Romans or the Gauls would consider the city to have truly fallen. Siege warfare was common, it had taken the Romans themselves a decade to subdue Veii, and often the difficulties facing the besiegers were as difficult as those within the walls. Lifted by the thought, Numerius remounted and began to skirt the edge of the forum.

The crowd had begun to calm as it became clear that the barbarians were not about to inundate the city after all, but Numerius drew his short sword and held it in clear view as he passed along the edge of the multitude. Although the sun was dipping away to the West now, the temperature in the crowded forum was stifling as the great stone buildings and the paved surface gave up their store of heat. Above them all, the bronze and gilded statues of the ancients became flaming torches in the evening glare, guiding the people to the hoped-for salvation of distant Caere.

Sullen looks marked his passage, and for the first time Numerius could feel the hostility of the crowd as they recognised him, if not for a military tribute, certainly as a member of the class which had abandoned them to their fate. Fortunately their numbers quickly thinned before the shouts and curses could threaten to become a physical attack, and he guided his mount along the frontage of the area which the people called the new shops. Most had been ransacked as law and order disintegrated and he took a firmer grip on his sword as he passed by the premises of wine merchants and *thermopolia.*

Without exception they were occupied by men and women who had long ago given up any thoughts of flight, succumbing to the temptations of Bacchus, beyond caring whether their last day had arrived. A particularly fine thermopolium stood at the head of the forum, opposite the Temple of Regia. Numerius knew it well, it was a favoured meeting place of the Senators once the business of the day had been completed, but as he grew closer it was clear that the standards expected of their customers had been relaxed somewhat. A wide dining area looked out across the gentle slope of the forum to the grandeur of the Temple of Jupiter high on the Capitol. Normally the terrace was witness to politicking and learned conversations, as the finer points of law were discussed and deals struck. This evening, Numerius could see from his elevated position, the area was awash with the lowest sort of citizen, each one desperate to live their final hours to the full. At least one of the visible bodies had been stabbed repeatedly and several couples were copulating in full view of the last families to leave the city, cheered on by the drunken mob.

Numerius steered his mount aside and angled away towards the road which led up to the *Domus Publicus* but his heart sank as bleary cries rose in his wake. Conscious not to inflame the mob he looked straight ahead and kept the pace of his horse steady but the sound of running feet forced him to turn and confront the rabble. He gripped his sword tighter and lay it across his lap where it could be plainly seen but kept his tone as pleasant as possible.

"Go back to your wine, friends. Enjoy yourselves before the Gauls arrive."

A bull of a man threw back his head and laughed.

"Oh, we are all friends now are we?" He turned his head as he reached out to grasp the bridle of Numerius' horse and the tribune saw that the man's neck was smeared with blood, his ear little more than a gory flap of skin. Fresh cuts and grazes covered the knuckles of his ham-like fists, and it was clear that the oaf had been taking full advantage of the unique opportunities which the current situation offered his sort. Numerius knew instinctively that one of them was about to die. The man turned back with a sneer, and Numerius locked eyes with him as he slowly brought the point of his blade across his thigh so that it pointed directly at the thug's pockmarked face.

"Well, friend," he snarled, "as you and your kind decided to run away this morning rather than fight, it looks like we are all in the shit!" A rumble of laughter came from the motley collection of lowlife which had gathered behind their leader and, although the thug smiled, his eyes were those of a drink fuelled killer.

"Come and have a drink with your new friends." He hawked and spat a gobbet of phlegm onto the flank of Numerius' horse before looking up, his lip curled into a sneer. "I insist."

The moment to strike had arrived, and Numerius waited until the man's gaze had risen level with his waist before the sword darted forward. As the man's head continued to rise, the point of the blade slipped effortlessly into his eye socket and on into the brain. As his mouth fell open in surprise and shock, Numerius withdrew the blade and swung it an arc, slicing easily through his victim's forearm. Freed from his grip, Numerius kicked in and drove his horse across the forum and into the shadows cast by the temples opposite.

A great cry of indignation arose in his wake but, casting a glance behind him as he slowed again, Numerius could see that the chase had been half-hearted, as he had suspected it would be. Even lowlife could see that there would be little profit in assaulting a well armed man, and, their erstwhile leader lying lifeless at their feet, they turned away as the call of Bacchus proved to be too powerful for them once again.

Numerius snatched a small banner down as he passed a shop and wiped his blade clean before sliding it back into its scabbard. He was entering the sacred grove which led up to the Domus Publica and its neighbour, the Atrium Vestae, and he gave a snort of irony as he thought on the gesture. Surely the gods could not punish the city any more, even if he did carry a bloodied blade into the Regia, the sacred heart of Rome. The grove had once covered the foothills of the Palatinus but the growing city had nibbled away at it over the centuries until the remnant had been incorporated into the environs of the Vestals.

Ahead of him the red brick archways of the pontiff's home rose to a height of three stories with, nestled in its shadow, the elegant stone portico of the circular Temple of Vesta. Mirroring this, the facade of the home of the priestesses, the Atrium Vestae, stood off to the right.

Numerius checked the shadows as his horse made its way towards his father's residence but any threat seemed to have been left behind in the forum. Even the most unimaginative thief or robber would know that his chances of profiting from his haul would be slight with the army of the Gauls all but in the city.

Arriving before the temple, Numerius paused and cast a look into the dark interior. The great bronze doors were open and light filtered down from the opening overhead but otherwise all was in shadow and he felt compelled to visit the sacred hearth. Swinging himself down from his horse he mounted the steps and made his way through the vestibule and into the atrium. An impluvium decorated the centre of the room in the common Roman style and the tribune skirted the shallow pool as he made his way further into the building. The temple was modelled on a typical Roman domus, to reflect the goddess' position as sacred deity of the hearth and home, and Numerius made his way to the rear of the room and gazed sadly on the cold remains of the sacred hearth.

Despite its proximity to his father's residence, it was the first time that he had entered the temple. Like most citizens, he would make an offering of food in the hearth of his own home to give thanks for every meal. It had always seemed to be the appropriate way to honour the goddess but to see the Temple of the Vestals abandoned, the sacred hearth cold and empty, felt like the heart and soul had been torn from the city.

A voice echoed in the great chamber causing him to start and reach instinctively for his sword, panic gripping him as he grasped at the empty scabbard. Despite the danger of the hour, he had followed custom and deposited his blade at the entrance to the temple, and he gasped with relief as he recognised the owner of the voice.

"I taught you well. Even as they move to smite us for my arrogance, you still treat the gods with respect."

Numerius absent-mindedly held out his cup for a refill as he watched the first pale light of the pre dawn creep reluctantly into the sky to the East. It was unusual for him to break his fast with several cups of the finest Falernian, but then this was to be a very unusual day, he reminded himself. It was the day that Rome would fall to the barbarian Gauls. He allowed himself a small smile as he remembered that his father had dismissed the staff and slaves the previous day. He would have to recharge his own cup, as they had had to prepare their own meal the previous evening.

Ironically, he had just spent some of the happiest hours of his life with his father. Shorn of the responsibilities to family and state, he had become the man Numerius had always wanted him to be as a child. Warm, humorous and relaxed he had even joked with him as they had explored the mysteries of the *culina*, and after much opening of storerooms and storage bins they had managed to prepare a simple meal of bread, eggs and cold meats.

He rolled across and poured more wine as his father reappeared. Numerius nodded in approval.

"You look magnificent, father."

Marcus beamed.

"Yes, I was rather pleased with it myself." His mouth curled into a warm smile. "And rather relieved too. It's been a good many years since I last wore it!"

The pontifex had explained the previous evening that those who had gained curule responsibilities during the course of their lifetime of service to the city had decided that they would wear the distinctive robes to greet the arrival of the invaders. Resplendent in the insignia and distinctions of their former rank, they would seat themselves before their homes on the ivory chairs of office and show the barbarians how a Roman patrician *should* die after the shame at the Allia.

Numerius glanced out into the peristylium. The skyline beyond the colonnaded garden was growing lighter by the moment, they would need to prepare for the day.

"Let us move your curule chair to the front of the house, father. I don't think that the Gauls will be here just yet," he quipped, "but it would be a shame to miss them after going to so much effort!"

Numerius rose from his seat and made his way across. As Marcus led the way, he glanced back for what he was sure would be the final time on the triclinia which they had always called the 'family room'. It had been the idea of his late mother to convert the room and her touch was evident in every detail. The story of his gens, from its inception when Hercules himself had visited the marshy valley and Rome had been little more than a collection of hills, ringed the walls. The god himself dominated the ceiling, watching over his ancestors as they relaxed and entertained after another day's service to the city. Numerius wondered who would next dine under his terrible gaze; perhaps Brennus himself?

Father and son clasped forearms and, in a moment of spontaneity which surprised them both, Numerius moved forward to hug the old man. After a moment's hesitation he felt Marcus' rigid posture relax and they shared a loving embrace for the first and last time. Paterfamilias, especially those as important as the pontifex maximus, were not known for outward displays of emotion towards their children but the old man smiled warmly as they drew apart.

"I am proud of all my sons, Numerius, but I am glad that you inherit the position of paterfamilias from me." He chuckled. "Perhaps a more expressive style would add a touch of spice to the old family!"

Numerius made to reply but a ball of emotion had gripped his throat, so he pulled a thin smile and dipped his head. As his father took his seat at the entrance to the domus and arranged his robes about him, Numerius mounted and skirted the Temple of Vesta without a backward glance.

The sun had broken free of the Apeninnus, painting the fine houses and temples which capped the hills of the city a fiery red, as he took up the small *lares* statue and placed it carefully in the bag. That was the last of them, and he was finally free to make his way to the meeting place in the hills to the South. His brother Quintus' *lararium* was a tasteful room and he made a note to commend him on the design when they met, despite the gravity of the hour. Perhaps, he mused, he could borrow the plans when they returned and rebuilt the city after the coming storm had blown itself out.

Rome may be about to fall and their homes ransacked, but he had ensured that the most valuable objects had been buried safely in earthenware pots for retrieval when they returned. To his surprise, the lazy German slave had remained when all others had seized the opportunity to flee, and the man had been invaluable in helping him hide the precious items. He had considered rewarding him with his manumission but, as the only other man to know the whereabouts of the hoards, he still felt a tinge of regret that that had not been possible.

The household deities of the three Fabii now in his safekeeping, Numerius recrossed the atrium. Hopping across the body of the German, he emerged back into the street outside. Quintus' neighbour, Marcus Papirus, was still sat opposite and Numerius walked his horse across to bid farewell to the old man. Papirus nodded a greeting as he came up, and Numerius shook his head sadly.

"To live to see such a day."

To his surprise the old man laughed as he ran his hand through his long white beard.

"This is a great day!" He tapped the ground with his ivory cane and smiled. "We met with the pontifex maximus yesterday and decided on this course of action together. Your father told us of Nemesis. The scales of justice will be balanced by our sacrifice and Rome will rise again, even greater than before." He cast a glance across to the neighbouring hill of the Capitoline, now sealed and ready for war. "The finest of our young people are safe under Jupiter's protection. They will remain once this dark tide has receded." He leaned forward and clasped Numerius' outstretched arm, throwing him a wink as he did so. "And we old has-beens get the chance to die a hero's death, instead of wasting away like some cackling old maid!"

Numerius shared a laugh which was cut short as a great roar rose in the North. Papirus indicated to the South with a jerk of his head.

"It is time for you to take your leave, general. May Jupiter, Optimus Maximus, hold his hands over you."

They were already waiting as his horse laboured up the rise and walked forward into the shade of the tree line. The morning was already hot, the sultry air drawing the moisture from their bodies, tunics clinging to them uncomfortably. The smell of pine infused the air as Numerius exchanged greetings with Quintus and Caeso and turned the head of his mount back the way they had come.

The track switched back and forth as it climbed away from the plain, and Numerius raised his gaze to look on the city in the distance. As the sun rose higher Rome shivered under a heat haze, as if attempting to draw a veil across its shame. Despite the conditions, the dark stain which marked the army of the Gauls was clearly visible on the northern horizon, the roars and chants mixed with the braying of their war horns seeming to shake the very earth beneath them.

Like the flow of water as it tumbled through the *clepsydra* which graced the forum, light winked and glittered on barbarian arms as they funnelled into the city through the broken portal of the Colline Gate, and Numerius wondered idly what the barbarians would make of the water clock.

The first lines of smoke were appearing above the city, arrow straight in the still air, each column marking the advance of the barbarian horde as it fanned out through the *viae* and alleyways in search of victims and plunder.

Numerius dismounted and crossed to the sow. The dedication to Ceres made, the knife flashed. Marcus Fabius Ambustus, Pontifex Maximus, would journey safely to Elysium.

The last duty for their father performed, the Fabii exchanged a look and hauled themselves back into the saddle. The first vultures were beginning to circle over the city, riding the waves of heat on their serrated wings as they gathered for the feast.

Wordlessly, they turned away. Passing through the shadows, they emerged on the far side of the ridge and cantered south.

NINETEEN

Berikos tore the shield from the dead Roman's grip and backed against the doorpost as the last of the men edged their way back into the passageway. Atis was the last one through, and Galba moved across to overlap their shields with a clatter as the pair faced down the mob. A surge pushed one of the Romans within his reach, and the Aeduan's spear flicked forward to take the man in the groin. It was the perfect place to strike, and Berikos watched with satisfaction as the agonised man thrashed on the ground among the detritus of battle. It would hamper those who crowded behind him, anxious for their own chance to strike at the retreating barbarians.

Shouts and cries came from the rear as their fellow clansmen cleared the tabernarium of the last of the drinkers and, their rear protected, the pair edged back into the passageway itself. The big circular Roman shields were too wide for the constricted space and Galba tossed his to the ground where it would prove a hazard to any pursuers and moved shoulder to shoulder. The rim of the shield almost touched both walls and the pair hefted their spears above their heads and prepared to stab down at any

Roman foolish enough to follow them into the tight, dark space.

Suddenly the gloomy interior was bathed in light as several of the Horsetails emerged from the main room with flaming brands and disappeared up the steep staircase. Drawing level with the doorway, the pair saw that the room was already well ablaze. Flames were licking hungrily from the broken tables, chairs and barrels stacked in its centre, and they exchanged a glance which confirmed that they were of a like mind. They would need to move quickly if they were to cross the room above and escape before either the mob or the flames overtook them.

Looking back along the passageway, Berikos' heart leapt as he saw that the knot of men there were hesitating to enter the building. Flames were already casting an orange glow on the wall opposite the doorway to the main room, and the pungent smell of woodsmoke filled the air. A deep *whoomph* came from the interior, and it was clear to all that the building had little time left as thick black smoke curled out to snake its way along the ceiling.

Berikos and Galba paused as they felt the riser of the bottom stair nudge the heel of their feet, just as a series of frenzied yells carried down to them from outside. Looking back, they saw the men there being lifted and thrown bodily to one side as a group of well armed Romans forced their way through. Their expressions were hard and determined and the Horsetails knew that the time to break and run was upon them.

Galba raced ahead, vaulting the stairs two and three at a time as the shouts and curses from the passageway rose to drown out the roar of the flames. Berikos prepared to drop the shield, it would help him to run and cause a further obstruction for his pursuers to negotiate on the steep staircase, but firmed his grip as a better idea came to him.

The stairs took a sharp dogleg to the left as they reached the doorway to the room above, and Berikos turned back as he reached the turn. Fixing his stare at the final few feet of passageway before they reached the foot of the staircase, he forced himself to remain calm as he tilted the shield and drew it across his body. Galba called on him to hurry from the interior of the room, but he put his friend's pleas out of his mind and concentrated on the spot below him.

The tips of a man's boots flashed into view and Berikos grunted with effort as he unwound his body and sent the disc spinning down the stairwell. The throw was perfectly timed, and as the upturned face of the man appeared at the foot of the stairs, the hard bronze edge of the shield smashed into it with bone crushing force. Knocked senseless by the blow, the Roman crashed to the floor with a grunt and Berikos spun away and darted into the room. Safe for the moment, he ducked down and threw himself through the hole and into the adjoining terrace.

Galba was waiting and he threw his friend a crazy grin at the unlikely escape. Men were moving around the room, breaking up beds and piling them against the hole through which he had just come, while others thrust brands into the roof thatch overhead. The dry stalks caught immediately and the men moved across to fire the bedding now that they were all safely through. Berikos glanced around the room, counting heads.

"Vortrix?"

Galba shook his head sadly.

"He fell."

Berikos pursed his lips.

"He died well?"

Galba nodded as cries started to carry to them from the room next door. The Romans were still in pursuit, despite the flames. They would need to move on.

"It took a dozen of them, but he went down in the end. Many of us saw it, the bards will sing of it around the hearth this winter."

Berikos gave a curt nod of satisfaction and ordered the men through to the next room. The jagged hole there was far smaller and easier to defend, and they needed to regain their bulwark outside before the Romans there moved on it. He smiled grimly; burning buildings were unhealthy places to gather for last stands.

The men pushed their weapons and brands before them and filed through as the burning bedding began to bow inwards behind them. Spear tips followed, and Berikos drew his sword and raised it, waiting for a hand to show itself. The first appeared as the bedding was finally pushed away and the blade flashed down. A cry of agony and the hand lay at their feet, darkening blood oozing out to sizzle in the flames. Berikos exchanged a grim smile with Galba.

"That should slow them down!"

Replacing his sword in its scabbard, Berikos saw to his surprise that he seemed to have picked up his chieftain's lancea from among those which littered the ground outside, and he wondered that he had not noticed that he had the distinctive spear before. His last view of Solemis had been as they melted into the passageway and he seemed to be surrounded by a wolf pack of enemies. Albiomaros was moving to his side and Berikos hoped that they had made it through. The chieftain had rescued him from slavery and restored his honour. No longer would he feel shame now that the time had come to take his place at the council fire of his ancestors, as it will to all men.

Frenzied banging came from the wall at his side and moments later the tips of several spears appeared like the beaks of angry birds as his pursuers began to widen the breach. It was time to go, and Berikos hurried across the burning room and dove through the small hole opposite. The room was already ablaze and he winced in the heat as burning thatch began to fall in blackened clumps among them. The men were looking to him and he called his last instruction to them.

"Fire every room and get back to the bulwark. You *must* hold the gate for the army or the men we have lost here will have died in vain. I will hold them here as long as I can."

Galba moved to his side, but he shook his head.

"I am the last of my clan. It is time for me to board the boat for the West."

Berikos held out Solemis' lancea.

"Here, return this to your chieftain or lay it at his side on the platform of death."

An ominous crack caused them to instinctively duck their heads as the roof beams shifted in the flames. Berikos grabbed at Galba's shoulder and spun him around, shoving him towards safety as a clump of burning thatch dropped into the room.

"Go!"

Galba shot through into the next room and turned back for a last look at his friend. The big Aeduan had hefted his broadsword and stood, rolling on the balls of his feet as he waited to see which of the attackers would be the first to break through. Arms and feet began to punch their way into the room and Galba reached for his sword hilt as he prepared to return. He *had* to help, despite the fact that it would almost certainly cost him his life. Suddenly, as Berikos swung, a high pitched *crack* rang out as the tortured roof beam finally gave way and the scene was blotted out in a cascade of fire. Thrown back by the blast, Galba just had time to roll aside as a jet of flames pulsed through from the next room.

Laying on his back he exchanged a sad look with his companions before his discipline reasserted itself.

"Come on, let's go. We have a gateway to hold."

The fire had spread now to engulf the entire terrace, and they ran doubled up through a tunnel of flame. Thundering down the final staircase, they spilled out into the courtyard. Figures were running all around and the noise was deafening, but the barrier remained intact and they raced across and snatched up their shields. They were just in time and, despite the desperation of their position, Galba noticed that the new day had finally arrived to stain the Roman temple on the hill opposite a bloody crimson. He gave a snort of irony at the grim humour of the Roman gods. Pushing the thought from his mind he threw himself onto the step and braced his shield to repel the onslaught.

Suddenly he realised that nothing was as he had expected it to be. The men before him were moving from right to left. There were war horns among them, their excited wails reverberating around the square. As Galba's exhausted mind scrabbled to understand the scene before him a man detached himself from the horde and walked across. Unfastening his helm, he eased it from his head and held it by the great raven which capped it and grinned.

"Sorry we took so long. We were taking the auspices."

*

Consciousness was returning, slowly, bit by bit, and with it feeling and senses. He found that he was disappointed.

If this is the Isles of the Dead, they still smell like sweat and shit!

He forced his lids apart and winced as the light stabbed his brain.

"He's awake!"

A face hovered over him, pale and blurred, a line of teeth fixed in a smile.

"Morning genos!"

Other people moved behind the owner of the face, shadowy and indistinct like trout in a stream. A great fire roared in the background, men swarmed around him. Faces crowded in as he attempted to drag his mind back from the abyss and he winced again as a burning dagger of pain forced him back under.

He lay on a bed of hay. Clean and fresh, not a trace of shit. This was better. His head still ached but not so much, and he grimaced as he raised his hand to touch the back of his head. There was a lump there the size of a pigeon's egg, and he could feel the blood matted in his hair as the memories returned. Snarling faces and darting blades, the dawn.

Confused by the grunts and snorts all around him, Solemis thought that he must be in a pig sty, and he raised himself on one elbow and grinned at the scene which met his eyes. The swine were his clansmen and they looked as if they had fallen into a deep sleep the moment that they had touched the hay. A soft chuckle carried to him and a shape detached itself from the shadows and came across.

"Welcome back, Solemis."

Caturix smiled and held out a rough wooden cup. Solemis took it gratefully, downed the contents in one and held it out for a refill. Closing one eye against the glare he squinted up at the Crow chieftain.

"How long?"

"Not too long, the sun has just passed its high point." He jerked his head as he returned the cup to the grateful Horsetail. "The Romans have blockaded themselves on the hill with the temple on top. Brennus has taken the army to attack them, but I don't think that he will get far."

Solemis gave him a look of surprise and winced again as the skin was pulled tight across his injury. "I am surprised that they still had the strength to climb a hill, the speed they ran away from the battle." Caturix snorted and squeezed Solemis' shoulder. "It is good to have you back."

Their conversation had awoken the others. All around them men were hauling themselves to their feet, the joy at seeing their chieftain awake and seemingly none the worse for the crack he had taken to his skull obvious from their expressions. Solemis scanned the room quickly.

"I saw Vortrix go down myself. It was a good death. Berikos?

Galba came across and shook his head sadly.

"He covered our retreat. He asked me to give you this."

Solemis nodded that he understood, wincing as the pain stabbed again. "I know that he would have gone down swinging. I wish that I had witnessed it!" He took the spear and used it to lever himself up from the ground as he turned back to Caturix. "Have you found the Fabii yet?" Caturix' eyes widened in surprise. "How hard were you hit? We watched them cross the river and march west, remember? They won't be in the city." Solemis flashed a cold-hearted smile. His hunter's instinct had returned, and he realised that their wolf pack was now within the fold. This was the greatest day of his life and he was determined that he would live it to the full; he could sleep later. "We saw the *brothers* flee, yes. What about the other members of their clan?"

Turning the corner Solemis gasped at the scene which met his eyes. A wide circular space was packed with Celts, all turned towards the approaches to the hill which he knew the Romans called the Capitoline, off to his right. A quick glance told him that another assault on the Roman defences had met with failure and the warriors there were tumbling back down the narrow passageway in disarray.

Other men had broken into the shops which stood hard on there and were helping themselves to the goods within. A man sauntered by gnawing at a ham, and Solemis was soon on his way to the source. Caturix tore a strip of flesh from a rib as he gazed around the statues and colonnaded temples which encircled the area.

"Where should we begin?"

Solemis indicated the hill opposite with a nod of his head.

"That looks a good place to start. We know that the brothers are tribunes so their people will live in the finest homes."

Dark lines of smoke were beginning to rise from city as the army slowly spread through it, but the homes which capped the hill opposite them seemed to be untouched for the moment. The high walls which surrounded the wealthier homes could be hiding any number of Roman soldiers and Solemis could understand the warriors reluctance to be drawn onto unfamiliar ground. Hefting their spears and shields Solemis and Caturix led their clans across to the foot of the Palatine and entered the shadows.

Climbing away from the mayhem in the forum, they soon left the temples which lined the lower reaches of the hill behind. The roadway channelled them upwards and soon they were among the homes of the wealthiest citizens of the city. The oppressive heat of the forum lessened as they climbed into the freshening breeze, the air teasing through the branches of the cypress which lined their route soft and calming, despite their murderous intent. The road curved away as it climbed and warriors ran on ahead, testing the great wooden gateways as they did so.

The doors were shut and barred against them and Solemis was about to order one broken down when Ferox, one of Caturix' Crow, called out in surprise.

"There are old men here!"

Solemis and Caturix exchanged a look and walked across. The road widened into a small square, a solitary beech tree at its centre, its ancient gnarled trunk and twisted boughs offering welcome shade to the space.

Skirting the square, several of the older citizens had obviously chosen death over flight and had arranged themselves on chairs before their domus. Dressed in their finest, the men sat and stared impassively ahead as the first of the Celts warily approached them.

Solemis ran his eyes around the doorways lining the square. Any one of them could be hiding an armed force, ready to spring out on them as they were distracted by the elders.

"Check the gates."

Galba nodded and, trotting past one of the elders aimed a hefty kick at the door to his rear. To their surprise the door swung open and Solemis indicated the others with a movement of his head.

"Pair up and check them all."

As his clansmen did as ordered, Caturix formed the men of the Crow into a dense knot across the roadway and Solemis nodded to himself as he recognised his kinsman's astuteness. If an enemy did surge out of the buildings they would immediately be faced by a wall of shields and spears. At worst they should be able to retreat in order, back to the forum where the army would overwhelm the attackers in moments.

Solemis used the time to study the men seated like statues before them. Every man among them wore the broad stripes on his tunic which Solemis had learned signified senatorial rank. Several togas also carried an edging in colour which he guessed must mean that they held, or had held, even higher rank. Each man sat straight backed, completely immobile, on his chair and Solemis found the dignity of the men impressive, despite the obvious contempt in which they held the barbarians before them.

Atis reappeared at a doorway and threw his chieftain a smile.

"Nothing here, Solemis."

Soon, others began to re-emerge and, satisfied that they were not walking into a trap, Solemis crossed to the first of the senators and addressed the man in Latin.

"Where is the domus of the Fabii?"

The man stared impassively ahead, contempt issuing from him in waves. Caturix sneered and drew his sword as he moved behind the Roman. The man attempted to ignore the act but Solemis saw him swallow as he fought against the desire to look. He took a step back to avoid the blood which he was sure was about to be shed and spoke again.

"Numerius Fabius Ambustus killed my friend's chieftain, his paterfamilias. He *will* take his revenge whether you live to see the sun set this evening or not."

Solemis watched as the Roman gripped the folds of his toga at the knees, his knuckles whitening, and knew the answer. Taking another pace back he nodded to his friend. Caturix swung and the senator's head spun from his shoulders and rolled in the dust of the roadway.

The chieftains moved on to the next man in line.

"You heard my question."

The Roman, an older man sporting a long white beard gripped his ivory cane a little tighter but remained silent. Solemis' head began to pulse with pain once again as the sun beat down relentlessly and, tiring of the Roman's arrogance he reached out and tugged at the senator's beard. The cane flashed and a searing pain shot through his head. Solemis staggered back and landed on the ground. Moments later he opened his eyes and recognised the head of his assailant as it rolled to his side. To his great surprise the Roman blinked before the light of life left his eyes and he kicked it contemptuously away as a further stab of pain forced him to wince. A shocked silence had descended on the square and Solemis snapped out an order.

"Kill them all!"

Heavy blades flashed in the sunshine. It was over in moments, bloodied heads ringing the hoary tree like macabre spring flowers. Caturix moved to his side and squatted.

"Tough old bastards. What now?"

Solemis blew out his cheeks and tried to think. Albiomaros came across with a skin of wine and pressed it on him. Solemis drank and felt better almost immediately. Shooting his friend a look of thanks he scrambled back to his feet.

"We'll get nothing from the patricians. We need to find a low class guide, a man with a less developed sense of honour."

Doros, the Crow champion cut in.

"There were a few of those drinking places in the big square at the bottom of the hill. We could have a look out the back and see what we could find?"

"Here…just along here, it's not far"

The man stumbled along, the collar of his tunic twisted in the grip of the big barbarian. Caturix marched ahead impatiently as the men of the clans hurried in his wake, scanning the grove for signs of danger as they went.

Ahead of them, a building, its frontage a series of red brick arches, cut into the roadway. At its corner sat a small circular temple of creamy stone, its colonnaded design almost dainty beside its massive neighbour.

"There!" The man pointed excitedly. " That's him!"

Caturix drew up as Solemis translated again and twisted the man towards him.

"You're sure?"

The Roman flicked an anxious look at Solemis. He smiled reassuringly.

"My friend wants to know if you are certain that the man is Marcus Fabius Ambustus, and that he is the father of Numerius Fabius Ambustus."

A short while before, he had been sleeping off the effects of a day and night drinking free wine in one of the darkest recesses of the tabernarium. Now, he knew, his life hung by a thread. The Roman nodded vigorously and spittle flew in long white tendrils as he blurted out the reply.

"Yes! Yes! Marcus Fabius Ambustus, the pontifex maximus. Paterfamilias of the Fabii. I watched him only yesterday as he performed the ceremony for victory on..." his voice trailed away as, even in his current hungover state, the man realised that he had said too much. Solemis completed the sentence for him. "The campus martius?"

The man gave a weary shrug and Solemis turned to Caturix.

"He's sure."

The Crow chieftain shoved his captive away and instantly forgot him. As the Roman scrambled away, Caturix hefted his shield and drew his broadsword. Advancing on the lone figure seated on the steps of the building, he clashed the pommel against the rear of his shield and called to his clansmen.

"Crow!"

The men of his clan moved forward and fanned out in his wake until they were a solid wall of bronze, leather and muscle, sweeping down upon the hapless figure of the pontifex. Solemis followed on with his own clansmen and, despite the enmity between them, he had to admit that the old man before them lacked nothing in courage.

Caturix reached the seated figure and Solemis moved forward to translate for his kinsman as he drew to a halt and pulled himself up proudly.

"Chieftain of the Fabii; Know that my name is Caturix, son of Crixos son of Catuvalos, Chieftain of the Crow clan of the Senone tribe. I come to take vengeance for the unlawful slaying of my father, our chieftain, Crixos by the hand of your son Numerius."

Solemis stood to one side and watched as Marcus fought to retain his self control. Although the old man's face paled, only the small erratic flexing and straightening of his fingers betrayed the turmoil within.

The Crow had formed a circle around his seated form, and they began to beat the rear of their shields as their chieftain dropped his own shield and grasped his longsword with both hands. Solemis raised his voice against the rhythmic clatter as Caturix spoke again.

"Blood for blood! Bone for bone!"

As the Crow chieftain drew back his sword for the killing stroke the members of his clan moved in to skewer the Roman with their spears. Solemis watched as Marcus' eyes went wide and his face contorted into a mask of pain. As Caturix' long blade swept in to take the pontifex' head,

Solemis heard the man gasp out his last agonised words through gritted teeth.

"Nemesis! The scales are balanced!"

TWENTY

"Here he comes! Remember, nobody laugh."

Supported by his clansman, the outline of the chieftain appeared in the doorway as he hobbled into view. Moments later the room had descended into a chaotic brew of raucous laughter and mad honking sounds as Sedullos eased himself in. He threw them all a sheepish grin and settled onto one of the long, low Roman chairs. A clansman lifted his leg carefully onto the cushion and Sedullos grimaced with pain, setting the laughter rolling around the confined space once again.

Brennus shook his head and snorted again as he ran his eyes over the scratches and cuts which covered the clan chieftain's face and arms. He indicated to Solemis that he follow him outside with a flick of his head, shooting a parting comment over his shoulder as he left.

"Stay for food, Sedullos. You'll like it, we have goose today."

The pair strolled out into the sun-washed peristylium as the teasing and laughter redoubled in the room behind them. Brennus shook his head as they sat on the raised lip of the water feature which dominated the space.

"We have got to get out of this place, Solemis, the men are going mad. Sedullos and his men saw a Roman leave the river and climb up to the others on the hill. Instead of telling me that he had discovered a route to the top which was unguarded, he went for glory and got chased away by a flock of geese, tumbled down the slope and broke his leg." He snorted in disbelief as he launched a pebble at a nearby statue. "Can you believe these people?" he wheezed. "They have got bloody guard geese!" Both men shared a laugh and Brennus stretched and belched. He rubbed his stomach and pulled a face. "We are all growing fat here, Solemis. This siege warfare is just not our way." He sighed and looked across to the dome of the Capitol. The seasons were rolling by as they had for all time. The smattering of trees which hugged the slope of the great hill were beginning to lose their sheen as the bread oven heat of summer lessened a little more with each passing day.

Brennus took a swig from the amphora and handed it across. "I wanted to talk to you Solemis before you leave again, because you don't think like other men. Most men think in a straight line; their life, their clan. But you stand back and see the whole. Despite the death of your father, what did you spend the winter doing before we attacked Clevsin? Most men would have raged about the murder and plotted their revenge, but you made friends with your Umbrian neighbours and learned how to speak both their language and that of the Latins. You saw the wider world, Solemis. That is a rare quality." Brennus placed a hand on his friend's shoulder and fixed him with a stare. "It is why I will be recommending that you replace me as Chieftain of the Clans when we return."

Solemis was thunderstruck.

"Where are you going?"

Brennus sniffed and tugged at his moustaches as he thought.

"I am not of the clans. I was raised in the North, among the Germans." He shrugged. "Things were done there and I had to flee when I was little more than a boy. Things that demand a blood price."

Solemis gasped out a reply.

"Then the Horsetails will come too. We all will."

The chieftain shook his head.

"No, I am a war leader, nothing more. The Senones are settled here now, they have made new friends but also powerful new enemies. The Romans and the Etruscans will not forget their humiliation at our hands. The people need a strong, intelligent leader and that man is you. The blood of my ancestors calls my sword home."

He handed across the wine and grinned.

"Drink on it?"

Solemis drank to steady his nerves as Brennus gazed into the distance. A dark cloud moved across the face of the sun and an owl ghosted across on silent wings. He knew that it was a sign but he was unfamiliar with reading portents. He was a warrior, maybe he would seek out a druid later and ask him what the augury signified.

"We need to go home, soon, before the snows return and close the passes over the Apeninnus. We have won a great victory here, men should be home in time to share the news with their ancestors at Samhaine. They missed that last year because we left it too late. I won't let that happen again."

Solemis returned the amphora and ran his tongue across the hedge of his own moustache, savouring the remaining droplets.

Brennus lowered his voice and looked about them.

"The Romans have offered to pay us to go away."

Solemis' eyes widened in surprise and his face lit up with a smile. They had all spent too long in the man-made canyons of the city. Celts belonged among trees and grass where they could ride everyday under the wide sky and their gods were close to hand.

"When? How much?"

"When you were out gathering supplies in the East. They came to the barrier and offered me six thousand pounds of gold to leave."

Solemis could barely contain his excitement. It had been months since they had been home. Aia should be heavily with child by now if the news which she had shared with him on his departure had been correct. Although there had been signs of a Roman led relief army massing in the far south, Solemis discounted the threat. He would lead the Horsetails back across the salt road and into Umbria. It would be far quicker than accompanying the army north, laden with the spoils of victory as it was, and he could honour his southern neighbour, Anastasios, and his sons for their part in Rome's humiliation.

"You accepted their offer, of course," he laughed, mischievously. "I would if I were Chieftain of the Clans, particularly if we were about to leave anyway!"

Brennus gave a sly chuckle.

"Eventually; I did say that I wanted to supply the weights which would measure out the tribute."

Solemis knew that there was more, and his mouth curled into a smile.

"And?"

Brennus laughed.

"Never a straight thought, my chieftain. I have had a smith make up some weights that are heavier than the stamps on them declare," he shrugged, "a sort of parting insult, if you like." He turned to Solemis. "What can I say if they object? Something in their language, something short and easy to remember."

Solemis reached across and took another swig from the amphora as he thought. Suddenly a smile lit his features as the perfect phrase came to him.

"How about, '*Woe to the Conquered!*'"

A wicked smile spread slowly across Brennus' face as he tested the phrase.

"Woe to the Conquered…"

"That will do," he beamed. "What is it in Latin?"

Solemis chuckled as he added an insult of his own. "If they complain that the weights are not true, throw your broadsword onto the scales, just for me, and say '*Vae Victis!*'"

*

Numerius shifted in his saddle, shading his eyes against the glare of the sun as he stared into the West. Away to the South the Roman army was clearly in view, and he pursed his lips as he began to fear that his hunch had been wrong. He turned to his brother.

"We shall have to leave and join Camillus soon." He cursed and struck the horn of his saddle in frustration. "I would have wagered anything that the barbarian would retrace his route. We can't let Camillus lead the army into Rome himself and steal all the glory!"

Quintus nodded but remained silent. Word had reached them several weeks before of the death of their father, and the flames of vengeance burned unchecked.

A decurion edged his mount across and raised himself in the saddle, squinting into the distance.

"Tribune! A rider coming in from the North!"

They turned as one and tracked the dust cloud down to its source. Numerius felt a kick of hope. It could only be one of the men he had placed on the ridge overlooking the city. He was certainly moving like he had important news to impart, and the Roman sent prayers to Jupiter, Hercules and Mars that he was correct. It seemed to take an age before the man appeared before them, and he waited impatiently as the messenger spat the road dust from his mouth and made his report.

"Tribunes! A group of barbarian horsemen have left the city and are heading in this direction."

Numerius spat out a reply.

"A group? How many man?"

The rider flamed and cleared his throat.

"About twenty, tribune; they look to be taking the via salaria."

Numerius made a fist and exchanged a look of triumph with Quintus and Caeso.

"It must be Solemis and his men!"

His horse caught the mood, skittering sideways as Numerius calmed it with a sweep of his hand.

"Right, you know what to do. The moment that we break cover they will see us. We *must* reach the bridge before them or they will escape." They brought their spear points together and hardened their expressions.

"For father!"

*

Solemis was elated. They were finally leaving Latium after a summer spent raiding and fighting among lands he felt he now knew better than his own. No Horsetail had ever been nominated to lead the tribe, and he was eager to return home and begin the feasting and distribute the *potlach* which would cement his following among the clans.

Brennus would be away as soon as the clans disbursed, heading north before the snows tightened their grip on the passes back across the Alpes. By Beltaine next spring he would be Chieftain of the Clans and, the gods willing, father to a son.

Albiomaros interrupted his thoughts as he drew his attention to the sky.

"The vultures are back, look."

Solemis looked away to the South. The dome of the sky was clear and bright, all the haziness of summer a memory. They exchanged a look.

"Let's pick up the pace. We know that they are gathering an army in the South, we can't afford to meet them here."

Solemis urged his horse on and Tantibus lowered his head and surged forward. The Horsetails were strung out now as they gained the salt road and flew eastwards. Suddenly a hand reached out to tug at his sleeve and Solemis looked across to find that Rodolfo had drawn level. He relaxed the reins and leaned across as the Umbrian cried out over the thunder of hooves.

"Dust, to the South."

Solemis narrowed his eyes and cursed. They still had about five miles to go before they gained the bridge across the River Anio where they had entered Roman lands. It would be a close run thing.

Cresting a fold in the land the riders came into view and he cursed again as he saw that they were outnumbered four or five to one. Solemis' eyes flicked to left and right as he judged the distance between the men who were clearly Roman equites and the bridge and relaxed a little. They were close to the crossing, but not close enough to intercept them before they crossed. How long they could stay ahead on tiring mounts would be another matter.

The blackened remains of the toll collectors hut came into view as they swept down and galloped onto the approaches to the bridge. Clattering across, Solemis hauled on his reins and came to a halt. As his clansmen and the Umbrian brothers copied his action, they looked at him in surprise and confusion. The Romans were approaching the crossing, hefting their shields as they prepared to give battle.

To the dismay of his men, Solemis threw himself from Tantibus' back and drew his sword.

"Go…quickly."

Their mouths gaped, but Solemis forestalled their protests.

"There is no time to argue. The bridge is narrow, I can hold them here. I won't be the chieftain who is responsible for the annihilation of the clan!"

Before they could respond, he slapped several horses on the rump with the flat of his sword and hastened across to the span. As he ran, a volley of *gaesum* whispered overhead to fall among the leading equites. The men and horses tumbled to block the entrance to the crossing as further javelins arced across the gap, skewering those attempting to pick their way through the mess of kicking, screaming men and horses.

The attack had bought him enough time to gain the high point of the bridge and broken the cohesion of the Roman charge and Solemis turned back and flashed his clansmen a last look of thanks. To his surprise they had formed a line to his rear and he felt overwhelming pride as they beat their last spears against their shields and cried out his name.

Sole-mis! Sole-mis! Sole-mis!

As he turned back, the final missiles whickered overhead to fall among the packed ranks before him and he rolled his shoulders as he prepared to face the onslaught. Shield less, he could wield the full sweep and power of the heavy broadsword and, clasping the grip with both hands, he swept the blade in wide, silvered arcs as he faced down the foe.

The rumble of hooves carried from behind, and he felt relief flood through him as he knew that the members of his clan had seen the sense in his decision, living to fight another day, perpetuating the clan. He sensed a figure move to his side and he snorted as he moved to his left, opening a gap for his right hand man.

Albiomaros laughed and planted his feet foursquare as he came up alongside, his own blade hissing as it cleaved the air in short, adder-like strikes.

Solemis risked a look at his friend as the Romans finally crossed the wall of dead and dying and began to form up behind their shields. The big Trinobante grinned as the dying sun reflected a flaming crimson from the plates of his owl-helm, and held up the palm of his hand to show the red weal which marked their brotherhood. Solemis was overcome with emotion as he returned the gesture and indicated the oncoming wall of shields with a flick of his head.

"They want us alive, genos."

Albiomaros looked back and noticed that the Roman soldiers carried no arms. They would close inside the sweep of the Celts' great blades and pin them against the parapet while they were knocked unconscious and trussed up. He threw Solemis a look of incomprehension and the chieftain indicated to one side of the bridge. Near to the remains of the toll hut the three Fabii brothers were sat astride their mounts, savouring the moment of final victory over their tormentors. Albiomaros looked back with a fatalistic smirk.

"They may well want us alive, Solemis." He kissed his blade and touched the pendant at his neck for luck. "But they will pay a heavy price!"

TWENTY-ONE

The ship wallowed in the swell as the crew began to release the ropes securing the small boat to the stern.

"This is as near as I dare take you. You'll have to row in from here."

Catumanda nodded her thanks and swung her legs over the side rail, thankful that she was back in the practical garb of a druid. With a last look up at the nervous faces lining the side rail, she lowered herself gingerly into the unstable craft and half threw herself onto the bench. The awkward part done, she took up the oars and struck out for the quayside and the war band which awaited her there. The warmth of the sun on her back and the rhythmic action of her arms lulled her mind as the nearness of the end of her journey caused her to reflect on the previous few days.

It had been a pleasant trip up the coast from Neapolis to Ostia. Despite the lateness of the season the dome of the sky remained clear, the winds light, and the druid had wondered at the beauty of the coast. Shattered headlands of creamy stone punctuated strips of golden sand, backed by marshland. Sweeping inland, lush green forests marched away, edged by a distant mountain range. It was the perfect place to contemplate what was beginning to look like the culmination of her life journey. Only the strange grey forest remained to be explained from the recurring dreams which had plagued her nights since she was a child.

Her sudden barking laugh had startled her hosts when one had inadvertently revealed that a people called the Senones, wild keltoi from hyperborea, had occupied a city called Rome to the North, and she had shared a knowing look with Demokritos across the table. It was clear now where her final destination lay, and she had requested that a ship be chartered to convey her there as soon as possible.

As she had expected, it was the old man's last meal with his family and she had watched as he stealthily set his affairs in order with them. As the head of the family his wishes were paramount, and he had insisted that Philippos remain at home for the remainder of his education. He was to be groomed to succeed him as a philosopher and mathematician and Catumanda had shared the boy's joy.

She had remained there out of respect for the full three days of the ritual which the Greeks called *prothesis*, as the female mourners washed and anointed his body and stood sentinel over Demokritos' remains in their dark robes. Following the laying to rest, she had hurried to the harbour and headed north.

A yellow legged gull, its strange chortle reminding the druid of a manic child, pulled her mind back to the present.

The Neapolitan ship was now stern on to the shore as the kubernetes worked the twin pedalia, swinging her head south for home, and, as a shadow passed across her, she realised that she had reached her destination. A rope thumped into the well of the boat making her jump and she looked up to see a row of grinning faces.

"Sorry druid; I didn't mean to startle you!"

Another warrior added his voice, and she joined in the laughter as a wave of emotion at the nearness of her own people threatened to overwhelm her.

"You'll be sorry when you spend the rest of your life squatting to piss!"

Catumanda ran her eyes along the cheery group as she began to realise just how much she had missed the sight of men in chequered trews and the sound of her own language in the year that had passed since she had stepped aboard the *Alexa* in Isarno. Another peel of laughter rolled along the quay as a tall blond warrior, his face and arms bronzed by the southern sun, bent forward with a gleam in his eye.

"Careful now druid, I am going to unroll this and there might be a splash."

The corners of Catumanda's mouth curled into a sweet smile as she hooked a little finger at the man. He winced and instinctively felt his groin as another voice called above the uproar.

"It must be your lucky day, Searix. She is going to make it bigger for you!"

Catumanda pulled herself across by the rope and soon she had managed to ascend the crazily swinging ladder, despite its best efforts at dumping her back into the sea. Willing hands were waiting for her at the top, and she reached out thankfully and let the men pull her onto the quayside.

Dwarfed by the stand of Celtic warriors, she had not noticed that their chieftain had joined them as she scaled the wall, and the warriors moved aside as he smiled a greeting.

"Welcome to Latium, druid. My name is Caturix." He leaned forward as the men crowded back around.

"Can I ask? What are you doing here?"

She patted a sealed cylinder which hung suspended at her side.

"I need to deliver this to a druid. How far is the city called Rome?"

Caturix jerked his head to the East.

"Seven or eight miles inland; the road is good, straight and fast, but you may already be too late."

She looked at him, aghast. The delay for Demokritos' funeral could have caused her to fail in her quest at the very last. Caturix saw the look which crossed her face and whistled to the big blond warrior.

"Searix! Mount up, we have finally found a use for you!"

Catumanda interrupted as the men stirred into action.

"I *must* get this to a druid. If Rome is only a short distance away as you say, I could be there within the hour, even travelling by cart."

Caturix looked back, his face serious.

"You don't understand druid, we are already leaving the city. They have paid us to go and we are more than happy to oblige. There were reports of a Roman relief army coming from the South and we were dispatched to check that none were arriving by sea. Unless you are it," he added, "it would seem that we have nothing to fear."

Caturix recognised her disappointment and smiled gently.

"We will escort you to the army, the druids will be with them."

She nodded in agreement despite the nagging feeling that her destiny was somehow linked to the city itself. As Caturix organised a party to scour the deserted dockside for a suitable cart and sent Searix racing off to find out if any Celts remained in the city, Catumanda remembered her blood brothers.

"Do you know a warrior called Solemis?"

Caturix turned with a look of surprise.

"What, *the* Solemis? The chieftain of the Horsetail clan?"

Catumanda snorted and shook her head. So her friend was a chieftain already. She was hardly surprised.

"Yes, I would think that that would be him. He may still have a big friend with him called Acco."

Caturix beamed with pride, and Catumanda found that she was absent-mindedly rubbing the welt of a scar which cut across her palm as she waited for his reply. The big chieftain checked that there was nobody within earshot, leaned forward and lowered his voice.

"Solemis is my brother-in-law. My sister, Aia, carries his child." He winked at her. "Solemis doesn't know that I know, but Aia told me so before we rode to war." As Catumanda's face broke into a smile, Caturix straightened up and shrugged. "I am a great friend of Solemis and proud to be so, but his best friend is his champion, Albiomaros. He usually calls him genos."

NEMESIS

Caturix rode alongside her, chirruping away about the great deeds done by her friends during the migration and the great battles which they had fought here in the new land. None of the blood-curdling tales surprised her in the least and she found that her mind was wandering to her last conversation with Philippos' grandfather, the Greek philosopher, Demokritos. His parting revelation concerning the gods made perfect sense of course. Different people did not have different gods. They were the same gods called by a different name. The Greek Poseidon *was* the Celtic god Manannan or the Egyptian god Yam. Ares *was* Camulos or Anhur. Zeus, Toranos or Baal. The gods used people such as herself to spread learning among them all, but what the gods gave with one hand they exacted a price with the other, and she knew that she would soon be taking her place beside the sacred hearth of her ancestors.

As they grew closer to Rome they joined the road which led through the hills to the city of Caere. It was here, Caturix explained, that the majority of Rome's citizens had fled at the beginning of the summer and the evidence of their panicked flight was all around. Abandoned belongings littered the roadside, alongside carts with broken wheels and discarded toys, corn dolls and wooden swords. It was the human side of the disaster which had overtaken the population, and the druid could not help but contrast it with the glory and pomp of war still proudly displayed by the men who rode at her side.

As the city hove into view, Searix returned in a rush with another warrior, their cloaks streaming, cloud-like, in their wake. Caturix urged his horse forward as his clansmen exchanged looks of concern. The pair came to a halt in a cloud of dust and scattered stones and Catumanda listened as the excited warrior reported to his chieftain.

"The last of the army have left, Caturix. Brennus sent Epacos here to tell us to keep away from the city and rejoin them via the bridge at Fidenae."

Catumanda stood on the footrest of the cart so that the warrior could recognise her clearly as a druid and called across.

"Epacos, are the Horsetails with the army?"

Epacos blinked in surprise as he noticed her for the first time and glanced at Caturix. The chieftain, his clansmen now in danger of being cut off by either the arrival of the Roman relief army or a sally by the garrison from the Capitoline snapped out.

"Well, answer her! We will need to find a route suitable for a cart. Druids aren't allowed to ride horses, lad!"

He shook his head as he recovered.

"The Horsetails left earlier. Solemis led them to the East."

Catumanda chewed her lip in disappointment as she thought. The death of Demokritos had delayed her long enough to make her miss both her brother druids and the reunion with her genos. The old Greek had clearly been an instrument of the gods like herself, his dreams had proven it to be so; it *must* be their will.

Catumanda's gaze instinctively drifted skywards as she sought a sign which would show her the path which the gods wished her to take, and she smiled as a heron, its curious bent-necked flight unmistakable even in silhouette, crossed her path. The bird of the underworld, the heron was a clear indication that the gods were seeking to guide her in her moment of indecision, and she watched as it dipped one of its great wings and flew off towards the river. As her eyes were drawn across to the city on the hills, the flash of sunlight on arms drew her gaze towards the highest point and she caught her breath at the sight which awaited her there.

Catumanda whipped the mule forward and raised her voice as she attempted to make her wishes known to Caturix. The chieftain was busy discussing possible routes to the North which would enable them to escort the cart bound druid, while still keeping clear of avenging Roman equites. Eventually she halted the cart and brought the heel of her staff down on the foot board with a crash. As the men finally quietened and turned their faces to her, Catumanda slipped the cylinder containing the precious *kalendae* over her head and passed it across.

"Caturix; See that this is given directly to the most senior druid among the Senones, *by you personally*." She fixed him with an earnest stare. *"Trust no other."* The chieftain made to protest but she cut him short with a chop of her hand. "Tell him that the druid Catumanda says that the contents have great power and they must be sent directly to a druid named Vernogenos on the Spirit Isle in Albion."

Caturix attempted a last appeal to reason but Catumanda refused.

"Caturix; You have a responsibility to one not yet born." She locked eyes with him as the warriors shifted uneasily around them. Their chieftain was beginning to argue with a druid, and the druid was making it plain to them all that she would brook no disagreement. It was time to go. Catumanda let her words sink in and then spoke slowly and clearly as she held his gaze so that there would be no misunderstanding.

"The boy will need a kinsman to tell him what happens here and teach him the ways of our people. When he reaches manhood, he will know then what must be done."

Catumanda drove on her mule, scattering the Crow and their mounts before her.

As she rounded a hill Rome came into full view for the first time, and she paused and stared in wonder. The sheer size would have been almost unimaginable to the girl from Eyam before she had begun her quest in the South, and she felt an overpowering sense of pride that Solemis and Acco had defeated such a foe and chased them from their fabulous city.

Closer now, she was sure that the temple she had seen from the road was the grey forest. Serene almost atop the highest point in the city, the building sparkled as the weapons of its defenders shone in the sunlight like shattered glass. High above a terraced bank of clouds raced away to the East, the undersides painted red by the lowering sun.

Catumanda dropped from the cart and unhitched the mule. Pressing her face close to the animal's neck she breathed in the muskiness as she fondled its ears. Finally she moved back and, with a gentle slap to its rump, sent it ambling away.

The mournful sigh of a war horn carried to her from the South, and the answering roar of men from the hill inside the city told her that the army of Rome had returned to their city. She pulled a wry smile.

NEMESIS

Yes, it is safe to return now. The big, bad men have gone!

Adjusting her crane skin bag, Catumanda took up her staff and stepped onto the bridge.

*

Rome heaved as its grateful citizens acclaimed their saviour and vent their fury at the captives. Numerius gritted his teeth and gave the rope another sharp tug out of anger and spite. Despite all his efforts on behalf of the city, it was his old enemy, Camillus, who had been reappointed dictator and accorded a triumph. Some were even beginning to call him the new Romulus, the second founder of Rome! He tugged on the rope once again and Solemis' head and shoulders shot backwards.

Nemesis! The injustice of it all! Have we not paid our debt?

At the head of the procession, the dictator, the red paint on his face appearing even starker than usual beneath the shock of white hair, waved happily to the crowd from the platform of his chariot as his escort struggled to shield him from their wild celebrations. Quintus leaned across as the crowd surged forward again.

"Let us hope that our dictator remembers who he could rely upon during the darkest days. At least we are in full view of the crowd, unlike that fool Sulpicius!"

Numerius finally pulled a wry smile. If Camillus had been incensed when he discovered that the tribune had paid a ransom to Brennus for the return of the city, he had been positively apoplectic when he discovered that, despite the discovery that the weights had been false, they had agreed to bring down even more gold from the capitol. Finally the barbarian had laughed and thrown his own great sword onto the scales and cried *'Vae Victis!'* Unbelievably the fool had actually sent for more! Even coming on top of all their humiliations that summer, it had been deeply shameful and Numerius at least took some comfort in the fall of his rival.

The procession wound its way down the Sacred Way, past the Temple of the Vestals and the Domus Publica and crossed the expanse of the forum. Numerius watched the two barbarians, Solemis and his big friend Albiomaros closely as they passed the home of the pontifex but neither man glanced that way. He was certain in his own mind that they had been present at the murder of his father but neither man had spoken a word to him since their capture, despite the attentions of some of Rome's more 'persuasive' citizens.

Camillus drew up at the foot of the Capitoline and, after a last wave to the adoring crowd, alighted and began to ascend to the Temple of Jupiter.

Solemis exchanged a look with Albiomaros with his remaining eye and, despite the pain from his broken body, he smiled inwardly as he saw the indomitable spirit which still burned within the big man. Grimy and lice ridden as they both were, they were determined to board the boat the Isles of the Dead with as much dignity and defiance as they could muster.

As they followed the procession past the temples and homes of Rome's wealthiest citizens, the fury of the forum was replaced by an icy hatred from the people who lined the roadway. Finally breaking out into the sunshine at the summit, they found themselves before the great temple itself. Albiomaros turned his way and spoke clearly, despite the certainty of the beating which would follow.

"We made it, genos. It took us a while, but at least we still beat Sedullos to the summit!"

As the guard set about his friend, Solemis' laughter caught in his throat. A gasp of shock escaped his lips as he gazed on the temple, and the memories of a fresh autumn day in a far-off land came tumbling back into his mind. Oblivious to the sounds of his friend's beating, Solemis pictured three children and he heard her words clearly again.

'The trees were a creamy colour but so was the ground and, looking up, we noticed that the sky was the same'.

He turned to Albiomaros with a sense of wonder.

"Genos, this is the place in Catumanda's dream! The floor, the columns and the roof are all carved from the same coloured stone. It's her strange forest!"

The guard had stopped his beatings and Solemis was surprised to see a smile play across his friend's swollen lips as he replied in a voice edged with wonder.

"She's here."

Solemis looked back and caught his breath as he noticed a small, brown clad figure for the first time. The procession moved forward again and drew to a halt at the steps of the temple. The Roman, Camillus, his face painted blood-red, crossed to a great white ox held by the Roman priests as others led Catumanda down the great steps towards them.

Solemis felt his eye cloud as tears came to it, and he blinked them away as she was led across. Obviously they were to follow the ox, now bellowing its last, into the next world, and Solemis felt a curious mixture of joy and regret that the three childhood friends were to end their stories together. Her hands and feet were shackled but she shuffled across, and they smiled and shared their first embrace in twenty winters.

Unaware of their relationship, Numerius ordered the guards to let them perform their religious rites before, rather more ominously, they were led across to the stone.

As they drew apart Catumanda held her hand out. They glanced down and saw the ridge of reddened skin which bisect her palm and copied her action. Clasping hands in an echo of that long off day, they renewed their pledge.

"Let us be joined for all days.
One blood…
One bone…
One clan…
Steadfast and true!"

Catumanda moved forward to kiss them tenderly, whispering sorrowfully as they drew apart.

"What have they done to you?"

They both grinned, despite the pain, and a rumble of laughter came from Albiomaros as Solemis replied defiantly.

"Not as much as we did to them."

EPILOGUE

It was growing late as Numerius guided his mount off the via ardeatina, back onto the track he knew so well. He had rebuilt the villa soon after the defeat of the Gauls with the money donated by a grateful dictator, and he snorted at the irony. Camillus, at least, acknowledged the debt owed to him for his efforts and sacrifices that summer.

The sun lay on the earth's rim, away to the West, the shadows lengthening by the moment as it shone its crimson light across his lands. Still a little fuzzy headed from the entertainments of the day, the old Roman sighed in anticipation as he thought of the relaxing bath which waited for him at the head of the track.

Almost twenty years had passed since they had driven the Gauls from the city. Rome had risen, phoenix-like, from the ashes of the destruction which they had wrought, and the aged senator reflected on the part which he had played in its rebirth. The walls of Servian had finally been refortified and the army had been reorganised so that the massacre of the higher echelons of society would never be repeated. Numerius had been instrumental in the reinforcement of the unwieldy phalanx style formations by the *triarii,* and he had seen to it that the soldiers of the new army had abandoned their long spears for the heavier bladed swords and body covering shields favoured by the Gauls.

He smiled to himself as he remembered the pride with which he had led the army against their old foes, the Volsci and the Aequi, his new formations crushing them both and adding their lands to Rome. Naturally, he snorted, Camillus had been acclaimed the victor and awarded a further triumph, but age had dulled his sense of grievance. He now found that the pursuit of comfort within the bosom of his growing family afforded him far greater pleasures than the pomp and ceremony of the city.

Each year now the numbers of veterans who attended the celebrations marking the refounding of the city grew fewer, although Camillus himself seemed to have the longevity of Jupiter himself! He had put aside his rivalry with the old dictator for the good of the citizens, and together they had worked on new formations which they hoped that the Roman army would adopt as it went out to fulfil its destiny. Camillus' idea of freeing the centuries from the rigid mass of the phalanx completely had been brilliant in its simplicity. The new *manipular* formations were akin to pummelling your enemies with a series of hard-hitting, mailed fists, allowing the army an ideal combination of flexibility and mutual support.

The old senator sighed once more as he wondered how his father would have reacted to the new alliance between the houses of the Fabii and Furii. It was obvious now that he had incurred the wrath of the gods by seeking to delay the advent of the Gauls. Camillus' action in bribing the barbarians to uproot themselves from their dank northern forests had clearly been their work, and Marcus had paid the ultimate price. Like a brushfire, clearing away they weeds and dead wood, the defeat of the army and the sack of the city had rejuvenated Rome. Now she was poised on the cusp of a great future, he was sure of it, and he hoped that Nemesis, the goddess of justice had rebalanced the scales to her satisfaction.

A crow cawed, and Numerius' mind came back from its meanderings. He glanced absent-mindedly up into the branches of the great cypress which lined the track and narrowed his eyes. There were three crows, one of which was the largest he had ever laid his eyes upon, practically the size of a vulture. The crow cocked its head, the white of its inner lid flicking across as it studied him, and the Roman froze in fear. It was the same look which he thought that he had seen the druid Catumanda give him all those years before, and he swallowed, only dimly aware that his guards had moved protectively to his side.

The men, both experienced ex-gladiators, drew their swords and Numerius looked at them in surprise.

"Stay between us, senator. If we can break their line, forget us and ride for the villa."

Numerius looked ahead and saw that a line of horsemen had formed up there, blocking their path. A horse snickered from the field beside him and the three men cast about to either side as more riders ghosted from the shadows.

Despite the lateness of the hour Numerius knew the men for Gauls, their size alone would have been enough, and he sighed in resignation as he recognised the horsehair plumes which fluttered softly from their spear shafts with each gentle caress of the wind.

A second line of Gauls walked free of the shadows and, sawing at their reins, took station behind the first. Numerius knew that the time for flight had already passed. Walking his own mount forward, he halted a dozen paces from them and pulled a wry smile.

"It's been a long time."

He looked along the line of warriors and gasped with surprise.

"You I remember!"

He gave a dry laugh as his mind wandered back to the day beside the River Allia.

"You led the charge which would have wiped us out, had it not been for Caedicius' *tribulus*. Very nasty things," he snorted, "those spikes!"

Caturix was unmoved.

"I watched you kill my father. He died well, sword in hand on the field of battle. Your father," he added with a snarl, "squatted like a woman as my blade took his head."

Numerius hardened his expression again. The barbarian was right. This was not the time or place for the reminiscences of old men. His gaze moved on and he paled as he saw the man who sat proudly at their head.

It cannot be!

The young man drew his sword and hefted his shield as the horse warriors at his side followed his actions. The Gaul edged his mount proud of the line as he began to pass judgement on the Roman.

"Chieftain of the Fabii; Know that my name is Solemis, son of Solemis son of Connos, Chieftain of the Horsetail clan of the Senone tribe. I come to take vengeance for the slaying of my father, our chieftain, and of Albiomaros and Catumanda, friends of our clan."

The Gauls rhythmically beat swords and spears against their shields, and the dark birds cawed and swayed with excitement as the men began to chant.

"Blood for blood! Bone for bone!"

AUTHOR NOTE

The few surviving sources which describe the events at this time were written several centuries after the events themselves, but they all agree that the Romans completely underestimated their enemy. Although it seems that the army of Rome may have been surprised whilst still in marching formation by the sudden arrival of the Senone army, it appears that they offered some resistance before they broke and ran. The Roman commander, Sulpicius, appears to have ordered his reserves to a low hill which stood at the right of their line, and it was here that the Gauls attacked first, outflanking the phalanx and causing the panicked flight which cost the Romans so many lives. Many managed to cross the Tiber, seeking safety behind the walls of the abandoned Etruscan City of Veii which lay a few miles to the North, and it was from here that the Roman recovery began.

The Romans did fortify the hill of the Capitol, remaining there as the Celts ransacked the city below them, although how much effort the Senones made to remove them is debatable, despite later claims by Roman historians. The Celts were not conducting a war for territorial conquest, but to reclaim their honour following the Roman insults of the previous year, display the might of their arms and amass as much booty as possible.

The famous story of the night attack which was thwarted by the sacred geese of Juno and the *'vae victis'* legends both come from this time, as does the tale of the deaths of the elder patricians, who, having decided not to seek sanctuary on the Capitoline, sat before their homes and awaited the coming of the Gauls. Legend has it that Marcus Papirus *did* cause the resulting slaughter by striking one of the Gaulish chieftains with his cane after the man tugged at his beard.

The sacrifice of prisoners and their arms is well attested in the sources from this and later periods. Many 'bog bodies' have been discovered in the Celtic and Germanic north, and large deposits of ritually destroyed weapons have been discovered in similar locations. The 'wicker man' sacrifices are of course well known from several modern films and they were described by both Julius Caesar and Poseidonius in antiquity.

The description of the *lunisolar kalendae* was based on that found at Colligny, near Lyon (Lugdunon) in present day France. Written in Gaulish using Latin letters, it has been dated to the first century, but the concept is global and far older. Principally, it enabled them to fix the correct time for the observance of religious rituals, essential to the druids.

The fishing village of Cale is the modern city of Porto, its Latin name, Portus Cale, is thought to be the origin of the name Portugal itself.

Numantia would of course eventually fall to a Roman army commanded by Scipio Africanus after a siege lasting nine months in 133 BC, but even this famous general failed to break the defences, starvation succeeding where the force of Roman arms could not.

The character, Demokritos, did live at this time. A pioneer of mathematics he is sometimes referred to as the father of modern science, not least due to his formulation on the atomic theory of the universe!

That the Romans recovered so strongly from their defeat is a mark of their civilisation. The Servian Walls were rebuilt at this time and the army reorganised so that the massacre of the patrician class at the Allia could never be repeated. Gradually the phalanx was replaced by the manipular formations of the later Republic and Imperial periods. Standardised sword, shield and armour was introduced on a Celtic pattern, alongside more advanced iron working and improved close-quarter fighting techniques.

The Romans never forgot the shame of the defeat and sack of their city by the Senones under Brennus, the Raven. It would take them almost four hundred years, but they would take their revenge on those who had inflicted the particular fury which they came to call the Terror Gallicus.

Cliff May,

March 2015.

CHARACTERS

AMA – Lindo's helper.
AIA – Solemis' *gwraig*. Sister of Caturix.
AIKATERINE – Wife of Hektor, mother of Thestor.
ALBIOMAROS/ACCO – 'Big man from Albion'. Solemis' 'blood genos' and champion of the Horsetail clan.
ALEXANDROS – Owner of the Greek ship, *Ksiphias*.
BERIKOS – An Aeduan warrior freed from slavery by Solemis. Adopted by the Horsetails.
BRENNUS – War leader and chieftain of the Senones.
AMBUSTUS, CAESO FABIUS – Tribunus Militum of Rome.
AMBUSTUS, MARCUS FABIUS – Pontifex Maximus. Paterfamilias of the Fabii.
AMBUSTUS, NUMERIUS FABIUS – Tribunus Militum, later paterfamilias of the Fabii.
AMBUSTUS, QUINTUS FABIUS – Tribunus Militum.
ANASTASIOS – Solemis' Umbrian neighbour.
ATTIS – A warrior of the Horsetail clan.
BRIZIO – An Umbrian warrior, son of Anastasios.
CACIRO – An Iberian carter.

NEMESIS

CAEDICIUS, QUINTUS – Centurion at the Allia, later commander of Roman forces at Veii.
CATUMANDA – A druid. One of the three 'blood genos'.
CATURIX – Chieftain of the Crow clan. Brother of Aia.
COTOS – Carnyx warrior of the Horsetails.
CAMILLUS, MARCUS FURIUS – Dictator of Rome. Leads the Roman relief armies.
CRETICUS, LUCIUS ANTONIUS – A decurion.
DEMOKRITOS – Grandfather of Philippos. Philosopher and mathematician, inventor of the *'lunisolar kalendae'*.
DOROS – Champion of the Crow clan.
DORSO, Gaius Fabius – A cousin of Numerius.
DRUTEOS – A Horsetail warrior.
FIDENAS, QUINTUS SERVIUS – Sulpicius' deputy commander at the Allia.
GALATUS – A warrior of the Horsetail clan.
GALBA – A warrior of the Horsetail clan.
HEKTOR – Husband of Aikaterine, father of Thestor.
LICINIA – Wife of N Fabius Ambustus.
LONGUS, QUINTUS SULPICIUS – Commander of the Roman army at the Allia and the garrison on the Capitoline.
OLINDICO O OLINOCO – 'Lindo', a druid at Cale.
PAPIRUS, MARCUS – An elder patrician.
PHILIPPOS – Catumanda's companion.
RODOLFO – An Umbrian warrior, son of Anastasios.
SEARIX – One of Sedullos' warriors at Ostia.
SEDULLOS – A clan chieftain of the Senones.
SOLEMIS – Clan chieftain of the Horsetails. One of the three 'blood genos'.
TERENO – Iberian owner of the fishing vessel, *'Dolfinn'*, rescuer of Catumanda and Philippos.

TERKANTU – Eldest son of Tereno.
TERKINOS – Deaf son of Tereno.
THESTOR – Baby son of Hektor and Aikaterine.
ULTINOS – Uxentio's son.
UXENTIO – An Iberian smith.
VERNOGENOS – Druid on the Spirit Isle.
VORTRIX – A warrior of the Horsetail clan.

PLACES/LOCATIONS

RIVER ANIO – River Aniene, Lazio, Italy.
ANXUR – Terracina, Latina, Italy.
APENINNUS – The Apennine Mountains, Italy.
ARDEA – Lazio, Italy.
CAERE – Cerveteri, Lazio, Italy.
CALE – Porto, Norte, Portugal.
CLEVSIN/CLUSIUM - Chuisi, Tuscany, Italy.
RIVER DUBRO – River Douro/Duero, Portugal/Spain.
EMPORION – Near L'Escala, Costa Brava, Spain.
FIDENAE – An abandoned Etruscan city in Latium, conquered by Rome 435B.C.
NEAPOLIS – Naples, Campania, Italy.
NEQUINUM – Narni, Umbria, Italy.
NUMANTIA – North of Soria, Garray, Spain.
OSTIA – Lazio, Rome.
PYRENES – The Pyrenees.
SPOLETIUM – Spoleto, Perugia, Italy.
RIVER TIBERIS – River Tiber.
TIBURUM - Latium, Italy.
TIRRENO SEA – The Tyrrhenian Sea.
VEII – Isola Farnese, Province of Rome, Italy.

VESBIOS – 'Hurler of Violence'. Mount Vesuvius, Campania, Italy.
VOLSINIA - Bolsena, Lazio, Italy.

ABOUT THE AUTHOR

Born in London and raised in Essex, I now live with my family near the Suffolk coast.

Visit my website at www.cliffordmay.com

Printed in Poland
by Amazon Fulfillment
Poland Sp. z o.o., Wrocław